Crowley lifted the cover to the case, barely aware of the lunging black shadow that shot out across four feet of open space, heading directly for Gordon. Gordon's face was a mask of frozen horror. The next instant, the black shadow fastened itself to Gordon's neck.

"Jesus Christ!" Crowley screamed. Gordon dropped his flashlight, but Crowley could still see the hideous head of the taipan, its fangs buried deep in Gordon's neck.

The snake launched itself out of the case even further, stretching an unbelievable five feet. Gordon fell backward to the floor. The snake's head glided into space and held itself steady three feet above the floor, defying gravity. Crowley could have sworn the eyes were glowing red from some self-contained energy deep within the snake. Its jaws dropped open. Rows of teeth showed, barely visible beneath a sheath of white flesh.

"Gordon," Crowley cried out in anguish. "Save me! Don't leave me!"

Another foot of the taipan's body flowed from the case. Crowley gasped and retreated until he found that he had backed himself into a corner!

DEATH BITE

MICHAEL MARYK and BRENT MONAHAN

ace books

A Division of Charter Communications Inc.
A GROSSET & DUNLAP COMPANY
51 Madison Avenue
New York, New York 10010

DEATHBITE

An ACE Book, by arrangement with
Andrews and McMeel, Inc.

First Ace Printing: December 1980

Published simultaneously in Canada

4 6 8 0 9 7 5 3 1
Manufactured in the United States of America

We wish to acknowledge the expert assistance of the following persons and organizations. All inaccuracies or exaggerations for purposes of literary impact are the sole responsibility of the authors.

- Dr. James Patterson Bacon, Jr., Curator of Herpetology, Klauber-Schaw Reptile House, San Diego Zoo
- Dr. John L. Behler, Curator of Herpetology, Bronx Zoo
- Dr. William Loery, Chief Pathologist, Princeton Medical Center, Princeton, New Jersey
- Col. Lawrence E. Spellman, Curator of Maps, The Richard Halliburton Map Collection, Princeton University
- Australian Consulate-General, Australian Information Service, New York, New York
- Eric Worrell's Australian Reptile Park, North Gosford, New South Wales, Australia

Foremost among snakes large and dangerous is the TAIPAN. This snake carries more than twice as much venom as any other Australian snake and has fangs much longer than those of the Tiger snake. None of the persons known to have been bitten has recovered, and a horse died five minutes after a bite. It will attack on sight, and its actions inspire dread.

Clifford Pope, *The Reptile World* (New York: Knopf, 1955)

Newspaper reports in Australia have endowed the taipan with almost supernatural powers.

Eric Worrell, *Song of the Snake* (Sydney: Angus & Robertson, 1958)

BOOK
ONE

1

KENJI TASAKI ordered a halt, then leaned his weight against a tree, physically and emotionally drained. He was too old to be hunting snakes. Next week he would be fifty-nine, if he lived that long. Just two months ago, no one could have persuaded him to take even a single step off his veranda to catch the most harmless reptile. Yet here he stood, waist-high in kangaroo grass, compelled to hunt a snake no one had ever captured. In fact, the snake was reported to be so large and fearsome that most hunters, including Tasaki, believed it to be nothing more than legend.

Squinting from the sun's merciless glare, Tasaki watched his five aboriginal hunters unshoulder their burdens and retreat to the shade of the acacia scrub. There they squatted on their haunches and traded words in short, disjointed phrases. The conversation never interfered with the abos' real attention—the savanna that sourrounded them. A cool dry breeze was fanning the grasses into a sea of restless, rustling motions. The abos searched the savanna with wary, practiced eyes, for any movements not caused by the breeze.

* * *

It rested within the shade of a boulder, testing the air with rapid flickers of its tongue. The glistening forked tip snatched errant molecules into its Jacobson's organ, two cavities in the roof of the mouth. The elementary brain analyzed the taste-smell.

It turned its head into the wind, its scales sliding silently across the surface of the stone. It sensed a combination of unknown odors. A strange animal was near. Prey.

* * *

Tasaki turned his weatherbeaten face into the wind. He looked back at the trail they had cut into the savanna, back to the forest which retreated down the steep slopes all the way to the island's shoreline. Through a breech in the forest's canopy he saw the grey ocean and, far off, hugging the horizon like a blue-green fog, the jagged contours of Papua.

Tasaki wiped his arm across his glistening forehead. Sweat had plastered his shirt and pants to his skin. It was maddeningly cold and clammy, and as fast as the wind evaporated it, his body pumped out more. Inside his boots, the moisture had dragged his kneesocks down to his ankles. Tasaki knew it was useless effort to hike them up. They would only slide down again.

Tasaki had given up his fabricated nerve the day he retired from catching snakes. Now, after four years of soft, city retirement, he could not easily resummon it.

He had grown too old and too fond of life to resurrect the role of fearless hunter. It hadn't been so bad this morning as he stood on the open beach, but all day long, as he pulled himself up the shadowy slopes, over the exposed roots and through the tangle of lianas and vines, fear had been climbing, too. Twisting its way up his spine, boring into his skull. But if he could not reclaim his nerve, he would at least master his fear, he told himself with great resolution. After all, he had captured and killed snakes for almost a third of a century. And a snake is a snake, no matter what the dark legends say.

Except for the fact that it was totally uninhabited, Naraka-pintu seemed little different from a hundred other Indonesian islands Tasaki had hunted on. Of course, it was part of the legend that no one could live here. The name, Naraka-pintu, meant "Door of Hell," and Satan's gateway was guarded by his demons in the form of gigantic, poisonous serpents. The snakes saw to it that all souls on the island belonged to dead men, whether or not they had arrived in that condition.

Tasaki was unruffled by native superstitions. In New Guinea legends flourished like bamboo shoots. What unnerved him was that visiting natives who claimed to have seen one of the demons often accurately described the savage Australian taipan down to the smallest detail. The Australian taipan, averaging less than nine feet, had killed grown men in less than five minutes. When the natives described the Naraka-pintu taipan, however, they never set its length at less than fifteen feet. Such a creature, legendary or not, commanded fear and respect.

◦ ◦ ◦

*The strange animal odors remained constant,
growing neither weaker nor stronger. It slithered out
of the shade, its muscles rippling in waves of lateral
contractions. If the quarry would not move to it, it
would move to the quarry.*

* * *

Fate can be brutal, Tasaki reflected. It can compel
a man to actions completely counter to his instincts
and logic. For thirty-one years he had hunted snakes,
selling their skins, bones, venom, and blood. Thirty-
one years of sloshing through leech-infested swamps
and jungle monsoons. Some days it would have been
easier to die than continue but for the dreams of security, of solid walls and floors and of a mattress with
springs. Finally, four years ago he had saved enough
to be done with snakes forever.

A year after he had quit, the crazy American
tracked Tasaki to his favorite haunt, a Djakartan gin
mill. There, between swigs of Japanese beer, Tasaki
heard yet again the legend of the Naraka-pintu serpent. But the American insisted that it was no legend.
Although he declined to say how he knew, he was certain the creature existed, and that it was a giant
taipan. He offered Tasaki ten thousand dollars to capture one alive. Why not offer instead a half-loaded
revolver, bid him press it to his temple and squeeze
the trigger for the money? That kind of offer, generous as it was, was meant for the totally insane or the
totally desperate, and Tasaki was neither. He remembered his great satisfaction on rejecting the offer. Ignoring the refusal, the American pressed a card into
Tasaki's hand, assuring him that the offer remained
open. On the card were three international addresses

and five telephone numbers. Tasaki tucked the card in his wallet and, for three years, forgot about it.

Suddenly, two months ago, the savings of a lifetime vanished. Not only Tasaki's but also most of Uncle Seiwa's savings as well. Tasaki's eldest son, Takeo, lost it in reckless speculations. Dishonor! Last month, with no money to block its view, Tasaki spotted the American's card in the back of his wallet. He called the first number, demanding twelve thousand for the job. The next day thirteen thousand sat in the National Bank of Indonesia, the extra thousand a bonus if the taipan measured longer than sixteen feet.

The wind had died down, leaving Tasaki's face covered with a network of beaded rivulets. A faint hissing brought his blood pounding to his head. It took Tasaki a moment to realize that the noise came from a distant waterfall, tumbling down the forest slopes.

* * *

The odors stopped, leaving it confused. It reared back along its sinuous length, lifting its head until it cleared the three-foot high grasses. The lidless amber eyes scanned the savanna. The prey was not in sight. It dropped its head to the ground and slithered forward.

* * *

Tasaki turned back toward the aborigines. Two had relaxed their vigilance and were teasing a centipede that had rolled itself into a tight, defensive ball. The leader of the natives, a well-muscled man named Oolloo, divided his attention between the savanna and the pump action of his much-prized shotgun. Tasaki knew the men of their tribe to be fearless snake hunters. He had no idea, however, how the abos would react if they actually found a taipan of giant proportions. He could not even guess his own reactions.

Sensing Tasaki's stare, Oolloo looked up at the Japanese bossman. Tasaki shifted his eyes to the savanna, aware that Oolloo could instinctively pick up the slightest gleam of fear. With a snap of his fingers and a wave of his arm, Tasaki brought the hunters to their feet. Nets, poles, and capture bags were collected, and the party moved forward cautiously through the grasses.

* * *

At last the ground began to vibrate, sending messages up through its ventral scales and thence to its nervous system. The signals were complex and confusing. It paused to reassess.

* * *

Oolloo had not survived twenty years of snake hunting by being careless. As he took the point position and waited for the others to fall in line single file, he checked the safety of his shotgun. It was off. He made certain one more time that the choke of the barrel was wide open to give his shot the widest possible spread.

Oolloo glanced up at the sun. He judged the hour to be four in the afternoon. With such brilliant heat streaming down on the savanna, the chances of running into a snake in the unshaded grasses were slight. Nevertheless, he grabbed his six-foot pronging stick by its end and, as he started forward, slowly parted the high grasses with a gentle pendulum motion.

The aborigine's objective was a rock prominence well into the savanna where the moist, shady crevasses would help a snake maintain a constant body temperature. If no snake were found among the rocks, the high ground would at least provide a lookout across the plain.

                o   o   o

A massive black shape towered above it. Flank quickly—attack!

                o   o   o

Oolloo's cry of warning wrenched Tasaki's attention from the ground. The abo leader had shifted into a blur of movement, both powerful arms pressing his long, fork-ended pole into the earth, his weight fully behind the action. Between the prongs, Tasaki caught a glimpse of a rounded, shiny blackness, squirming through the fork. Then, for just an instant, one of the abos stepped in Tasaki's line of vision as the abo reached up to loosen his half of the capture net. The next moment Oolloo was in full view again, still bearing down upon the pole. But now, to the abo leader's right, looming up out of the tall grasses, was the head and neck of the most fearsome snake Tasaki had ever witnessed. It was a giant taipan. Five voices shouted out to Oolloo in unison. He had not seen it, intent on pinning the snake's body to the ground.

Tasaki's mind reeled. Could this be a second snake, a mate? If not, Oolloo must have pronged the back end of a monster at least sixteen feet long, easily capable of winding to strike at the victim's flank.

The snake's head continued to rise until it came even with Oollo's eyes. At last the abo saw it, but before he or any of the group could master their shock, the massive reptilian head shot forward across a meter of space, jaws agape, and buried its fangs in Oollo's face. It snatched and ripped viciously at the man's nose, cheek, and eye socket. The horrifying sight paralyzed the hunters. Even more gruesome, the snake did not strike once and retreat. The head reared back on its slim neck for a fraction of a second, then struck again. Blood spurted along Oolloo's cheek, mingling with a white, viscous venom, dripping down the rips in the flesh. The shotgun sling slipped from Ooloo's shoulder, and his weapon clattered to the ground. Ooloo dropped the pole and reached out blindly for the snake, his muscles tensed in a single-minded determination to strangle the monster whose venom was about to kill him.

The snake lashed out a third time, tearing into the native's right wrist with its fangs, then whipping its neck left and right, back and forth in a frenzy. It yanked back, drawing Oolloo off balance and down to his knees. His wrist ripped out of the snake's jaws. The taipan stared at the immobile party of hunters with amber, evil eyes, dropped quickly to the ground, and disappeared into the grasses.

Not ten seconds had gone by since Oolloo had shouted his warning. With the snake out of sight, the abos regained their senses and hurriedly set about the motions of capture; they backed away from the stricken man and pulled the net open, careful to keep their bodies well behind it. Tasaki studied the terrain. To their left and slightly behind them lay a patch of barren rock, about thirty feet in diameter. Tasaki directed the abos toward it, but he held his ground. The grasses near the fallen hunter quivered, alive with malevolent hisses.

Tasaki stood about twenty feet from the wounded abo. Oolloo had dropped to his hands and knees, feeling for the shotgun. The blood ran thickly from his right eye socket. Already the native was showing symptoms of neurotoxic poisoning, much swifter than Tasaki would have thought possible. All muscle tone had vanished from Oollo's face. His lips and jaw hung flaccid. His breathing had become rapid and shallow. It would have been merciful for Tasaki to raise his revolver and end the man's agony abruptly, but he could not bring himself to do it.

Oolloo pulled himself up along the length of the shotgun, raised the weapon slowly, as if in a trance, and took two faltering steps into the grasses. Thick, white excretions began to bubble from his nose and mouth. He took two more halting steps, raised the shotgun butt to his shoulder with a superhuman effort and fired. The kick of the blast sent him crashing backward into the grasses where he disappeared from Tasaki's view. A covey of startled birds fluttered into the sky. The low, angry hissing continued.

Tasaki watched the tops of the grass stalks intently. He drew his revolver from its holster and cocked it. He now stood halfway between the fallen native leader and the four remaining abos, who had fanned out to the four corners of the open area and were stamping the earth contiguous to the rock with their feet. Their eyes, alive with fear and excitement, searched the grass with unwavering attention.

Oolloo's half-brother, Boomi, was the first to spot it. The vegetation trembled in rapid, erratic waves, heading directly for the natives. Boomi cried out and pointed with the tip of his machete. The two abos with the net pulled away from one another. The top of the net lifted off the rock surface, stretching upward to neck level. Their action trapped Boomi between the snake and the net, and he quickly backed away from the churning grasses. The men with the net inched forward; the last man readied his snaring pole. The knots of hemp drew taut. Boomi stooped under the net, twisting his body to the side, his machete dragging the rock.

The snake sprang out of the grass as if catapulted, biting into the native's trailing foot. Boomi kicked back in pain and astonishment. His fingers caught in the net and prevented the others from throwing it. The taipan released its hold and reared up, hissing at each native in turn while they darted in and back, taunting it with the free ends of the net. The fourth native pushed his snaring pole over the net directly at the open jaws. With mad fury, the jaws snapped shut around the pole.

Tasaki watched Boomi free himself from the net and claw his way back along the rock surface. His bites were not so terrible to look on as Oolloo's, but already the abo's head lolled and his eyes were unfocused.

The taipan released the pole and hissed madly at the encircling cords. Tasaki could not believe what he was witnessing. He had been wrong. This snake was more than a snake. It was the Devil incarnate. Ordinary snakes hid from the heat of the afternoon. Ordinary snakes fled at man's approach. Ordinary snakes struck if cornered, but then only once. This demon stood its ground fearlessly, even pressed the attack. It would not apparently be satisfied until every man lay dead. The abos feinted backward to lure it from the grasses. At last the full length of the taipan was exposed. The snake was at least nineteen feet long.

Tasaki holstered his revolver, picked up an abandoned pole, and circled cautiously into the grasses.

2

THE REVOLVER lay in his friend's right hand, its barrel close by the hole in the right temple. The opposite side of his head was scattered across the forest floor. Blood spattered the nearby leaves. *It* had vanished.

The muted thumping and the distant cries swelled in Scott Miller's head, dragging him from sleep to consciousness. His eyelids snapped open. He sat up. His heart battered against his ribs at a sprinter's pace; the sheets were saturated with perspiration. The cries had ceased but the thumping continued, from the other side of the bedroom door.

"Scott? Are you all right?" a female voice called from the hallway. It took Miller's sleep-fogged mind a moment to recognize the familiar timbre.

"Yes, Ioka," he replied, staring in the direction of the shadowy door. "Yes, I'm fine. Go back to sleep."

"I heard you crying out. May I come in?"

"There's no need. I was just having a bad dream."

"The same one?" Her softly spoken words hung in

11

the air. When Miller did not answer, she persisted. "About the taipan, Scott?"

"No. Not the taipan," Miller lied, as a bead of sweat trickled from his brow. "You go back to sleep. It was nothing." For some seconds he heard no sound from the other side of the door. Then he caught the sound of her slippers scuffing along the wood floor.

Miller nervously ran his tongue along his upper teeth, thinking of the dream. He sighed deeply, then willed the dream back into the black recess of his mind from which it had crawled. The clock on the bedside table read five forty-three.

He pulled on his bathrobe and crossed the hall into his study. As he shuffled through the stacks of papers on his desk he sensed a presence in the room. He looked up. Ioka stood in the doorway, her slender figure haloed by the hall's bright lighting.

"I put the coffee on," she said.

"You know me too well," Miller noted. "No more sleep today." The young woman made a clucking mother-hen sound, then shook her head disapprovingly. Miller laughed gently "You're going to lecture me about working too hard, right?"

"No," she said, unfolding her arms. "I decided last night that if I could not change you in six years, I should give up trying."

"I don't believe that for a minute," Miller replied, flipping open his appointment calendar.

Ioka sighed with an edge of exasperation.

"I can't help saying it. You go to sleep at two in the morning, and when you finally get to sleep you have bad dreams that wake you, and you have the dreams because you are working too hard." Her words spilled out in a swift verbal flood.

Miller laughed again. He pushed his chair back

from the desk and raised his hands as if to take an oath. "I promise. Once the park is open and in full swing I'll get to bed before midnight every night. But there are still four more days to go before we open."

Ioka stepped into the study. "You must let me do more of the work. What do you have in your appointment book today that I can take care of?"

"First order of business is meeting with Mayor Gardner about lengthening the accessways into the park."

Ioka perched on the corner of the desk. I know the changes you want to make, Scott. We discussed them yesterday at dinner. Let me talk to the mayor."

"I don't know, Ioka. I've got a feeling he's hoping to weasel a bribe in exchange for speeding things up at City Hall."

"And that is why I should talk to him instead of you," Ioka persisted.

Miller looked up at the exquisite Eurasian face. The mayor would have to be carved from granite not to succumb to Ioka's persuasive charm. "All right. See what you can get him to promise. Gardner's scheduled for nine, so if you take care of him that gives me an extra hour to prepare for the reporters."

"How many in this group?"

"About two dozen. Some of the most influential pencil wielders from here to Richmond. They can help put the Great Scott Serpentarium on the map before we sell the first ticket. That is, if I can persuade them to write about us favorably."

"You can," Ioka said confidently. "What else will you let me do for you?"

"How about getting me that cup of coffee?" said Miller.

◦   ◦   ◦

"Now, ladies and gentlemen, let's move from the Western diamondback rattlers in their Arizona habitat to the Eastern diamondbacks." Miller stepped from the snake pit and led the way along a seamless curve of the protective wall. The walkway was dappled with puddles from an early morning shower. At his side walked a handsome, long-legged woman with keen emerald eyes and cascading blond hair. Directly behind them trailed four of the park's tour guides, reviewing the facts they had memorized for their new jobs. The reporters brought up the rear, some in raincoats, others carrying umbrellas. They stretched out behind the guides like pulled taffy.

Miller looked at the sky. The clouds were breaking up, and the sun shone through intermittently. "We're running late, Lilla Sue," Miller said to his blonde aide," so if they have more questions, you'll have to field them."

"Fine, Scott," Lilla Sue replied. She leaned toward her boss, lowered her voice, and said, "I've already gotten a dinner invitation from the celebrated Earl Jackson 'to discuss the fine points of the park.' I think the only fine points he's interested in are the ones on my chest."

Miller nodded, the hint of a smile tugging at the corners of his mouth.

"You can decline that invitation if you want, Lilla Sue. That's service above and beyond the call of duty, even for a public relations agent."

"I can handle him, Scott," Lilla Sue said. "If he gets too grabby, I'll file for combat pay." She laughed and dropped back to talk to the reporters. When the group had regathered along the concrete wall Miller announced: "This is the last pit in our tour, ladies and gentlemen. As a point of information, regular tourists will be seeing the park exactly the reverse of the way you saw it: North America first, then South and Central America, Australia, Asia, and Africa, and, finally, the Rotarium. We started in the Rotarium to avoid that little shower, and it was simpler to wind our way backward than to come again to the front of the park. We've put the North American area first because these are the snakes our tourists are most likely to encounter."

One of the reporters took a cigarette from his mouth and said, "I'm almost fifty, Mr. Miller, and I've done a good deal of hiking, fishing and camping. Yet I've never seen a live snake in the woods. Aren't they becoming pretty rare in the U.S.?"

"Far from it," Miller replied. "Last year over four thousand people were bitten by snakes, and more than thirty died. Three-quarters were rattlesnake victims. We had a reporter visiting from New York a few days ago, who told us that last month a hiker was struck by a rattler in Harriman State Park. Less than forty-five miles from Manhattan Island." Miller paused for a moment while pencils and pens scribbled in notebooks. As the reporters' heads came up, he nodded in the direction of the pit. "In fact, this diorama reminded the gentleman of that incident."

The scene below was a reproduction of a deep-furrowed country road, flanked by small oak trees and evergreens. On one side of the road stood a wooden signpost that read, "Pittsburgh—10 mi." On the other side, the chassis of an ancient Packard lay rusting in magnificent decay. In the shade of the half-open trunk a rattler lay coiled, absolutely motionless but for the flicking of its tongue. The tail of another protruded from the car's left front wheelwell.

Miller said, "Rattlers can and do live very close to

populated areas. Many Americans also share the mistaken notion that rattlesnakes only live in the deserts of the Southwest. They're actually found in every continental state except Maine and Delaware. The Eastern diamondback rattlesnake is the largest and most deadly of snakes within the United States. The longest recorded specimen measured eight feet nine inches, but the average length is about six feet."

"How come the hiker didn't just run when he heard the rattles?" another reporter asked, still interested in the Harriman State Park incident.

"He may have had no warning," Miller answered smoothly. "Rattlesnakes don't always give a warning before striking. However, if they do, it's unmistakable." He withdrew a rattle from his pocket and shook it. "The rattler is the only snake in the world equipped with such a device, although some other snakes, when approached, do whip their tails through the leaves and grasses surrounding them, and this can sound very much like a rattle. Also, it may interest your readers to know that rattles are added with each shedding of skin. But, since rattlers don't shed their skin at uniform intervals throughout their lives, the rattles do not accurately indicate the snake's age. Now, ladies and gentlemen, that concludes the formal tour. I believe most of the facts I covered on the serpentarium are contained in the information packets you were given at the start of the tour. Any more questions?"

"Yes," a young, bespectacled woman said quickly. "I read an article about your immunity to snake bite. Does it have anything to do with your size or your excellent physical condition?" With the tour completed, inevitably the questioning shifted to the owner of the park. Scott Miller seemed almost as fascinating to the reporters as his new venture. The man stood six foot-three inches tall. Even though he dressed in loosely fitting trousers and a long-sleeved shirt, one could tell that he possessed a phenomenally developed physique. The well-defined muscles of his neck were so huge that his head seemed to grow out of his shoulders. He was forty-five, but his energy led most people to believe him a much younger man. His beguiling smile and conspicuous intelligence more than compensated for his lack of good looks. But Miller's most startling features were his eyes. The irises were coal black, so dark one could see one's own reflection in them. But of the personality behind the eyes one could read nothing. Peering into them was like staring into a pair of black voids.

Miller answered the woman's question: "Physical condition and body weight do affect an individual's reactions to venom. However, I've built up my own immunity artificially with a series of desensitizing shots." He rolled up his right sleeve, exposing his thick forearm. It was laced with white scars, some mere dots, other gashes as long as an inch. Farther up his arm, just below the elbow, were two fresh puncture wounds, slightly swollen and surrounded by red-purple discoloration. The reporters murmured with respect.

"However, my immunity is only to the most prevalent group of poisonous snakes in our hemisphere, the Crotalidae. This includes rattlers, copperheads, moccasins, and the South American bushmaster, which is what bit me yesterday." This time the reporters reacted with pronounced interest.

"Didn't you just tell us the bushmaster is the most deadly of all American snakes?"

"I did." Miller flashed his beguiling smile. "Of course, the idea is to avoid getting bitten. Not only is it a painful experience, with or without immunization, but one can develop infections from the bite itself. Unfortunately, it's very difficult to keep the bushmaster alive in captivity. We have some of the only specimens in the United States. Recently we discovered that bushmasters thrive in high altitudes, with lower atmospheric pressure and cooler, damp weather. Because specimens had been captured in lowland, equatorial regions, it was assumed for a long time that this was their preferred habitat. So, to get our bushmasters to feed, we must take them from their pit and put them in a special pressurized chamber every few days. Naturally, they strongly resent being disturbed, and few of my snake handlers want to volunteer to go into the pit, so . . ."

"Did I hear you say you aren't immune to all snake bites?" a voice interrupted.

"That's correct," Miller replied. "There are hundreds of venoms, each with a unique combination of protein poisoning agents. Some attack the nervous system, others the circulatory system."

"I also read that you donate your blood to help snake bite victims recover," said the young woman, removing her glasses. Miller failed to respond. His attention had been diverted to a solitary figure who had separated himself from the group and was striding toward another pit. He wore mirrored sunglasses and carried a Nikon camera, the neck strap wound around his wrist.

"You *are* the one who donates his blood, aren't you, Mr. Miller?" the woman asked. Hearing his name, Miller turned back to the reporters.

"Yes, that's right." He beckoned to a tour guide and said in a low voice, "Get that man back with the group, Marcy. I don't want overcurious people wandering alone through the park." The guide nodded and walked after the man.

"Mr. Miller, just how does a millionaire playboy from Long Island wind up running a snake exhibit in the Deep South?" The blunt question came from a bearded gentleman with a pronounced English accent.

"Well, Mr. Davies, for amusement it certainly beats the backgammon tournament at the Northampton Country Club." Miller kept one eye on the exchange between the guide and the errant reporter. Miller's glib answer pleased many in the group, for it was common knowledge that Kenneth Davies was an incorrigible needler.

"And the actual reason?" the Englishman persisted. Miller continued smiling, but he was no longer in the mood for questions.

"Two pages in your packets are devoted to my biography and the reasons that led me to build the Great Scott Serpentarium. If I may make a suggestion, you probably have all your questions answered right there. But, if you find some things still unanswered, please feel free to call me or Miss Davis." Miller shifted his attention once again to the distant pit. The man had busied himself with snapping pictures. The tour gude was returning with a look of bewildered defeat written plainly across her face.

"Just one more question," the Englishman said. "The pit that man is photographing is empty. When we walked by it before, you made no explanatory comments. I assume it will be filled by opening day, since it is situated directly in front of the main gate.

What will it hold?"

"Nothing, Mr. Davies," Miller replied. "Absolutely nothing. For the moment, it's there to arouse curiosity, as it obviously has in yourself. Eventually, it will be occupied, but for now that occupant is a secret."

"Why?" another asked.

"Well, I see no point in shooting off all the big guns in one salvo. When enough of the public has seen the park and our attendance begins to level, the contents of that pit will bring people back for a second look. Now, I thank you all for coming, and I hope you'll be kind to our new venture when you write about us. We've prepared a lunch for you in the cafeteria. Miss Davis will be there to answer any other questions."

As the tour guides shepherded the group in the direction of the cafeteria, Miller turned toward the empty pit. In doing so, he nearly bowled over one of the reporters, a happy-faced character who had blazoned his lapels with "I love snakes" bottons.

"Wonderful presentation, Scott. Just wonderful!" the man said enthusiastically, thumping Miller on the back.

Miller forced a smile. "Thanks, Ward. I appreciate that."

"I could tell the boys were impressed. Bill Cooper and Carmine Di Donato expecially. And that girl reporter, Linda Whats-her-name, the one with the wire-rim glasses, obviously has the hots for you. She'll give you a great writeup."

Although no one was standing nearby, Miller lowered his voice.

"Listen, Ward. You know just about every reporter here today. Who's the fellow taking the pictures over there?"

Ward shrugged. "Never saw him before. Gotta go,

Scott. Good luck!" He hurried off, still beaming.

Marcy, the guide, had been waiting to report her exchange. As Miller headed for the empty pit, she trotted along, one step behind, like an eager puppy. "He said he wouldn't cause any trouble. He just wanted to take a few more pictures."

"What's his name?"

"I didn't ask."

"O.K., Marcy, Get some lunch." The girl took a few more steps, realized she had been dismissed, and slowed to a halt. Miller continued across the pathway to the empty pit. The man noticed his approach. He lowered his camera and dropped the sunglasses off the crown of his head onto his nose.

"Nice park, Mr. Miller. Beautifully designed."

"Thank you, Mr. . . ."

"Carouthers. *Charlottesville Herald.*"

"You've come a long way for our presentation."

"It was worth it."

Miller instinctively disliked the stranger. He believed that people who wore silvered glasses usually were hiding behind them. "I'm glad you liked it. However, the tour is over, and lunch is being served, Mr. Carouthers."

"So I see. I wanted to get a few pictures of this pit. I notice it's much deeper than the others and also much better protected from the public. That *is* why you have these plexiglass shields up, I assume: to protect the snakes from the kids and not vice versa."

"Exactly. Now, if . . ."

"What's going into it?" Carouthers asked, pushing his sunglasses farther up the bridge of his nose.

"If you'd stayed with the group, you'd have heard."

"Heard what?" Carouthers asked, not in the least chastised.

"It's a secret."

"Judging from the size of this pit, it must be a big one," Carouthers remarked, in an off-handed manner as he fitted the cap over his lens. "Well, I'll be listening for news of your secret." He held out his hand. Miller shook it without feeling. "So long," Carouthers said. He turned smartly on one heel and strolled away, whistling a tune Miller had never heard.

3

THE TELEPHONE jangled three times before Scott Miller entered the study and reached for it, a tumbler of bourbon in the other hand.

"Hello," he said, setting down the drink and switching on the desk light.

"This is Western Union," said a female voice, accenting each first syllable. "I have a cable for Mr. Scott Miller."

"This is he."

"Will you accept the message over the telephone, sir?"

"Yes, I will. Just one moment." He reached for a pad and pencil, then sank into the thickly padded chair behind the desk. The white paper's brilliant reflection made him squint. "O.K., go ahead, operator"

"The message reads: TAIPAN NEARLY SIX METERS ARRIVING SNOWBIRD MAY NINETEEN LONG BEACH CONFIRM. TASAKI. Would you like me to repeat the message?"

"No, thank you. I have it, operator."

"Would you like to wire the confirmation now, sir?"

"Yes," Miller replied. "Just hold on a second, please." Miller set the receiver on the desk and stared at the words he had scribbled on the paper. His mind reeled giddily. Nearly six meters; nineteen feet! The Naraka-pintu taipan was all but within his grasp. He marveled that the culmination of six years' planning and preparations could be successfully distilled to a dozen words on a sheet of paper. His heartbeat quickened, powered by the adrenalin of exultation. His only obstacle lay in smuggling the taipan into the country. Damn that Ensign Hilton! Just when Miller needed him, the man had to pull a one-year assignment in Alaska. Out of spite or frustration, a lesser man than Miller might have exposed Hilton's lucrative black market dealings to the naval authorities. But that was not Miller's operating style. Moreover, Hilton might still be of use to him. Who knew what Miller might someday need by-way-of Alaska? Marcus Wrightson now had to be his man instead, and San Diego the place.

Miller lifted the instrument. "Yes, operator I would like you to use the information on that cable to return a message immediately. The message is to read: NEGATIVE LONG BEACH. CAN SNOWBIRD DIVERT MAY NINETEEN TO BEARING OFF COAST OF SAN DIEGO. REPLY IMMEDIATELY. And sign it MILLER" He repeated the message, but the operator had gotten it the first time. Miller returned the receiver gently to its cradle.

Marcus Wrightson, Miller thought. An inconsequential neurologist working in San Diego. A scientist who wrote to him last month, desperate for a donation of snake venoms so he could continue his research. Desperate was the key word. That was the kind of man who could serve him without question. However, even if Wrightson possessed an especially high moral character, as Miller suspected a research scientist might, he was certain he had the wherewithal to buy off Wrightson's conscience, one way or the other. Now that the taipan was on the way, no problem seemed insurmountable.

Miller came out of his chair like an uncoiled spring. He unlocked a grey, metal map cabinet nearby and flipped through piles of U.S. Topographical Survey maps. He located the quadrant adjoining San Diego on the Pacific side, laid down a ruler, and plotted a distance from the shoreline to a stretch of seabed labeled "La Jolla Canyon." Satisfied, he sat back again and rocked in his chair, staring at the silent telephone, willing it to ring. After an interminable minute his overcharged nervous system pulled him upright and to the windows. The moon had risen high into the night, casting its borrowed light down on the gently lapping waters of the swimming pool. Miller gazed at the swirling, transitory silver glimmers for a few moments, then turned back into the room to pace.

The telephone rang as Miller drained the last of the bourbon from his glass. He snatched up the receiver before the first shrill sound had died.

"Scott Miller."

"Mr. Miller," the now-familiar voice said, "this is Western Union. I have a reply to your cable. It reads: CAN DIVERT. NAME COORDINATES. TASAKI. Would you like to wire an immediate reply?"

"Yes. The reply is: LONGITUDE ONE HUNDRED SEVENTEEN DEGREES THIRTY MINUTES FIFTEEN SECONDS

WEST BY LATITUDE THIRTY-TWO DEGREES FIFTY-SIX
MINUTES TWELVE SECONDS NORTH. PAYMENT WILL BE RE-
LEASED TOMORROW YOUR NAME. Sign it MILLER."

After he hung up, Miller stood motionless by his
chair. Then he rushed to the cabinet and withdrew
another map. The map's accordion pleats widened as
he pulled it through the air until, with a deft flick of
his wrist, it fluttered completely open across the desk.
He ran the nail of his forefinger along the multicolored folds to flatten them. If the taipan were to
arrive in San Diego instead of Long Beach, a new airport must be found. Preferably something in the suburbs of the city, small enough to assure privacy but
large enough to accommodate a four-engine cargo
plane. Miller rubbed the back of his hand absent-
mindedly across his chin, staring at the details of the
map. He found an airport in an excellent location, not
too far out. The Mission Bay Marina was also coin-
cidentally well situated. Marcus Wrightson would
almost certainly have facilities for storing a snake in
his laboratory. As far as Miller was concerned, everything was working out perfectly.

°   °   °

Warren Crowley took one last puff on his cigarette,
then dropped it on the floor in the general direction of
the ashtray. He rolled across the mattress and reached
for a huge stack of magazines piled precariously at the
edge of the night table. He lunged for the top maga-
zine but only succeeded in toppling the entire pile
onto the floor.

"Son-of-a-bitch!" Crowley swore as he tried to
reach the scattered pile without having to reshift his
weight. Just as he was about to string together a line
of choice expletives, Crowley heard a metallic noise

across the room. His tape recorder had automatically engaged itself. For a moment he stared at the plastic reels circling its face at different speeds, catching and reflecting the sparse light in the motel room. Then he rolled off the bed and sauntered over to the dresser where the recorder nestled in the midst of momumental debris. Crowley pushed aside a half-eaten sandwich and a pair of mirror-lensed sunglasses and picked up his earphones. As he fitted them to his ears he heard Scott Miller's unmistakable bass-baritone voice say: "O.K., go ahead, operator."

Crowley pulled his last cigarette from its pack. He searched the cluttered dresser top for a match while he listened to a female voice respond: "The message reads: TAIPAN NEARLY SIX METERS ARRIVING SNOWBIRD MAY NINETEEN LONG BEACH. CONFIRM. TASAKI."

Crowley put the cigarette down and forgot about the match. He listened to the rest of the conversation with rapt attention, propped against the dresser like a department store mannequin. Even when Miller paused to collect his thoughts, Crowley remained motionless, scarcely breathing. When the recorder clicked off, Crowley came to life like a boxer responding to the first round bell, dashing across the room to the telephone. A minute later, another phone rang in Atlanta, Georgia. Crowley shifted his weight, listening impatiently to the uniformly spaced buzzes.

"Come on, Thanner, goddammit," he muttered. Finally the phone was lifted on the other end.

"Yes," said a voice.

"It's me, Crowley. You were right, Mr. Thanner. The pit *is* for a taipan. It's about six meters long. I just intercepted a cable to Miller from someone called Tasaki."

"Is the snake in the country?"

"No. Must have been an overseas message. It's supposed to arrive at Long Beach on May nineteenth. On something called the *Snowbird*. A boat, I guess. But Miller wants the *Snowbird* diverted to a location off the coast of San Diego. Same date."

"Nice work, Crowley," Thanner said. "Stay there and keep monitoring Miller's private line. I'll check out the *Snowbird* tomorrow."

"Miller's waiting right now for a reply to see if *Snowbird* can be diverted."

"If Scott Miller wants something diverted, it will be diverted," Thanner stated matter-of-factly.

"Do you want to hang on and wait for Miller's reply?"

"No. Call me tomorrow morning with a report on the whole night's calls. Same as usual."

"Right. And do you still want blowups of those shots I took at Miller's park?"

"Certainly. If it proves impossible to steal the taipan in San Diego, you may have to steal it from under Miller's nose."

"Makes no difference to me, Mr. Thanner."

"For what I'm paying you, it shouldn't. Look, Crowley, gears are starting to mesh now, so stay by your wiretap and don't take any more short vacations, huh?"

"I won't, Mr. Thanner. Good night."

Crowley hung up and retrieved his cigarette. He found a new matchbook, lit the cigarette, and drew in a lungful of smoke. "Don't take any short vacations!" Hey, fuck you, Thanner, Crowley thought. He'd been cooped up in this stinking motel room for five weeks, and once, just once, in all that time had he taken off for three days to do some drinking, gambling, and whoring in Miami Beach. And Thanner wouldn't let him forget it. It really got to Crowley when a client implied that he wasn't thoroughly professional about his work. If you call this work, he thought bitterly. Christ, you've fallen on hard times when you're reduced to snakenapping. Six meters. Let's see. A meter's about forty inches. Six times forty, two hundred-forty inches. "Holy Jesus!" he said aloud. "I'm about to steal a twenty-foot snake!" The cigarette hung loosely from Crowley's slack lips. An involuntary shudder ran down his spine. The tape recorder clicked back on.

4

LILLA SUE DAVIS picked up her purse and moved toward the airline information booth, her taut, rounded hips describing erotic sine waves through the terminal waiting lounge. One passenger had left the deplaning throng and was walking uncertainly toward the booth. Marcus Wrightson? The man's bewildered look was her first clue.

Lila Sue slowed her pace to study the man's appearance. She judged him to be about thirty, and roughly six feet tall. His build was lank but wiry. He had a healthy head of blond hair and honest blue eyes. Their wide-open, perplexed look lent an innocent appearance, contrasting pleasingly with his high cheekbones and the strong angularity of his jawline. She noted that he carried a summer-weight jacket over one arm, and wore a light-blue shirt, serviceable for both casual and formal wear, well-tailored black trousers and black loafers. His left hand, bearing no wedding ring, clutched a thin attache case. She read his overall look as professional but not businesslike.

Definitely the waiting lounge's leading candidate for college professor and medical researcher.

"Hi," she heard her candidate say brightly to the information booth agent. "I'm Marcus Wrightson. I heard a public address call for me."

The agent smiled and nodded over Wrightson's shoulder toward Lilla Sue. She stepped forward, her hand extended. "Yes. I asked them to page you, Dr. Wrightson. Welcome to Florida. I'm Lilla Sue Davis, from the Great Scott Serpentarium. I've been waiting to drive you there."

Wrightson stared at her, bewildered. He hesitated before confessing, "I had no idea someone would be picking me up. How—how did you know which flight I'd be taking?"

"Oh, it's no great mystery." She steered him out of the lounge's traffic pattern. "Today, through the wonders of modern computer technology, you can find out who's aboard any flight in the U.S. I just checked with the commercial carriers that fly direct from San Diego until I found your booking. In your letter, you did say you intended to be here on opening day. That clued me you'd be on a flight last night or this morning. So, *voilá*, here I am to fetch you!"

"I'm impressed," Wrightson admitted. "And grateful, Miss Davis."

"Lilla Sue is fine." The man was genuinely handsome.

"I'm not used to this kind of treatment, Lilla Sue. I expected to rent a car and just mingle with the crowds until I could figure how to meet Mr. Miller."

"It's all been taken care of by yours truly. I'm the park's PR agent, official greeter, chauffeur, and whatever else is needed at the moment." Her smile fetched a pair of appealing dimples. "Let's pick up your luggage and be on our way."

As they waited at the baggage carousel, she asked him how his flight had been. "Tiring," Wrightson replied. "I hate night flights. I never get a wink of sleep. But what else could I do? I had a three o'clock class yesterday and finals are coming up. But never fear; I'm resilient. I'll roar through the day like a cyclone and probably conk out before the sun hits the yardarm."

"Oh, you can't do that," she said seriously. "You've been invited to the opening night party, which begins at nine."

"And me without my dancing shoes!" Wrightson exclaimed. "All kidding aside, this is really a shock. Talk about red carpet treatment. Are you sure Mr. Miller doesn't have me confused with Frank Lloyd Wrightson?" They both laughed at the joke.

Lilla Sue was delighted to find a sense of humor in the well-favored visitor." You must be one hell of a letter writer, Dr. Wrightson."

"Marc is fine." His blue eyes lit up. "Amazing! Here comes my suitcase."

Lilla Sue watched the suitcases dropping one after the other down the chute. She shook her head skeptically. "Don't you believe it. They're probably left over from last Tuesday's flight."

As they walked through the automatic doors toward the parking lot, Wrightson turned to Lilla Sue and said, "If the park is half as beautiful as its PR agent, Mr. Miller is sure to have a success on his hands. I know you must hear this ten times a day, but you could be a model." His guileless compliment pleased her, be she dismissed it with a snort of contempt.

"I was a model in New York City for five years. Or at least that's what I kept telling them down at the unemployment office."

"Not an easy life, huh?"

"Not for a girl who loathes perpetual starvation diets. Or who dislikes coping with clients' ad reps who expect to be slept with for a lousy two-hundred-and-fifty-dollar modeling job. Do you know what a cattle call is, Marc?"

"No."

"You're lucky. So I stopped torturing my ego and found this nifty job."

"How does one hop from modeling to public relations?" Wrightson wanted to know.

Lilla Sue shrugged. "By hopping into the right bed with the right guy."

Wrightson had been putting down his bags to rest his arms. He paused a moment, not sure he'd heard the woman correctly, then looked up. She looked back at him wih eyebrows raised but otherwise quite composed. "Lilla Sue," Wrightson marveled, "you are one up-front lady!"

"Yeah," she agreed. "That I am. They don't make 'em more up-front than me. Need help with your bags?"

"No."

"Great. Hey, don't go into shock, Marc. I was dating a nice guy, off and on. He worked for a big public relations firm. He taught me everything he knew and vice versa."

Wrightson made a small bow in respect to her candor and picked up his suitcases. Lilla Sue found herself rather pleased by his Victorian reaction. She stopped in front of a Mercedes-Benz.

"Everything first class at the Great Scott Serpentarium." Her voice took on a sharp, clearly disparaging edge. "I talked Mr. Miller into getting this bauble

for our taxi. I figured we needed some class to coun-
teract our park's very commercial and very unchic
name." After they stashed the luggage in the
Mercedes trunk she climbed behind the wheel and
started the engine. Leaning toward Wrightson, she
confided, "Don't tell the boss, but personally, I hate
snakes. They make my skin crawl."

"To tell the truth, I'm not overly fond of snakes
myself," Wrightson admitted.

Lilla Sue looked at him in happy surprise. "No kidding! So, why do research on them?"

"Well, I really don't have that much to do with the
snakes, actually. In fact, I have a work-study student
who does my milking for me. My interest is in their
venoms and how they relate to neurological diseases."

"I'm afraid I really don't know anything about
what you do, Marc," she said.

While she paid the parking fee and maneuvered
the Mercedes into the heavy weekend traffic, he
said, "There's not that much to tell. My father was
a medical doctor; my mother was involved in poli-
tics on the community level. They both provided
me with role models. By the time I got into college
I knew I wanted to pursue a career in service to
mankind. I've always been interested in the sci-
ences so it was natural that I got into teaching and
research. I teach part time at the University of California at San Diego. The rest of the time I do research at the university and a local hospital. The
research is funded by the federal government."

"And you say your research is neurological?" asked
Lilla Sue.

"Right. I'm studying the effects of toxic substances
on human nervous disorders and diseases. You may

know that many plants and animals, apart from snakes, have developed poisonous chemicals, either as a way of catching food or in self-defense. We've found that some of these poisons can actually be beneficial to man. Take, for example, a poisonous toad found in Asia. Thouands of years ago, somebody discovered that the poison from its skin glands could treat sores and toothaches. Scientists have since found that those curing agents are steroid hormones. As a local anesthetic, it can be ninety times as effective as cocaine. One of its hormones also seems to inhibit certain forms of cancer. And yet, it's a poison to enemies of the toad.

In the same manner, toxins of certain animals, especially snakes, inhibit the degenerative processes of certain human nervous diseases. For example, amyotrophic lateral sclerosis . . ." Wrightson's voice trailed off. "Hey, I'm sorry. I can't seem to get the chalk out of my veins. I've reverted to a professor."

"In broad daylight, too," Lilla Sue commented, a gleam in her eye. "My God, you should have a slide rule driven through your heart!" They both laughed. "Really, I'd like to hear more. You don't know how pleased I am to learn that snakes can serve a useful purpose."

"Where was I? Oh, yes—amyotrophic lateral sclerosis. Maybe you've heard it called Lou Gehrig's disease. It was named after the famous baseball player who died from it. It paralyzes the motor nerves in the spinal cord and brain so that you gradually lose control of your muscles. In two to six years, death is inevitable."

"And you want Scott Miller to donate venoms for this research."

"Exactly. He may be my only hope for keeping the

research alive. I'm mapping the proteins and enzymes within certain powerful venoms, tracing their effect on the chemical processes within the nerves themselves. And I think I'm very close to some big answers. My main problem is that my research substances come from rare snakes. Even common krait venom costs about six thousand an ounce."

Lilla Sue nodded. "That much I know."

"And we can use up an ounce in twelve days. Something like the venom of the King cobra is beyond our budget altogether, especially since the government may be cutting back its funding for neurological research this year in favor of cancer."

Lilla Sue looked in the rearview mirror and checked her professional makeup job. She was well aware of her growing attraction to this man. Despite the abundant animal magnetism Wrightson radiated, he wasn't the macho woman-killer type. That was fine with her. In fact, her sexual image of Marcus Wrightson was the reverse, more like the sheep in wolf's clothing. He didn't seem to think of his good looks as a privileged lever for prying off women's pants. He appeared quite easy about relating to her as one human being to another. By the time Lilla Sue was nineteen, she had been subject to every permutation of every devious come-on ever fabricated by the male psyche. The only approach that aroused her now was the non-approach, in short, a situation in which she could play the aggressor. To be perfectly certain that his charm wasn't a conscious ploy, she said, "I don't mean to interrupt, but, speaking of King cobras, Mr. Miller will be presenting one in the auditorium at ten o'clock. It's the park's first live demonstration." She gave him her best dimpled smile. "Now, we can either settle you in at your motel or drive right to the park and catch the show. You're the honored guest, so the decision is yours."

Wrightson glanced at his watch. "Well, as long as we can make it, Lilla Sue, I'd really like to see the first show." Lilla Sue smiled to herself. The chase was on.

Once out of Orlando and heading west, it wasn't difficult to find the way to the Great Scott Serpentarium. Every five miles or so, Wrightson noted a giant serpent looming out of a marsh or from a clump of cypress, its two-dimensional fangs and coils pasted onto the warped surface of a roadside billboard. Next to the coiled snake was emblazoned the name of the park and the direction "Straight Ahead."

Arriving at the park's entrance gate, Wrightson noted: "The parking lot's only about one-third filled. Seems like a small crowd for opening day, especially with this beautiful late-spring weather."

Lilla Sue assured hm: "By noon the place will be mobbed. It's too early for the average sightseer."

"Sure," Wrightson granted. "Even a snake needs a couple of hours in the morning sun to get its blood circulating." While Lilla Sue parked, Wrightson checked out his surroundings. The park was huge and Miller would need a great many customers to pay off his investment. Palm trees of various heights and shaps graced the entrance. On the edges of the two buildings flanking the main gate, high chain-link fences curved gently out of sight, inscribing an enormous circle. Through the fence, Wrightson could see the multicolored crowds of visitors, moving in slow, counterclockwise waves, led by uniformed tour guides. High overhead floated giant green balloons in bloated, sperpentine shapes. Red, forked tongues hung off the top ends. Black eyes had been stamped onto the rubber, as had the legend, GREAT SCOTT SERPENTARIUM. Multicolor bunting and streamers festooned the lampposts.

Wrightson was reminded of his VIP status as Lilla Sue whisked him past the lines at the main ticket office. His companion picked up a map of the park and shoved it into his hand. "For later," she said, as she linked her arm with his and led him straight ahead toward a large, white-domed structure. Wrightson checked his map. The building was labeled "Rotarium."

"Is this the auditorium?" he asked, trying to glance into the pits as they hurrid along.

"Right. And we made it here with four minutes to spare!" Lilla Sue said as they passed under the concrete eaves. "I want to make sure they're still holding two seats for us down front. You wait here." She disappeared through a door marked "AUTHORIZED PERSONNEL ONLY."

Alone, Wrightson looked curiously at the pits that lay across the path from the building. The wall separating the pits from the visitors was continuous, of poured concrete, and about thirty inches high. Two feet of inwardly-curving plexiglass atop the wall served as a second protective barrier. Wrightson stood too far away to see down into the pits, but some of the taller vegetation was visible, backed by another wall with counterweighted ladders poised at its top.

"O.K. We're all set," Lilla Sue said, slipping her hand into his. Wrightson was surprised by her boldness, but not displeased. They entered the Rotarium and mingled with the crowds outside the doors to the arena. The walls were enlivened with large illustrator's cartoons, depicting the more fanciful snake myths and legends. Without approaching the written explanations beneath each panel, he recognized a number of superstitions: that a snake can roll like a hoop by taking its tail in its mouth; that a snake will drink milk from a cow's udder; or that a snake will swallow its young to protect them.

Two sets of doors on opposite sides of the waiting chamber opened. The crowds pressed forward. Wrightson and Lilla Sue allowed themselves to be swept along. As they edged their way up the entrance ramp into the arena, Wrightson was able to comprehend the total architectural concept of the Rotarium. From the outside it resembled a gigantic igloo, a perfect, white concrete hemisphere. In its absolute simplicity it was at once ancient and modern—in a word, timeless. The waiting area as well bespoke functional simplicity. Beyond this lay the arena, the innermost circle in the park's multi-concentric design. A curving glass wall, ten feet high, divided the arena in two. The spectator's side wrapped itself around the stage in a large semicircle, rows of seats climbing backward to the outer wall at a steep rake. Wrightson counted the capacity. Ten rows. Thirty seats in each row. Across the glass divider, the arena took on the aspect of a hospital operating room—white floor, white walls, white doors. The arena floor lay lowest where it touched against the concave glass wall. From there it pitched upward on a shallow, even incline toward a small central hub. This highest point in the arena was a circle no wider than eight feet in diameter, its rear arc just touching the wall farthest from the spectators. In the center of the circle, rising like a flat-topped mushroom, stood a white table. A lone beaker sat on its glassy surface. The surface of the floor, as well, appeared glassy. Probably one of those superhard, supersmooth acrylics, Wrightson guessed as Lilla Sue led him into the front row, stepping over the outstretched legs of two extremely relaxed gentlemen, apparently reporters. One had already set a pad on his lap and was scribbling indecipherable notes.

As Wrightson took his seat adjacent to one of the men, he overheard the scribbler say, "No, no. Di Donato's already written a two-pager for tomorrow's weekend section, and he's covered all the shit about the snakes. Miller's my story. You know, what kind of showman he is—that sort of angle." The reporters had aroused Wrightson's curiosity. He leaned toward Lilla Sue. "Tell me about Miller."

"He doesn't have much to do with the staff on a personal level. Basically, I can only tell you what he reveals publicly."

"Go ahead. I'm interested."

"He's a multi-millionaire. Inherited, not self-made. Born on Long Island; grew up there. Got his undergraduate degree at Princeton. His MBA at Harvard. For years he led a playboy existence and took little interest in managing his fortune. Two brief engagements, no marriages. That info's not on the bio sheet. He's not saying why he's built this place other than the stuff you read in the article that got you interested: as a tourist attraction and for selling snake venoms. I do know that he became interested in snakes from a trip to Malaysia. Claude Marengasau, some big-deal snake hunter, taught him to hunt and capture snakes. You'll see Claude's daughter in the arena with Mr. Miller. She's his main assistant and also his constant companion."

"You mean his mistress?" Wrightson asked.

"Nobody knows. It's a strange relationship. She seems more like a daughter than a mistress, and yet he's never seen in the company of other women. Anything's possible. Ask me the same question in a month. I'll bet I have the answer."

"I'll bet you will, too. But what I need are some clues to Miller's personality. You must know something about him first hand."

"You mean, how can you play on his personality to get that donation out of him?"

"Smart girl."

"Just be yourself. He likes honest, intelligent people. And he's said to be quite generous. You'll have to play the rest by ear."

As Lilla Sue finished her last sentence, an exotic oriental melody floated from hidden speakers. An oboe's hollow, plaintive timbre conjured up cliché images of Hindu snake charmers. Wrightson looked around to gauge the audience's reaction. The music had quieted them considerably, but he could sense their expectation mounting. Their desires to be entertained were now definitely palpable. The arena remained empty another minute. Then, as the tension peaked, the music diminished and a male voice filled the auditorium.

"Ladies and gentlemen, the renowned adventurer, explorer, and writer; the creator and director of the Great Scott Serpentarium: Mr. Scott Miller."

Wrightson listened to the audience's resounding applause. One of the doors of the arena swung open. The man stepped out of the darkness beyond into the light. The applause continued, but it tapered off more quickly than Wrightson would have expected. Then, looking carefully at the individual, he sensed the reason. Scott Miller was awesome—more a presence than a man. Wrightson glanced over at the reporter's notes, curious to know what adjectives might capture this Miller's essence. "Commanding?" "Hypnotic?" Definitely "Powerful." His imposing figure was dressed in white shoes, white slacks, and a white cotton long-sleeve shirt. His sleeves were rolled back, exposing a phenomenally developed pattern of muscles traced with a system of dilated veins. Somehow Wrightson knew that, beneath his clothing as well, Miller possessed a superb masculine physique. The image that flashed through his mind was that of the central figure in the Greek Laocoön Group sculpture.

"Welcome and good morning," Miller said, pivoting to address the entire crowd. "I hope you've enjoyed viewing our snakes at a distance in the outdoor pits. Now it's time to see one up close." Without forcing and apparently without amplification, Miller's resonant bass-baritone voice was clearly audible. "This particular creature will require careful handling, so I'll be assisted this morning by Miss Ioka Marengasau."

A young Eurasian woman stepped into the arena, holding a capture pole. She was extraordinarily beautiful, and Wrightson was captivated at first glance. Regretfully, he shifted his gaze to a second assistant, a burly, uniformed man who entered through a second door, hefting a hamper-sized wicker basket. As he set down his burden, the haunting sounds of the oboe drifted once more through the auditorium. The uniformed assistant flipped the basket's cover off with a quick motion and then backed cautiously out of the arena, pullng the door shut as he withdrew.

All eyes focused on the basket. A massive reptilian head emerged from the open top, gradually clearing the edges by almost three feet. The audience gasped. The basket stood almost three feet high, and the snake inside, only partially visible, had already lifted itself to the level of a grown man's eyes. Tongue flickering, it dropped its neck and curled down the outside of the basket toward the gleaming white floor.

"This is the King cobra, reputed to be the largest venomous snake in the world," Miller said with calm understatement. "It can be extremely aggressive. Some herpetologists give it its own separate classification, *Ophiophagus*, because it feeds entirely on other snakes. It has been known to eat smaller members of its own species."

The snake had all this time been curling out of the basket, crisscross bands of black seeming to slide along a stationary undersurface of yellowish brown. And yet, unbelievably, its tail had not yet appeared. Its rapidly emerging length was further accentuated by its relative thinness, the body never thicker than three inches in diameter.

Miller stepped back to the far wall to allow the audience to concentrate on the snake. "The King cobra, or hamadryad, is found in India, southern China, and throughout Southeast Asia, and the Philippines. It is an excellent swimmer and climber." At last the tail dropped out of the basket and flopped to the floor. "This specimen is nine years old and measures just an inch shy of fifteen feet."

The cobra's gliding undulations carried it closer and closer to the agitated audience, until its head banged lightly into the glass wall. Surprised, it reared back on its powerful neck, its impressive hood spreading wide, displaying an orange-tinted throat and neck. Hissing fiercely at the glass, it swayed back and forth on its pale belly. A woman in the front row screamed. Most of the audience laughed, less from derision than from a need to release their own pent-up nervous tension.

The snake swayed not three feet from Wrightson.

But for the glass wall the reporter next to him could have reached out and touched it. Wide-eyed, the reporter turned to his companion.

"They're fucking crazy! The pair of them!" he declared with pat conviction.

Wrightson turned in Lilla Sue's direction to hide his smile. "I wonder," he whispered, "how many people here can appreciate how cleverly this arena is designed. That cobra is literally fighting an uphill battle." The floor's incline and its slippery surface worked with gravity to pull the snake constantly toward the crowd. To approach the handlers, it had to put forth a determined and prolonged effort. Neither was the snake able to pick up telltale vibrations through the solid concrete. Moreover, the all-white room had to be extremely disorienting to the creature, offering it no points of reference. Other than the few inches of tanned flesh that Miller and the woman had chosen to expose, the snake was the only dark object in the arena. Wrightson also noted that the air in the arena was cool. If they had exposed the cold-blooded creature to a lower temperature prior to the demonstration, all of its bodily functions, including its conscious actions would be proportionately slowed. Finally, Wrightson was certain that Miller had King cobra antivenin on hand in the next room, just in case something went wrong. Still, aware of all these advantages and precautions, Wrightson reflected that there was no way they could get him in there with a monster like that.

The snake was poised motionless, allowing Wrightson to return his attention to Miller's beautiful assistant. She was in her early twenties, he guessed, and wore a white silk cheongsam, exposing a slender neck and deep cleavage. Two long lateral slits in the

shift revealed expanses of flawless thigh. The shift
hung straight from her ample bosom, which betrayed
her European heritage, as did her long, thin nose and
rounded eyelids. Her oriental stock showed in her delicate bone structure, fawn-colored skin and lustrous,
straight shoulder-length black hair, as well as in the
controlled grace of her bearing. Wrightson stole a
glance at Lilla Sue for comparison. Both women were
quite beautiful, but Wrightson knew that much of
Lilla Sue's beauty was artifice, a calculated blend of
makeup, dyes, diets, speech and movement lessons,
and big city savvy. In contrast, the Eurasian girl-wom-
an was completely natural in her beauty. Wrightson
suspected the fundamental difference was that elusive
quality known as vulnerability. Looking at Miller's assistant he experienced a much more direct appeal, a
sensation he had never remembered feeling.

Both Miller and his assistant wore special shoes
with rubber crepe soles. She handed Miller the capture pole as he rolled down his sleeves. The music
stopped. The cobra had left its back unguarded long
enough. It twisted and faced the center of the arena,
hood still spared.

The woman moved first, stepping sideways down
the incline to the snake's left. As she did, she began to
croon to the snake in throaty, sing-song syllables. The
slit in her cheongsam widened, exposing her leg up to
within a few inches of her hip. The snake's eyes
fastened on the dark, elongated triangle, poised in the
alert, hypnotic attitude legendary to the cobra. The
woman pursed her lips and made coaxing sounds as
she rotated her leading leg slowly. The snake moved
forward, head high, opened its fearsome mouth and
hissed, baring a double row of glistening white fangs.

Miller closed in from the opposite side, angling

around to the snake's back. He pushed out the capture pole, bracing it with his left hand. His right hand curled lightly around the pole's pistol grip and trigger mechanism.

The cobra spotted the movement instantly and twisted around in Miller's direction. It slithered forward, tracing an endless series of esses on the floor. It was definitely bothered by the slippery surface. Its tail searched out a rough place where it might grab for purchase, but there was none. Frustrated, the snake dropped its lower jaw, drew up its head and lunged at the pole in a lightning-quick feint. Miller withdrew a bit. So did the snake. The woman used the moment to move closer, almost within striking distance. She continued to draw the snake's attention with steady movements and her strange sing-song. Wrightson smiled wryly. He knew the sounds meant nothing. The cobra, like all other snakes, was stone deaf. But silence did not create an exotic impression. Milk the spectators before you milk the snake, he thought.

The cobra's head swung down and up in a great shape as it consolidated its length into a tightly coiled mass. In another moment it would launch out at the woman with all the concentrated energy of its massive masculature. It tensed.

Miller's capture pole shot forward. The rubber-covered tongs encircled the snake's neck, then clamped in tight. The woman rushed to Miller's side, grabbing the pole with both hands, while first one, then both his mighty arms took hold of the snake's neck, just behind the head. She released the pole. Immediately, the enraged snake began to lash its body in Miller's direction, fighting to entwine itself around his legs and then, securing its purchase, to wrench its head free. Bending quickly, the woman grabbed the cobra's

tail in both hands. She slowly walked away from
Miller until the snake's near-fifteen feet stretched
across the arena, waist-high above the floor.

The audience, delighted and relieved, responded
with thundering applause. Miller raised his arms
above his head and triumphantly offered the
monster's gaping jaws to their view. A number of pho-
tographers caught the moment, the press with their
Hasselblads and Nikons, the tourists with their pocket
Instamatics. Wrightson studied the reporters. Their
eyes glistened with excitement. Miller had caught
their fancy. When their reports hit the newsstands,
the Great Scott Serpentarium would have all the visitors he could handle.

The snake continued to writhe, helplessly sus-
pended in the air, as its handlers worked their way up
to the milking table. Miller lowered the fearsome
head flatly to the beaker and pressed skillfully on the
juncture between the snake's neck and head. He
looked out at the audience through black, un-
fathomable pupils and waited for them to become
quiet. An involuntary shudder coursed along
Wrightson's spine. He saw in Miller's face the unblinking, impassive stare of the King cobra. The audience fell silent. Miller turned his attention to the
snake.

"By pressing behind the neck and depressing the
upper part of the head, the cobra's venom is squeezed
out of the glands that produce it. The membrane you
see stretched across the beaker prevents contamina-
tion of the venom by the air and by the snake's
saliva." A viscous white liquid oozed down the side
of the beaker, partially obscured by the snake's lower
jaw. "You can see from the color and thickness of the
fluid why we call this process 'milking.' "

Wrightson's attention kept slipping away from Miller's lecture. He found it impossible to stop his eyes from drifting to the other end of the cobra, where the young woman stood with patient poise. More kudos for Miller as the showman, Wrightson reflected; he'd skillfully made use of the classic beauty and the beast relationship. At least the ploy was working on *him*. Suddenly, the crowd was beating their palms together once again. Wrightson had daydreamed through the entire milking.

Miller and his assistant carried the subdued serpent to the wicker basket, dropped it in, and clapped the lid down tightly. While the burly attendant removed the basket, Miller approached the audience, standing halfway down the glaze-bright floor.

"I hope you like our demonstration. Please enjoy the rest of the park, and tell your friends to come visit us. Thank you." He raised his hands to signal that he had finished and bowed slightly to cap off the performance. The audience responded one last time as exotic orchestral music filled the auditorium. Miller led his assistant forward to accept her applause, and together they backed out of the open door, leaving the stage once more a barren whiteness.

"So that's Scott Miller," Wrightson said, watching the crowd mill out.

"The one and only," Lilla Sue replied. They stood and waited for the row to empty.

"When do I get to meet him?"

"He must have some time penciled in for you, but I'm positive it's not before the party. I tell you what: I'll take you to the park entrance. While I'm doing some other work, you join one of the tours and pretend you're just another visitor. At twelve-thirty I have my lunch break. I'll meet you in front of the cafeteria. We can have something to eat, then I'll drop you off at your motel."

"Sounds great."

Lilla Sue smiled. "I'm sorry to have to ignore you, but it *is* opening day. I promise that tonight you'll get the attention you deserve." Before he could respond, she was guiding him out of the arena and toward the bright daylight.

5

"HEY! DID you die in there? Marc?"

"O.K. I'm coming," Wrightson called at the motel room door, as he stepped groggily into his pants. The door rattled on its hinges, reacting to a forceful battering. "I'm coming," he repeated in a louder voice, not sure his voice was carrying over the resounding blows. He zipped up his fly and unlocked the door. Lilla Sue Davis stood in the hall, wearing a white evening dress that did full justice to her slim figure and her bronze tan. Her golden hair swept backward and up, defying gravity in a triumph of hairstyle engineering. She looked rather unhappy.

"You're quite a sound sleeper, aren't you?" she said, brushing past him into the room.

Wrightson dug the sleep out of one eye. "Yeah. I am. I'm sorry, but I really needed a nap. I must have forgotten to wind my clock. You look really nice."

Lilla Sue sat down on a corner of the bed. "Thanks. You look like hell. The party starts in two minutes, and I have *got* to be there. How soon can you get your act together?"

51

Wrightson stifled a yawn. "Ten minutes. If you help. While I'm showering, could you lay out the suit hanging in the closet? You'll find a shirt, tie, and socks to go with it in the suitcase." Wrightson ducked into the bathroom, stripped and climbed into the shower. The water shot out of the nozzle in fine needles, massaging life back into his muscles. He felt wonderful after his nap. As he lathered up, he reviewed his arguments once more, this time with the knowledge he had gained in the Rotarium. Suddenly, the stream of water stopped beating against his shoulders. He pivoted to face the fixtures and caught sight of a delicate hand tugging at the shower curtain. It swished back. Lilla Sue stood just outside the tub with a bath towel in her other hand. While Wrightson gaped in stunned surprise she took a swift visual excursion of his undraped body, beginning at his bewildered blue eyes, following the glistening trails of water along the muscles of his neck, down his matted chest and along the confluence of hair that bisected his taut stomach, vaulting over his deepset navel and running directly into his suddenly tumescent groin. As her gaze lingered on his burnished gold pubic hairs and the moisture-bejeweled flesh distending beneath them, her pert Madison Avenue smile broadened into a randy Cheshire Cat grin. Her impudent eyes rolled back up to meet his, and, as they did, she drew her lower lip into her mouth behind her dazzlingly white incisors, moistening it tantalizingly with the tip of her tongue.

"You asked me to help," she said. "You're running two minutes behind schedule. I'd dry your back, but you've turned this place into a steambath. It's killing my hair."

Wrightson tried to speak but for a moment couldn't find his voice. "I'll hurry," he managed at last, wrapping the towel around his middle. He could feel the heat of his blood suffusing the surface of his skin.

"You must be quite athletic," she observed.

"I, uh, run," he said.

"That's a nice body. I'll bet you're a health food nut, too," she remarked as she turned for the door. "You can take a nice leisurely shower after the party," she said over her shoulder. "I might even join you." She was gone before he could reply, so Wrightson said nothing, grabbed another towel and began to dry his hair.

*   *   *

As Lilla Sue steered the Mercedes into the Great Scott parking lot, Wrightson checked his watch in the pale yellow moonlight. They were about thirty minutes late. Then, seeing two other cars following in behind, he felt a little better.

The park looked different by moonlight. Day's hard, brilliant colors had been replaced by the soft interblendings of light and shadow, except around the cafeteria, where glowing reds and oranges spilled out of the rectangular windows, staining the night. Above the curving fences which defined the park, like jewels set high in a crown, multibulbed light poles cast down pools of purple-whiteness. Above it all, bathed in cool white, the dome of the Rotarium rose above the walls and the other buildings, completing the image of the crown.

They hastened through the gates. Once again, in Lilla Sue's care, no invitation was required. The party was in full swing. Tables had been pushed from the center of the room and up against a far wall. At one end a band played a current ballad. Dancers crowded the floor, pressing their bodies close to their partners.

Spiraling patterns of hot colors swept slowly across their swaying shapes. While Wrightson waited for a gin and tonic, he saw Miller engaged in an animated conversation with a wisp of a woman. The woman's white gloves waved through the air like a pair of fluttering doves, punctuating her words. He searched the room for the Eurasian beauty. She was nowhere to be seen.

"Time to get you and the boss together," Lilla Sue said, taking Wrightson by the hand and dodging the couples who whirled across the open floor. When they reached Miller, the man next to him was saying, ". . . At a masquerade ball / Dressed in nothing at all / To back in as a Parker House roll!" Miller laughed, deep and resonant. Lilla Sue tapped the big man on the shoulder and said, "Scott Miller, I'd like you to meet Marcus Wrightson." Miller held out his hand.

"Good evening, Dr. Wrightson." Reflections of the overhead lights danced on the surfaces of his glistening, black pupils.

"Good evening, Mr. Miller. Thanks for inviting me to the party. And thanks also for Miss Davis. She's been taking excellent care of me."

Lilla Sue said, "Well, the excellent Miss Davis has to take care of some other people, so I'll bow out for a while." Wrightson was about to lavish more praise on the PR agent, but the man next to Miller said, "Listen, Scott. I have to get back to the little woman, but we really must talk about that export deal soon. Another week'll be too late.

"First thing next week, Harry. I promise."

The man's face lit up. "Great! Just great. I know how busy you've been lately. We're gonna dance some, then head home. Church is early, y'know." Harry, the good Christian, nodded amiably a few more times as he backed away. Miller turned to Wrightson.

"I'm so glad you could get away from your research, Dr. Wrightson."

"Please, call me Marc. Dr. Wrightson was my father, and I can't get used to the title."

"And I like to be called Scott, although for some reason most people insist on calling me 'Mr. Miller.' Why don't you put down that glass of, what is it, gin and tonic, and come on back into the kitchen where I've got the good stuff." Wrightson followed his imposing host. If Miller had shown up at scrimmage, the Rams' front office would have had him playing offensive tackle the next Sunday. They passed through a swinging door to a table cluttered with liquor bottles.

"'Nother gin and tonic?" Miller suggested.

"Please."

While he fixed the drink, Miller asked, "How do you like the park?"

Wrightson leaned against a counter. "I'm very impressed. Not only by the design and execution of the park, but also by the fantastic collection of snakes you've assembled. The only question that ran through my mind this morning was: 'Why no crocodiles or alligators? Why no crowd-pleasers such as the dragon of Komodo or other lizards?' "

Miller handed Wrightson the drink, then began one for himself. "The snake is my only interest. I feel that the introduction of other reptiles would detract from a group of creatures that deserve their own special attention. After all, many cultures have worshipped the snake since the dawn of civilization."

"Granted," Wrightson readily acceded, "but why do you display only deadly snakes and exclude the interesting, nonpoisonous varieties?"

Miller laughed. "Because, to the average man all snakes are deadly anyway, and that's why they come: to stand within arm's length of Death. After all, Death is man's ultimate fear, his constant obsession."

"Not mine," Wrightson countered brightly, swirling the cubes in his drink. "I'm too involved in living to give death more than a fleeting thought."

"Good for you!" his host shot back, the energy of his reply keeping his words from sounding too patronizing. "Your research, in fact, is geared precisely to the saving of lives, which is another way to say the cheating of Death. But it's all semantics anyway, isn't it?" He raised his glass. "To your research!"

"To your park!" Wrightson responded. They clinked glasses and drank, eyeing one another.

"So you need venom," Miller said as he lowered his glass, coming right to the point. Wrightson left his glass at his lips so that he only needed to reply with a nod of his head. No use sounding desperate, even if he was. "Well, Marc, as I explained in my reply to your letter, we're not a large snake-milking farm."

"I know. But you see, I'm not interested in poisonous American snakes. My research has centered on more exotic, Australian and Asian snakes. We've been getting kraits, for example, through a woman in Hong Kong who buys them from various snake hunters. Of course, each krait's secretion is very low, so we need a large number, and that's where all our money's been going. At least the krait isn't rare; we get them through China, where at present we don't have importation problems. Researching the properties of the rare, powerful venoms is straining our budget. For example, you have four Australian Tiger snakes in your collection. As you know, since the 1975 and 1977 importation restrictions on foreign animals, we haven't been allowed to bring the snakes in. And the Australian farms want an arm and a leg for their venom."

"Ah, yes," Miller sighed. "The laws of the International Union for Conservation of Nature and Natural Resources. How well I know them. They were a strong impetus to the construction of this park, believe it or not. I first learned of the impending conservationists' congress in 1974. I had a strong suspicion they'd convince their governments to embargo the flow of native wildlife. So, I set out immediately, buying rare snakes from farms on four continents. I sent hunters into the field for whatever I couldn't buy. Since I had no park yet, as soon as the snakes arrived in the States, I loaned them out to parks, zoos, reptile farms, even private collectors. Now, I've recalled almost all of them."

That was very clever," Wrightson responded with geunine admiration. "I wondered how you could get around the international laws to amass such a collection. You never had to, did you?"

Miller shook his head. "I find that it's always better to work within the law. If you can. Others disagree. Every year, animals are being smuggled into the country by the thousands.

"Now, Marc, you want the venom from our rare snakes, and I'm the one that has to be gotten around, right? I'm afraid this is not a nonprofit organization. In fact, part of our income is derived from the sale of venoms. I have a rather large full-time staff to pay, as well as the mortgages on the park, taxes, . . ."

"But surely the park will be a financial success from the tourist trade," Wrightson argued. "And such a donation can be a considerable tax write-off."

Miller nodded, his impassive face devoid of emotional clues. "Still, I'll have to consider the idea, then consult with my lawyer and accountants." He gestured, taking in the full sweep of the park. "I no longer speak as a private individual." He rose. "Well, I'm the host for this bash, so we'd better get back outside and circulate." He walked to the swinging door and held it open. As Wrightson passed through, Miller said, "Of course, there is one way you could sway a donation."

Here comes the catch, Wrightson thought. "Oh. How?"

"I still have dealings with various zoos and parks on the West Coast, as well as with importers from Southeast Asia and Australia. I need someone out west to handle my business for me."

"I'm a medical researcher," Wrightson protested. "I have no business experience."

"Yes, but I don't need a businessman. I can handle the paperwork from here. What I need is someone with common sense, who's responsible and dependable. Naturally, there'll be a cash retainer with the job. Shall we say ten thousand a year?"

Wrightson was pondering the kind of favors Miller might ask for such a figure when his eyes focused on Ioka Marengasau, Miller's exquisite assistant. She had just made her entrance to the party. The crowd parted for her, as though swept aside by the force of her aura. Except for a few lengths of clinging black silk she might have been standing nude in the middle of the crowd. The gown had scant room for undergarments. She was lucky to have found a few spots to daub on her perfume. Halfway up her bosom the gown stopped, two narrow bands of silk wound across her flawless breasts, over her collar bones, and around her elegant neck. Lacquer combs pulled back a swirl of black hair, revealing a pair of starburst diamond earrings. Her jewelry was discreet yet obviously cost a small fortune. That was all she wore, but that was enough for Wrightson. For him, she was the real show.

"You know, if you don't start breathing in a few moments, old boy, you'll pass out," Miller said in his ear. "She dances very well. Ask her!"

Wrightson quickly negotiated his way through the crowd. Ioka turned suddenly and fixed her eyes on him while he was still at a distance. Then she shifted her gaze past Wrightson to Miller. A look of apprehension clouded her face. Wrightson looked back, attempting to glean from Miller's eyes the relationship between the man and the woman. Miller smiled benignly, nodded his head at her, then busied himself with another fawning sycophant.

Wrightson stopped at arm's length from Ioka. "Good evening, Miss Marengasau. I'm Marc Wrightson, from San Diego." She bowed her head, in oriental fashion. Thank God she's smiling, Wrightson thought. "May I have this dance?" he asked and suddenly felt like an awkward teenager. She nodded again, still silent.

The band played an old standard. Wrightson put his right hand lightly around her waist and took her hand in his left. She moved against him. His cheek brushed against her hair, its freshly washed smell mingling with the heady fragrance of her perfume. Her body felt warm, her hand cool. His body pulsed feverishly.

"I'm glad they're playing a fox trot," he remarked softly. "I'm afraid I don't know any of the new disco dances." Her cheek pressed against his chest. She responded with a slight nod of her head. Is it her, me, or my brand of mouthwash, he wondered half-seriously, vexed at her silence, and determined to know the woman better. "You dance very well," he said honestly.

"I learned in a young ladies' school in Singapore," she said, but made no attempt to maintain the dialogue. Her accent was slight. Her tone reminded him of wind chimes. They danced silently for another minute, jostling against other couples with gentle, random motions. "You know, I was watching you very closely at the demonstration this morning," he admitted.

"I know," she said. He had intended to surprise her, but had himself been surprised. She looked up at Wrightson. "Isn't it considered rude in your country to stare at someone?"

Wrightson thought fast and said, "Not if the one being stared at is so naturally beautiful."

"Thank you," she said in a whisper. The song ended, but the band segued into another slow melody.

"You handled that cobra with such ease. And courage.. I understand your father was a great snake hunter."

"Yes. I helped him hunt snakes even when I was a child."

"You really are stunning in that dress," Wrightson said, after noting a number of glances from both men and women in the crowd, "but I'll bet every man in this room is mentally slipping it off." He felt her body stiffen beneath his fingers.

"Please excuse me. I must leave," she said suddenly, pulling herself away. Before he realized it, she had slipped past the swaying couples and headed quickly for the doors. He caught up with her just as she stepped into the night air.

"Ioka, I'm sorry, I certainly didn't mean . . ."

"No, please, Dr. Wrightson. You did nothing wrong. I just could not stay in there." Considering the height of her heels and the tightness of her gown, Ioka moved at a rapid pace, heading toward the rear of the park. Wrightson cursed himself for making the remark. Lilla Sue would have appreciated it, but Ioka was not Lilla Sue.

"Would you mind if I walked with you?" Wrightson asked, anxious to mend his faux pas.

"If you wish," she answered brusquely. Then her pace slowed and her expression softened. She smiled at Wrightson. "I'm sorry. Now I am being rude. Yes, I would like you to walk with me." Wrightson shoved his hands into his pockets and regulated his step to hers.

"You shouldn't be upset because people were staring at you. You should accept it as a compliment to your beauty."

She shook her head. "I do not feel right in this dress. When those people looked at me, they made me feel I was not a respectable woman. I once read a play about Americans in Japan after World War II. One of the players, a Japanese man, said he could not understand Americans. If they put up a statue of a woman in a park wearing no clothes, she is nude and this is art. But if the real woman stands without clothes in the park, she is naked, and they arrest her for being shameless." Ioka shook her head again, obviously bewildered. "Maybe I am being silly, but I will feel better if I change."

Wrightson found it impossible to respond, knowing he was as guilty as any other man of regarding her as a sex object. He redirected the conversation to literature, asking if she read many American plays and novels. Ioka confessed that she had inherited a love of reading from her father. He had taught her English when she was very young, and it became her habit to read at least a dozen novels in English a year. She spoke of the works of Conrad, Melville, and Shakespeare. Wrightson dredged up all he could remember from his high school and college literature courses and threw out other people's opinions on classics in the English language. Ioka's responses were intelligent and unique, and had Wrightson impressed.

"You know far more about our literature than ninety percent of the people born in this country. How long have you been here?"

"Only three years," she replied. "When my father died I had no relatives I could live with. Scott was a friend of my father. He has taken care of me for the past six years."

"I know how tough it is to grow up without parents. I was what we call a change-of-life baby. My mother was forty-one when I was born. My dad died when I was twelve and my mother when I was sixteen."

Ioka's look bespoke her empathy. "Marc, I am sorry. That is why Scott means so much to me." She turned off the path and walked through a gateway bearing a "no trespassing" sign. Wrightson trailed behind and found himself on a pool deck surrounded by beautiful landscaping.

"And you must mean a great deal to him," Wrightson remarked in an off-hand manner, hoping she would volunteer information about her relationship with Miller. Her pace quickened as she reached the sliding doors of the main house.

"I am going to change," she announced, ignoring his comment. "The bar is next to that bookcase if you want to fix a drink." Then she was gone. Wrightson looked around. From where he stood in the living room, he could see the dining room and part of the kitchen as well. Miller's version of Xanadu was not bad at all, he mused. An interior decorator might call it "understated elegance." Wrightson walked over to the Steinway grand and lifted the lid. Faint brown discolorations on the edges of the keys told him the instrument was played and did not sit there merely for display. The books on the shelves had obviously been read, their spines showing cracks of fatigue. Many of the titles were in French. On a far wall hung half a dozen framed photographs. All had people as the subjects. One was of Miller as a young man, flanked by a girl and backed by a man and a woman—a very distinguished-looking group. Probably a sister and parents, Wrightson guessed. Another showed Miller at the summit of a snow-covered peak, bundled in sophisticated climbing equipment, holding a flag. The precipitous drop and the rugged panorama behind him indicated quite clearly that Miller and the photographer had conquered a very high and formidable mountain. The largest photo was of Miller, Ioka, and a middle-aged Eurasian man, taken at the stern of a boat. All three were smiling broadly. Both Miller and Ioka looked considerably younger.

"That's my father," Ioka said from across the room. Wrightson turned. She was dressed in sneakers, jeans, and a light-blue cotton jersey. She had loosened her hair so that it hung luxuriantly about her shoulders.

"That was quick! And you look just great this way," Wrightson said. "Feel better?"

"Yes," she said, approaching him. "Do you want a drink?"

"No, not really."

"Then let's go outside, Marc. I would like some fresh air." Ioka crossed to the sliding doors. Wrightson followed.

"How old were you when that picture was taken?"

"About sixteen."

"And how long ago was that?"

"Six years."

That meant Ioka was twenty-two. What else could she be but Miller's mistress? Wrightson felt a twinge of jealousy.

"Did Mr. Miller pick that dress for you?" he asked, watching her face carefully.

"Yes," she answered.

"And the earrings?"

"Yes."

"And you wore them to please him?"

"Tell me about your family, Marc," Ioka said, after a pause. He had pushed too hard. Perhaps she didn't mind Miller treating her like an object in private, but she had clearly resented his putting her on public display. Time to lighten up your act, Marcus, he thought. As they walked he fabricated an improbable tale wherein his father met his mother in a circus. He told Ioka that they became clowns, doing a horse act together, and that one night they had to fill in for a real horse that had suddenly died.

"They were so good, in fact, that no one could tell them from the other horses. Even the horse trainer was fooled. He locked my mother and father in the horse trailer and sent out a real horse to get him pizza and beer."

Wrightson's bizarre ideas, coupled with his ridiculous gestures and imitations had touched Ioka's sense of humor. "Marc, you are a silly man," she said, laughing.

"No, honestly," he declared, swearing with his hand raised above his head, fingers crossed. "Every other word is true. Of course, having been locked together all night in the trailer, my father had to marry my mother to save her honor."

"I don't believe you."

"Oh? Well, if my mother were alive, she'd tell you herself she married a horse's rear end." Ioka laughed aloud.

"I think you are a clown."

"Absolutely," he replied, and took her hand. She did not pull away, but instead squeezed back at his light pressure. They walked in silence for a minute, waiting for the other to speak.

"You are rather like my father," she said. "He loved to make other people laugh, even if he had to make himself silly. I remember, when we went to market he would juggle the fruits we bought. Oranges, and tambourines, and . . ."

"Oranges and what?" Wrightson asked.

"Tam-bou-rines," Ioka repeated in unsure tones.

"You mean tangerines," he said gently. "Tambourines are hand drums, about this big with little cymbals on the side."

Ioka blushed. "I have much English to learn."

"No, not very much at all," Wrightson insisted. "Why am I correcting you? I can't say even 'yes,' 'no,' or 'how are you' in your language." Then he turned to talking about his research, his life goals, and how important the rare venoms were to the realization of one of these goals. He described his letter to Miller, the prompt reply, and how they had begun to talk about a deal at the party. With each passing minute, Wrightson liked the young woman better. When Ioka listened, she really listened. He could tell from her responses. She expressed herself clearly and intelligently, like someone more mature, and yet she retained a fresh, youthful quality in her bearing and her outlooks. He also sensed a mutual relaxation of defenses, walls crumbling. They had meandered through the park, walking toward the front gates. Faint sounds of the band floated in the cool wind, out of place among the trees and the smells of nature. Wrightson paused at the pit closest to the entrance gates.

"I noticed today that this one pit is empty," he observed, leaning on the guard rail as far as he could. "It's also much deeper, and has a higher plexiglass than the others. Why is that?"

Ioka bit her lip nervously as she gazed into the pit. Her mood was suddenly somber, in a quicksilver change. "It is a secret."

"You can't even tell an old friend?" Wrightson asked. His tone was purposely cheerful.

"No. I'm sorry," she said, her hands straight at her side, as if all the energy had drained from her body. She stared blindly into the pit. Wrightson was pained by her sudden unhappiness. Impulsively, he gathered Ioka into his arms and kissed her firmly. She accepted his kiss passively, with a tiny whimper escaping from deep in her throat. With great reluctance he withdrew his lips and relaxed his embrace. She averted her eyes. Her right hand brushed lightly across her lips.

"Marc, I must go. Today has been a long day. I must get some rest." He was certain of her attraction for him, but he knew that she was being sensible, realizing the futility of the kiss. In a matter of hours he would be on a plane bound for San Diego. They would probably never meet again. And yet he could not let go.

"Look, I have to finish my talk with Scott tomorrow. Can't I see you for a little while?"

She smiled lightly. "The staff eats breakfast in the cafeteria between seven and seven-thirty. I will leave word with the guard to admit you." She took his hand in hers. "You are a good person, Marc." She stood up on tiptoe and brushed his cheek very lightly with her lips. Then, as she stepped back, Wrightson saw that her eyebrows had furrowed and her expression had hardened to one of grave concern. Her eyes turned from him to the empty pit.

"When you talk to Scott tomorrow, be very careful for yourself," she said ominously. Then, at a run, she disappeared into the blue shadows. Wrightson stared into the darkness for a minute, and shrugged. He decided to take on the next day when it arrived. He wandered back toward the sounds of the music. A number of people were leaving the party as he stepped inside. While he watched the couples dancing happily, he suddenly felt the pressure of a hand on his hand, warm breath in his ear, and the unmistakable softness of a woman's breast against his left shoulder.

"Here you are," Lilla Sue said, moving impossibly closer to him. "I've been looking all over for you." She pressured her groin firmly against his thigh, a maddening proposition. Wrightson felt the muscles of his rear end contract involuntarily and the heat flash again into his hips. He turned to face the woman. His shoulder plowed into her décolletage, nearly displacing her firm breasts from their concealment within the thin garment. Her hand had fastened into his far shoulder, making the turn impossible. "I had intended to save the last dance for you," she said seductively, her free hand flipping open the third button on his shirt, then insinuating itself among his chest hairs, "but I'm totally danced out." She hooked a lock of hair around her forefinger and gave a playful tug. Wrightson gasped. Lilla Sue laughed giddily, lifted herself to the limits of her toes, and planted her mouth against his ear. He felt her warm breath brush the fine hairs of his lobe. "I could really go a hot shower though," she whispered.

6

THE POLICE car cruised slowly down the oak-tree-canopied street as Nate Gordon turned the corner in his pickup. Instinctively, Gordon's foot went to the brake to check his speed. The policemen had a searchlight which they were shining on the facades of the street's overblown, immaculately manicured antebellum mansions.

As Gordon drove past, he saw that both officers were black. That didn't help to put him at ease. They were working for whitey in his neighborhood, and they probably noted him well as he drove by—a poorly dressed black in a battered pickup on "rich man's row" after midnight. He was surprised that they didn't turn the patrol car around and follow him when he pulled into the driveway of one of the biggest mansions.

Gordon stopped his truck in front of the columned portico. The warm night breeze carried the musty odor of boxwood to his nose. He approached the front door and rapped its knocker with the bearing of a stoical martyr walking alone and unarmed into the lion's den. Gordon's dour attitude was not modified when the door was answered by a black man. The butler was just another one of those blacks he would never understand—the ones who could live with ease and assurance in the white man's world. Sure, he, Gordon, often worked for whites, but he always went back as quickly as possible to his own life. He worked for The Man simply because The Man held the purse strings; he neither understood nor trusted whites, and whenever he straddled the two worlds, as he did tonight, he invariable did so with apprehension and discomfort.

Without a word the butler ushered Gordon down the central hall, past the antique Brobdingnagian furniture and the time-misted mirrors to the double doors of Fritz Thanner's study. While the servant knocked softly on one of the doors, Gordon looked at the grandfather clock standing against the opposite wall. Its golden hands pointed to 12:20. When there was no reply from inside the study, the butler opened the door and announced, as quietly as he had knocked, "Mr. Gordon." Over the servant's shoulder Gordon saw Thanner seated behind his desk, listening on the telephone. Thanner gestured him in with his free hand and indicated a wing-chair directly in front of the desk. Gordon sat down self-consciously.

Thanner raised the telephone's mouthpiece to his lips and said, "Look, Richards, that's not a valid excuse. There's always a war going on in some part of Africa these days. Just get the lion cubs from somewhere else, if you have to, but see that I have them by the end of the month." He paused and listened, obviously vexed. Gordon swept the entire room with a swift glance, noticing that the butler had closed the door. "Richards, if you can't meet my requirements

I'll cross you off my list and find someone else who can."

Gordon listened with barely mild interest. He had heard variations of this conversation several times in the past. Tonight the subject was lion cubs. Tomorrow it would be about tiger cubs, or parrots, or monkeys, or alligator hides, or ocelot skins. Nate Gordon was one of the very few people who knew Thanner's occupation and, at that, his knowledge was fragmentary and confined to a specialized area of interest. He served as Thanner's reptile expert. Gordon had grown up and still lived in the Everglades. He was a large man, built lean and powerfully, and at home with nature. By choice, he lived a simple near-primitive existence and as such had made himself intimate with the lives of the turtle, the alligator, and the snake. He had studied their behavior, caught and captured them. Occasionally, when he could find no other suitable work, he would wrestle alligators in reptile parks. His life had improved considerably since he'd been spotted and recruited by Thanner. Not only did Thanner pay well, but, because of the white man's worldwide business, Gordon's knowledge of reptiles had gradually become more catholic. Yet, despite the fact that Thanner had improved his lot in life, Gordon trusted him less and felt more ill at ease with him than with any other white man he knew.

Fritz Thanner had the monopoly on professional animal importation in the United States, apparently sanctioned by organized crime. It did not matter to him whether the animals he was importing were legal or illegal, dead or alive, whole or in part; the only laws he obeyed were the laws of supply and demand. Thanner had grown rich and powerful harvesting the world, catering to the human passion to possess other living creatures or their skins.

"Vera Cruz," Thanner said, nodding at the phone. "Right. I'll take care of the connection into the States. You just see that they get safely to Mexico. And, Richards, this time make sure they have all their shots before you ship them off." Thanner skipped the farewell and slammed down the phone as if it carried a communicable disease.

Thanner was a small man. Part of his diminutive stature was due to the fact that he was well into his sixties, but he had obviously been small in his prime as well. When he spoke, he made his desires known in an equally small but very distinct voice. His well-chosen vocabulary, along with his mane of white hair and his horn-rimmed glasses gave him the distinguished air of a college professor. Thanner studied Gordon, slumped in the wing chair.

"I'm a real night owl. I should apologize for asking you to come here so late."

"I don't mind," Gordon responded laconically.

"How long have you worked for me, off and on?" Thanner wanted to know.

" 'Bout five years."

"And most of it's been pretty boring work, right?"

"I don't mind," Gordon said again.

"As long as the money's good, eh?" Thanner smiled. Gordon never liked when that happened. "What's the worst snake you know, Nate?"

"Meanest or deadliest?"

"Both."

"Mamba maybe."

Thanner gave Gordon a sly smile and slowly shook his head. Gordon sighed and folded his hands in his lap. The little man had started his habitual question and answer game, which always made him feel like he was back in sixth grade. "Then, I guess, Tiger snake."

Thanner shook his head again. "Look at these!" He pulled a few glossy blowups from a manila envelope and handed them across the desk. "They're photos from a new snake park called the Great Scott Serpentarium. Did you ever see a snake pit so well protected? It's hard to see from the photos, but it's about ten feet deep." Thanner paused expectantly, eyebrows raised. "Aren't you curious to know what it's supposed to hold?"

"What?" The game was already starting to get to Gordon.

"It's for a taipan. Never heard of it? Don't feel badly, Nate. Very few people in this world have. It's a unique snake. I've got a story to tell you, and I know you'll find it as fascinating as I do.

"In Australia and parts of New Guinea there lives a species of rather ugly, brown-black snake called the taipan. It grows to about eight feet when mature, but has been known to reach eleven feet. It belongs to the Elapid family. You know, the kind of snake that has rigid fangs, the ones that tend to chew on their prey to work in their venoms. Like the Tiger snake you just mentioned. However, there the comparisons stop. The taipan's fangs are twice as long as the Tiger snake's, and it injects twice the venom." Thanner slid two books from the corner to the center of his desk.

"I've been doing careful research on the taipan." He pushed his glasses up the bridge of his nose as he began to read aloud. " 'An average yield from milking one taipan is 100 milligrams of dried venom. It takes only .0023 milligrams of venom, administered intravenously, to kill a 100 gram-weight mouse. One bite can kill 173,912 mice.' Think of that, Nate! Dried taipan venom the size of one grain of sugar could kill a horse. In fact, I've read that one horse died less than four minutes after being bitten. And men in less than three." Thanner looked down at the text. " 'It is slender and very athletic as snakes go, moving quickly on the ground. And it has an extraordinarily swift striking capability.' Now, this other reference book informed me that the taipan's poisons are both hemo- and neurotoxic. Listen to this: 'Bite symptoms are typically as follows: abdominal pain and faintness, followed by vomiting, then blindness and finally massive muscular paralysis, resulting in certain death when not immediately treated with antivenim.' " Thanner shut the book. "From all I've read, the taipan is the most aggressive of all snakes, probably the most intelligent, and certainly the most deadly. Now what do you think, Nate?"

"Bad!" Gordon shook his head earnestly. "That don't sound like no snake. That sounds like the devil himself."

Thanner, not tuned in to the serious undercurrents in Gordon's tone, nodded and continued. "Fortunately it's rare. Since it's not a pretty or an especially large snake, nobody's been interested in bringing it into this country. Now, Nate, you should be asking me why the owner of this new park is building a special pit to exhibit a taipan." Gordon failed to pick up the cue, so Thanner plunged on undaunted. "Well, he didn't. Not for a normal taipan anyway. And that's where my story really begins.

"A number of years ago a Malaysian snake hunter who was very well known and respected in the animal trade, Claude Marengasau, started talking about a giant taipan, twice as large, twice as vicious, and three times as deadly as the normal Australian taipan. He claimed that it lived on some obscure, uninhabited island in that corner of the world. He vowed to bring one of these creatures to civilization. To insure that he would be the first, he refused to tell anyone the location of the island. Frankly, most people thought he was making the whole thing up.

"Six years ago Marengasau was killed in the jungle. Rumor had it that he was attacked by one of these giant taipans. Around the time he died there was a white American with him constantly. A man by the name of Scott Miller. Now, in 1974 Miller returns to the States. He immediately begins importing a phenomenal number of snakes from all over the world. That's when he first came to my attention. Here are some photos of him. He's the big one in the middle."

"He looks strong."

"That's the word. Physically, intellectually, politically, financially. You name the category and Scott Miller's strong in it. He's a multimillionaire with plenty of connections. That's what's going to make this operation such a challenge. As soon as he began importing snakes, I had one of my agents contact him and offer my services. He politely refused. Said he had his own hunters and agents. Told my man he was going to build a snake park and was hurrying to stock it before the importation laws went into effect. I decided I couldn't put pressure on him, and I assumed he'd pose no threat to my business. But within six months Miller was glutting the country with his snakes. He had no place of his own at that time to keep them so he was farming the snakes out everywhere, offering other snakes as payment for storing his collection. You remember my telling you?"

Gordon nodded. He remembered vividly just how furious Thanner had gotten over the matter.

"Even though I'm sure it was unintentional, Miller cost you and me a good deal of income, Nate. What's more, when he brought those snakes in without going through me, everyone else suddenly began privateering. That's why I had to put that contract on Lacy. I lost a great deal of face, but Miller was too big to 'reprimand.' You understand?"

Gordon nodded.

"However, when I heard the story of Claude Marengasau, Miller, and the ill-fated giant taipan expedition, I began to see how I could get back at the man. First, I had another agent approach him with a large cash offer if he would reveal the location of the taipan's island. His reaction was quite pronounced, but the agent said he recovered quickly. He denied knowing anything about any such expedition. From then on I was sure that the giant taipan was very special to Miller and that he intended it to be the central exhibit in his park. Ever since, I've been keeping tabs on Mr. Miller. When he began building the park I put an operative at the location full time. Warren Crowley. He's the one who took the pictures of the snake pit and Miller. Crowley also has a tap on Miller's private phone. That's how I know a giant taipan has finally been captured and is right now on its way to California."

"*Where* in California?" Gordon asked.

"San Diego. On board ship. It's scheduled to arrive on May nineteenth. I can't give you all the details of this operation because we still don't know anything about Miller's California agents."

"You keep sayin' 'operation.' What do you mean?"

"I mean, Nate, that I want you and Crowley to steal that giant taipan."

Gordon squirmed. "I don't think I want no part of this, Mr. Thanner."

Thanner's palm shot out to silence his guest. "I promise you, Nate, it's not going to be dangerous in the least. If Miller has the snake well guarded we'll either try to take it out of his park or forget the idea altogether."

"That ain't what I mean, Mr. Thanner. If this thing is really as mean and as deadly as you say it is, then it ain't no snake. You say it's three times more powerful than a regular taipan, right? Well, nature don't make a creature what could kill half a million mice. If it does live, it's an evil spirit. Or the devil himself."

This time when Thanner heard the phrase he was listening to the man. He looked also and read in Gordon's face the primitive respect for the supernatural. "No, Nate, you're wrong," he countered. "It's super deadly just as the dinosaurs were super big. If somebody found a live dinosaur, would you call it the devil just because it was so much bigger than any other reptile?"

"Maybe you're right," Gordon admitted, "but I wouldn't move it. I'd let it stay right where it was."

"I should think you'd be anxious to handle it."

"Not me," Gordon replied with conviction.

"Well, chances are you won't ever see it," Thanner assured him. No doubt it will be kept in a heavy box. Crowley will handle the spy stuff, the actual breaking and entering of the warehouse or wherever they store it before transfer to Florida. I want you along to keep the snake safe and to keep a tight rein on Crowley. He knows nothing about snakes, how to keep them at the correct temperature, or how to move them safely. He also doesn't know the way I work. You do."

Gordon said, "Tell me about this guy, Crowley."

"He's very competent. Got his training in the Army as a professional eavesdropper, with a unit they call 'electronic countermeasures.' He's a wizard at wiretapping and surveilance. He also worked briefly for the CIA."

"How come he don't work for them no more?"

Thanner looked Gordon straight in the eye. "He got a little overzealous in his work. He was put in charge of a team assigned to assassinate some political figure in South America. He wired up the guy's car with dynamite. It was supposedly a beautiful job, except that two pro-U.S. politicians were in the car with the guy at the time it went off. He was either extremely unlucky or he didn't do his homework."

"I don't like working with other men," Gordon said, an edge working into his voice. He burned to ask Thanner if Crowley were white, but refrained.

"I know you prefer to work alone, but this isn't an ordinary smuggling and transporting job. It's a complicated theft. Crowley's very good at this kind of thing. Trust me. Granted, the official who recommended him to me did say Crowley tends to become a little unstable under stress conditions. But that shouldn't pose a problem, Nate. When you're both in San Diego, if it looks like the job is going to be too difficult, I'll give you full authority to scrap everything. You, not Crowley. O.K.? He can't possibly handle the snake without your expert help, and I trust you to be the judge of whether or not the job can be done."

"Why can't I wait and steal it myself from the man's park?" Gordon's question verged on a plea.

"It's the element of surprise," Thanner replied. "Miller doesn't think anyone knows of the taipan's arrival. He won't be expecting any trouble clear across the country. Once in Florida, he may have a complex security system for the taipan. Furthermore, if you got caught in his park he'd no doubt have all the local politicians and judges in his back pocket. They'd throw the book at you."

Thanner stood, crossed to the front of the desk, and sat on its corner. "I want that snake very badly. Miller's relying heavily on it to make his park a success. Imagine how helpless he'll feel when he learns it's been stolen! Who can he complain to, the customs authorities? It's the perfect revenge, Nate. Now, I'm willing to pay you very well for this job. I've never asked you for a favor before. I would look very dimly upon our future relationship if you refuse me this. What do you say?"

Gordon sighed ruefully and gazed up at the ten-foot-high ceiling. "As long as I can say if the job's too dangerous."

"Excellent!" Thanner exclaimed. "You'll fly to San Diego on the seventeenth of May. Crowley will go out as soon as he learns the rest of the details of the snake's arrival."

Gordon stood. He rubbed his forehead slowly, as if he felt a headache coming on. "I'll go. But you be damn sure I don't open that snake's box for no man!" Then, very quickly, he was gone, closing the door after him.

Thanner walked back to his chair and eased himself down into it. He lifted the telephone handset from its cradle and began dialing with the other hand. A few moments later he was saying, "Hello, it's Fritz Thanner. Yes, for a *very* good reason. I was certain you'd want to hear the good news as soon as possible. I'm receiving it on May twentieth. The operation has been a bit more expensive than I anticipated, however, so the price of the vial of venom is twenty percent more than I quoted you. No. Believe me, it'll be worth it. He'll die in a matter of minutes, and no one will be able to figure out how. That's right, I'll still have the snake. And somebody will be grateful as hell to pay a fortune for it, but that has nothing to do with what you want. No," he said, listening to a lengthy argument. "No!" he interrupted. "Listen, if you want a cheap kill, buy a bow and arrow. I tell you, nobody's ever survived without an almost instantaneous injection of the specific antivenin. Excellent. I'll expect it in the mail, then. Good night."

Thanner hung up the phone and interlaced his fingers behind his neck. As he leaned back into the chair, a smile of intense pleasure illuminated his face.

7

NILS JONSSON, first machinist's mate, lay motionless in his bunk, listening. His ears strained to separate the subtle, sleeping sounds of his two bunkmates from the incessant, throaty throbbing of the *Snowbird's* engines. Holding his breath, Jonsson picked out first one, then both the slow, rhythmic exchanges of air rising from the lower berths. The other mates were totally oblivious to the wakeful world, dead drunk. Their condition had cost Jonsson a quart of Scotch, an investment he had gladly made for his own peace of mind.

For the sixth time since tumbling into his bunk Jonsson reached quietly into his pillowcase and pulled out his watch. The faint, green glow of the hands told him he had to wait six more minutes before it would be two A.M. He strapped the watch to his wrist, deciding to forget the few minutes. If he waited any longer he might lose his nerve. Jonsson pushed in the watch's tiny alarm stem, then reached for the khaki shoeshine bag he had stashed between the mattress and the bulkhead. He stuck his hand into the bag and made a blind check of the items inside: a tiny flashlight, a staple puller, a stapler, a plastic resealable pouch half-filled with powdered sugar, an empty plastic pouch and a jacknife. Satisfied that the contents were all there, he lowered himself stealthily to the deck, grabbed the khaki bag, and stole from the room.

As he made his way down the corridor toward the cold storage lockers, Jonsson calculated just how much heroin he could safely steal and how much money he could get for it in the States. Provided, of course, that it was actually heroin Captain Sjömann had personally carried aboard in that large bamboo box just before they left Djakarta. Right up the gangplank in broad daylight. That was Sjömann's style, the cool bastard. It was no secret among the crew that their captain was forever transporting illegal materials from one port to another. Many of them including Jonsson, did a bit of smuggling from time to time. It was a private matter, not open for discussion. Jonsson had the clear idea he would be risking his job, maybe his life, if he got too curious about Sjömann's extra business; ordinarily he tried hard to look the other way.

Last year, however, when the captain came up the gangplank with a black lacquered case tucked snugly under one arm, Jonsson sensed that this item was worthy of investigation. His instincts had proved right. After a week of furtive snooping, Jonsson had found the lacquered case well hidden at the bottom of the meat freezer; it held fifty plastic packets of heroin inside it. The next night he replaced heroin from ten of the packets with powdered sugar. Not totally. Just a bit from each.

Enough to earn him some very pleasant shoreleave memories. Now, each time the *Snowbird* docked in an Asian port, Jonsson trained his predatory eyes on the captain's every movement. Tonight would tell if his vigilance would be rewarded. Only yesterday he had tracked down the mysterious bamboo crate in an unused food storage locker, then quickly retreated to formulate a plan. Tomorrow morning, if anyone asked, Jonsson and his two bunkmates had gotten themselves paralyzingly drunk on a quart of Scotch, tumbled into their bunks just after midnight, and slept soundly until awakened. All three would swear to it.

Jonsson's head still swam a bit from the alcohol he'd been unable to dump down the sink or the toilet. He leaned against a wall for support, hoping the adrenalin coursing through his veins in ever-greater quantities would momentarily sharpen his senses. He took a few deep breaths, then slipped into the deserted galley.

The unused storage locker lay on the other side of the cooking area; an unlit red bulb hung above the heavy door. Jonsson paused, listening for the footsteps of the night watch. Hearing nothing, he unlatched the door and placed the handle of a soup ladle next to the jamb so that he wouldn't lock himself inside. With the door closed, the locker took on the aspect of an unlit cave. Jonsson could not risk turning on the light because the same switch activated the red, outside bulb, a signal to anyone in the galley that someone was in the locker. Jonsson reached into his khaki bag, withdrew the penlight, and switched it on. The weak shaft of light barely cut the darkness to the opposite wall. Jonsson saw a pile of boxes, waist high, obscuring the deck on the far end of the locker. Behind this barrier, he knew, lay the bamboo crate. For the first time, he noticed that the storage room was not particularly cool. He trained the light on the thermostat behind him. It had been set at 68°. Jonsson's spirits rose. Certainly if the crate contained heroin, it would need no critical storage temperature. He made his way through the pile of boxes to the bamboo crate. The crate was a rough but very sound-looking affair, its corners strengthened by brass fittings. Two hemp handles poked from either side. The crate was encircled by two stout leather straps, held in place by half a dozen hemp guide loops. The crate was almost twice the size of the captain's lacquer box, a little smaller than a foot locker. Jonsson hoped it held twice the heroin. He set down his kit and carefully lay the knife, staple puller and stapler by the side of the crate. He directed the light's beam with one hand and worked clumsily on the massive strap buckles with the other. His fingers, numbed by alcohol and fear, struggled against the security of the heavy gauge metal. When the straps finally flopped open against the deck, Jonsson rocked back hard on his heels and ran a shirtsleeve across his forehead. He slowly lifted the lid of the crate, shining the light's beam along the opening. At first he thought the crate was empty. All he saw was blackness. Then he realized he was staring at a very black bag which almost filled the confines of the crate. The bag was lumpy, cut from a rather coarsely woven, heavy material. At its end, the bag's mouth was bound tightly by a length of strong cord. It became apparent to Jonsson that he would need both hands to undo the knots. He put down the penlight and grasped the cord in both hands.

A sudden noise froze Jonsson in place. It sounded like steam escaping from a pressure release valve, very close by. He remained still, trying to remember which pipes, if any, ran through the storage locker. With a shrug he dismissed the noise and continued working the cord off the bag. Because he struggled blindly, it seemed to him as if he had been in the locker for an hour. In the total darkness the small room closed in around him. He tore at the last knot in a rush to grab his flashlight.

At last Jonsson felt the cord come loose. He unwound the slender coils from the neck of the bag and laid the cord on the lip of the crate. Then, with both hands, he grabbed the open end and spread it. Before he could reach inside, he heard the hissing sound again and, simultaneously, felt a blow to his right hand. His nerves already primed, Jonsson reacted like lightning, yanking his hand out of the inky folds of material and slamming the crate lid shut in one swift motion. He grabbed a box that lay alongside his leg and threw it on top of the bamboo crate. Then he snatched up the flashlight and looked at his hand. He found a scratch, beginning to well with blood, about one inch long on the fleshy part of his thumb.

"Fan också!" Jonsson swore, more loudly than he intended. "Det är levande!"

Jonsson's brain burned with anger and disappointment. What the hell was Sjömann doing, smuggling a beast into the States? It must be something exotic or rare, worth a great deal. Jonsson tried to imagine what kind of wild animal it was that had either clawed or bitten him. One thing was certain—he was not about to open the crate again to find out what it was.

Jonsson examined his hand more closely. The scratch did not seem that bad, although it was beginning to really burn. He had been pretty lucky, he guessed, as he pulled the cord from the lip of the crate and stuffed it in his pocket. He chuckled to himself despite the fact that he was shaking. Whoever opened the crate the next time was in for a big shock. He put down his penlight with much reluctance and, blood pounding in his ear, rebuckled the two leather straps. As he did, the creature inside hissed again.

"Håll käften din djävel!" Jonsson hissed back at the beast, shoving the crate roughly against the wall. He restacked the pile of boxes in front of the crate, hurriedly gathered his tools and sugar pouch into the khaki bag, anxious to cleanse his scratch of infection.

By the time Jonsson had bent himself over the galley sinks, searching for some soap, he began to feel queasy. While he worked a good lather around his thumb, which curiously continued to bleed unabated, he realized that his salivary glands were pouring out great quantities of secretions, readying his mouth and throat for regurgitation. Jonsson fought the feeling. He had a stomach of cast iron; very rarely did he throw up. He shut off the taps, wrapped his handkerchief around the wound and stood without moving for a moment, breathing deeply. His nausea was rapidly getting worse. What was more, his head felt dizzy again. Could all this be caused by a little scratch, he wondered. No, it was impossible that any bite or claw wound could have such a swift reaction. It must be a combination of the shock he had just received and the alcohol still in his system. That had to be it.

Jonsson tucked his kit under his arm and walked slowly from the galley into the corridor. He reasoned that fresh air might be of help, or, at least, when he vomited he could heave into the ocean and not have to clean up afterward. With unexpected difficulty he climbed the stairs to the upper deck. He stepped into the open air and turned his face into the sea breeze. It felt alarmingly cold. He put a hand to his forehead. It was warm and beaded with perspiration. Now the nausea in his abdomen had contracted into a fist-sized ball of sharp pain, matching that of his throbbing hand. Jonsson stumbled toward the rail, gritting his teeth. He prayed for the relief that vomiting would bring. He hung his head over the rail, and let his mouth hang open. The ship was beginning to pitch and roll beneath him, as if riding through a typhoon. Jonsson clutched the rail with all his might, his knuckles showing a lurid white. His insides burned and bubbled like a boiling cauldron while perspiration burst out of every pore of his body. At last, with projectile speed, the contents of his stomach rushed upward and out of his mouth. Grateful, Jonsson leaned far out over the rail. He never remembered feeling so sick. He began to gag. Some of the vomit lodged in his throat; he could not control his mouth or tongue. His hands clutched his neck instinctively. His elbows unlocked. Nearing unconsciousness, Nils Jonsson was not aware his weight was slipping forward over the rail. His legs relaxed, and he executed a graceful somersault. He hit the water spreadeagle, parting the waves with a resounding splash. Ten seconds later, when the night watch arrived at the rail to investigate the sound, the ocean had reformed its surface, leaving no trace of the poisoned man.

8

MARCUS WRIGHTSON entered the Great Scott Serpentarium cafeteria at full steam, his body and the newspaper he carried backlit by the golden sunshine of the Florida morning. "Good morning everybody," he sang out cheerfully as he headed for the table where Ioka and Miller sat eating. He unfolded the newspaper and held it out between his extended hands. "Have you seen this?" Beneath the banner headline was a close-up photo of Miller holding the King cobra in the air, grinning at its hideous, gaping jaws. Wrightson peeked around his hand to read the caption aloud. "VIP and Viper. Great Scott Serpentarium owner, Scott Miller, handles King cobra. Story on A4.' Then he noticed a thick pile of newspapers on the chair next to Miller, halfhidden by the table. "I guess you've already seen it."

"Yes, and quite a few others," Miller said amiably, rising from his seat with outstretched hand. "Sit down, Marc. Let me buy you some breakfast." He intercepted a passing waitress, and Wrightson ordered orange juice, fried eggs, and black coffee.

"You're in a good mood this morning," Miller observed.

"I'm delighted about your opening day," Wrightson replied. "From what I read in that paper it really looks like you'll have a success here."

Miller nodded, unsmiling. "Provided the word-of-mouth is as good as the press coverage. To make sure we're pleasing the visitors, we'll have pollsters at the exit gates collecting their comments and criticisms."

As Miller talked, Wrightson stole a glance at Ioka and found her studying him. He smiled in response. She instantly refocused on her empty coffee cup. The silence had grown awkward by the time Wrightson realized Miller had stopped talking. Feeling obliged to say something, he said, "You, uh, don't miss a trick, do you?"

"I don't miss very much," Miller replied, looking first at Ioka, then at Wrightson, and back again to the woman. "Ioka, would you see that Dr. Wrightson gets better service than we did this morning?" She nodded, excused herself, and walked toward the kitchen. "Our breakfasts took forever and arrived lukewarm," Miller said in explanation. "Our cafeteria help serve the park crew from six-thirty to eight. I believe, in their not-too-subtle way, they're trying to tell me they resent double-duty." His words had a tone of disgust. "What'll you bet Monday morning a delegate from their union comes banging on my door?"

Wrightson listened without comment while his eyes followed Ioka out of the room.

"At least we both approve of one of my staff members, eh?" Miller remarked.

"She's quite beautiful," Wrightson stated candidly.

"Yes, she is. Inside and out. She's a very special person, Marc. I've drawn a great deal of strength from Ioka in the past few years. I'd like to think I've done as much for her. She inherits the park, incidentally, if anything ever happens to me. But you didn't fly across the country to listen to my personal life story, did you? In fact, you may be in a hurry to get back to California. What's your schedule?"

"My flight's not leaving until 1:30 this afternoon."

"Great! Then we can finish last night's discussion at a civilized pace. Have you thought over my offer?"

Wrightson leaned in and placed his hands on the corners of the table. "The ten-thousand-dollar retainer for representing you?"

"That's right." Miller fixed Wrightson's eyes with an hypnotic, fathomless gaze.

Wrightson cleared his throat. "Yes, I've thought about it. Excuse me for putting it so bluntly, but I gather what you're saying is 'no representation, no venoms.'"

Miller shook his head emphatically. "Putting it less bluntly, I'd say you're considering my offer with the wrong frame of mind. Representing my West Coast interests and being supplied with venom from another of my ventures are two separate matters. Naturally, however, you would be doing me a great favor by representing me. I, in turn, would feel a strong obligation to return the favor in kind."

"I guess my decision really hinges on what you expect of me. I certainly don't object to earning that kind of money so long as I understand exactly what the job entails," Wrightson admitted. "I'm afraid my conscience won't let me accept money for work beyond my capabilities."

"You needn't worry about that," Miller assured him. He paused, reading Ioka's return in Wrightson's eyes. She set down a tray with Wrightson's breakfast and an extra cup of coffee for Miller and remained standing awkwardly. Wrightson rose and pulled out her chair.

"I'm sorry, Marc. Ioka can't stay," Miller said. "She has a number of important matters to attend to over at the Rotarium. We were talking about them when you arrived. Right, Ioka?" He looked at the woman. She nodded woodenly.

Wrightson made a disappointed sound in his throat, then said to Ioka, "I was hoping to share a little more time with you today. I thought perhaps, if you weren't busy this moring, you might show me the local countryside."

"I am not working this afternoon," she offered.

"I'm afraid my plane leaves at 1:30," Wrightson said, crestfallen. He looked at Ioka in silence. If she was disappointed her face betrayed no emotion.

"Unfortunately," Miller broke in, "all of us have pressing business commitments." He raised his hand in an imperative gesture. "Make sure Burt has shortened the shaft on the capture tongs. The audience will never fear for our lives if we snare the snakes from the opposite side of the arena." She nodded understandingly and started toward the door. Then she turned and said to Wrightson, "It was very nice to have met you, Marc. Perhaps we shall meet again."

"I hope so," Wrightson replied.

Even before Ioka had gone, Miller asked abruptly, "Do you know what a taipan is?"

"Yes. It's a rare Australian snake."

"Right. Rare and extremely poisonous. It produces precisely the kind of venom you're interested in."

"And you're about to receive one, aren't you?" Wrightson said, more statement than question.

Miller raised his cup of coffee and blew across the lip. "Yes. You sound as if you've had this information for a while. Did Ioka tell you about it?"

"No. I didn't know it was a taipan until you told me, but I don't think it's any secret that you're expecting something special. You've got one empty pit in the park, and that's the one nearest to the front gate. Does any other park own a taipan?"

"Not anything like this one, but I'll get to that."

"A feather in your cap, I imagine."

"You're a very observant young man," said Miller. "Now you see why I want to engage your services?"

"Yes, I think I do. But it's not because of my mental acumen." Wrightson replied quickly. "I believe you've got that taipan coming into the country illegally through a California port, and, for some strange reason you think I should be the one to handle the matter for you. And that's the string that will pull the venom contributions, isn't it?"

Miller's face was impassive. He sipped at his coffee, then said, quietly, "Last night I made a point of telling you how I stocked this park. Nobody is completely aware of how I acquired my collection of snakes. For all anyone knows, I could have had a taipan in this country for years. When it arrives, I'll simply announce that I waited a few weeks after opening the park to display it to get the customers back for a second look. Face it, Marc, no one cares about ugly, deadly snakes when they talk about wildlife preservation. Those international agreements made a few years back were meant to preserve beautiful things. Siberian tigers. Koala bears. Even if people knew such a creature as the taipan existed, which most don't, nobody in their right mind would worry about its endangerment. The only concerned people are a few overzealous import inspectors. Naturally, they're the ones I must avoid dealing with."

Wrightson shook his head. "But why ask me to get involved in this?"

"Why?" Miller said dramatically, looking at Wrightson as if he were slow-witted. "Aside from the fact that you live in San Diego and know how to deal with poisonous snakes, because you stand to benefit as much from this creature's importation as I do. Consider the value of its toxins, Marc, the good you may be able to do with them. If you help me with this *one* job, I'll guarantee you in writing all the venom milked from the taipan. I'll also guarantee a minimum of eight ounces of rare venoms per month from my other specimens for one year."

Wrightson screwed up his mouth and looked around the cafeteria at the workers who went about their uneventful lives, oblivious of the schemes of the ones in power. He wished he were once again in their ranks.

Miller reached across the table and lightly touched Wrightson's hand. "I'm going to tell you something about this particular snake that you must promise never to repeat. Do you remember how big the cobra in yesterday's demonstration was?"

"About fifteen feet, I think you said."

"One inch short of fifteen feet. Not a small specimen. Well, this taipan is almost five feet longer!"

"Bullshit!" Wrightson exclaimed incredulously. "Taipans are more like ten feet."

Miller shook his head seriously. "This is not the Australian taipan *Oxyuranus scutellatus*. It's closer to the Papuan subspecies, *scutellatus canni*, but it's much larger and much more fearsome. It exists only on one island in the gulf between Papua and Australia. Imagine the amount of venom secreted by a snake that size. You'll be the only one ever to have analyzed its venom, Marc. In exchange for ignoring a law no one cares about, I'm offering you the chance to make a major breakthrough in neurological research, to help make your sacrifices really pay off. If nothing else, you can introduce this subspecies to the scientific world. That alone should guarantee you enough publicity to get all the research funding you need."

Wrightson shooed a fly away from the edge of his plate. "What would I have to do?"

"Just see that the taipan gets from a boat lying a few miles off the San Diego coast to a cargo plane on the outskirts of the city. Rent a motorboat or a sailboat, pick up the snake. Bring it ashore and hold it a few hours until you can transfer it to the cargo plane. This snake means a great deal to me. Believe me, I'd be out there handling the transfer personally if there were any way. I must stay in Florida in the event of later questions. It's a very, very simple plan."

"Simple for you," Wrightson agreed, "but dangerous for me."

"I won't tell you this involves no risks, Marc. But living itself is dangerous. Getting on that plane to San Diego is dangerous. You're spending years of your life working with only a slim hope of discovering a cure for one nervous disease. Don't tell me you're not a gambler. Marc, I have money and influence. If, by some ridiculous turn of fortune you should be caught, I would see that you got no more than a legal slap on the wrist. What judge would deal harshly with a scientist who was importing a snake for purely altruistic reasons?" Miller laughed heartily, and Wrightson found himself doing the same. "Am I right?"

"You did pick the right guy in me." Wrightson conceded. "In fact, even *that* kind of publicity might not be so bad. I do have a close friend who owns a thirty-foot Pearson. The problem is that I've only mated for him a few times. I couldn't very well ask to borrow his boat for deep-sea sailing with my limited experience. And I certainly couldn't ask him to come along, I guess I could rent a motor boat."

"Not necessarily. I can supply a first-rate skipper," Miller replied. "Ioka. She was raised on a sailboat." Miller watched Wrightson's face carefully.

"Ioka?" Wrightson said, clearly not expecting the woman to become part of the discussion.

"Of course. She's also one of the most skilled snake handlers I know. I'm not sure you'd want to deal with the taipan by yourself."

Wrightson nodded. "That's true. I certainly wouldn't."

"Twenty-four hours would see the job through from start to finish." Miller had been reluctant to throw out the queen of hearts as his trump card, but it seemed to be necessary to guarantee Wrightson's assistance. He decided to press the heart's suit. "And, come to think of it, Ioka needs a vacation. She's been a virtual prisoner here for months. She's always wanted to see Southern California, but we never got around to it. You know, Marc, I think the little girl in her would love to compare the old Disneyland with Disney World."

"I don't know, Scott. I'd much rather get my venoms legally," Wrightson said. "My gut reaction is not to get involved in this, and I'm sure if I have to say yes or no right now it's got to be 'no.' Would it be possible to call you in a day, or two?"

"If that's what it takes, I have no choice, do I?"

Miller replied. "You think about everything I've said, and I'm sure you'll decide to help me."

"We'll see," Wrightson said as he received the vaguely disquieting impression that his will was being inexorably drawn into the black vortexes of Miller's eyes.

9

THE SEAGULLS were circling noisily overhead and the sandpipers were darting back and forth with the waves as Wrightson walked down the cottage's weathered steps toward the beach. Dawn had just begun mixing pastel color into the gray washes of sea and sand. Wrightson kicked off his moccasins and ran barefoot down to the hard-packed, saturated sand. The birds raced out of his path with nervous, nimble starts. Wrightson looked back at the cottage with a twinge of sadness. In less than three weeks he would have to surrender it for the summer so the family he rented it from could begin their vacation. The cottage was small, but beautifully furnished and in an enviable location, snuggled into a narrow stretch of land between the mountains and the Pacific. He had procrastinated in his search for a summer place, and he made a resolution to take care of the matter during the week.

Wrightson stretched and flexed his muscles, then started down the beach at a trot, weaving in and out with the flow of the waves. He felt good. The trip to Florida had been a change of pace from the tedious routine of classroom and laboratory. He had met a number of interesting people, and he now had at least one option for preserving his research program. Even the return flight the afternoon before had been pleasant, since, for once, he slept most of the way.

Wrightson lengthened his stride, feeling the sun's rays on his cheek. Every time he began to mull over Miller's offer, the image of Ioka Marengasau drifted into his consciousness. He suspected that Miller had offered her assistance as a final gambit to elicit his help. What would Miller have said if he had told him about Ioka's warning the night of the party? Wrightson longed to learn more about their relationship, and he had to admit to himself that he was extremely curious about this new species of taipan. In the final analysis, however, he would be involving himself in an illegal activity. For a man whose worst offenses to date had been two speeding tickets and a parking violation, illegal importation represented a considerable escalation in criminal activity. He was so engrossed in weighing the gains against the risks, with Ioka's lovely face drifting in and out of his thoughts, that, before he knew it, he had reached the rock archway formation that indicated he had run a mile. He shortened his stride to catch his second wind. Wrightson made up his mind to delay his answer to Miller until the last minute. Perhaps a favorable reply from one of the funding institutes had arrived over the weekend, making it unnecessary for him to involve himself in Miller's scheme. Wrightson glanced at his watch. He had plenty of time to shower and cook breakfast before he was due at the lab. The pain in his legs had vanished. His thoughts were so positive that the mental euphoria carried into his muscles. He picked up his pace on the return run and grinned at the sun's growing brightness, now warming the opposite side of his face.

◦   ◦   ◦

Wrightson stepped into his lab room and stood for a moment, surveying the familiar surroundings. His graduate research assistant, Jeremy French, sat at the desk, bent over a mechanical project. The look on his face was that of total preoccupation.

Wrightson moved to the coat tree beside the door and exchanged his jacket for a lab smock. "Morning, Jeremy. How's everything?"

"O.K. Have a good trip?" Jeremy asked, borrowing just enough attention from his project to frame the question.

"We'll know in a few days," Wrightson replied, fighting his way into the lab coat. "What are you making there?"

"A noose," Jeremy replied, quite simply.

Wrightson walked over to the desk and peered over his assistant's shoulder. Jeremy's clumsy fingers were methodically looping a length of white string into a miniature hangman's noose. Wrightson stepped around to the side to study the assistant's face. His transfixed eyes focused through grime-speckled glasses and his tongue hung halfway out of his mouth, pressed tightly between his lips.

Wrightson shook his head disbelievingly. "May I ask you why you're making a noose?"

"Gonna hang the mice."

"Why?" Wrightson persisted, determined to make sense of the macabre scene.

"Another krait got bitten. The mouse I fed it on Friday night must have been a shrew in disguise,"

Jeremy said, after licking his forefinger and rolling the loose threads of the string together. "As soon as I dropped it into the cage, the crazy mouse ran up to the krait, sniffed it once and then bit it right on the tail."

"Did you have the cage temperature set too low?"

"Of course not."

Wrightson strode over to the cages. The bitten krait lay motionless. The wound looked bad. Wrightson sighed. "It's infected."

"Yeah. I think we're gonna lose this one, too."

"Son-of-a-bitch," the neurologist swore softly. "That's the second one this semester." Wrightson pondered the curious paradox wherein the very creatures whose venoms caused such violent reactions in other animals, themselves had almost no immunity to bite infections. It was probably nature's prerequisite to the development of their awesome toxins. "It never rains but it pours, right?"

"Sorry," Jeremy said lamely, looking up and blinking through his thick lenses. Wrightson picked up a computer readout sheet. "Forget it. These things happen. But, dammit, how come always to us and just when we can least afford to replace the snakes?"

Jeremy pointed a finger heavenward. "Somebody's got it in for us up there."

"Just as long as the government keeps backing us, I'll take my chances with the people upstairs," Wrightson replied. "Speaking of the government, any word about funding?"

"Don't know," the assistant murmured, back to monosyllabic replies. "Oh, there's a memo from the dean. Wants to see you right away."

Wrightson set down the readout and started toward

the door. "This may be it, Jeremy. I funneled the last batch of foundation requests through the dean's office. More clout that way. Keep your fingers crossed."

"Uh-huh," Jeremy replied, oblivious. Wrightson looked at the young man's uncrossed fingers. They had finally fashioned a workable noose. He dangled it in the air and eyed it critically.

"Are you serious about hanging the mice?" Wrightson asked.

Jeremy stuck his thumb in the noose and drew it tight. "It's the best way I know to keep them from biting the snakes. We can't afford a gassing chamber like first-class serpentariums have, right? I think I'm ready for my first victim. Wanna watch?"

"No, thanks," Wrightson declined, starting again for the door. He shook his head in wonder as he headed up the stairs for the dean's office. "That boy's got to move on soon."

* * *

"Come in, Marc," Dean Franklin said, looking up from the orderly stacks of paper on his desk. He failed to smile, and Wrightson prepared himself for the bad news. "Have a seat."

Wrightson rested his shoulder against the door jamb. "If it's bad news, maybe you can just say it quickly and let me get back to work," he suggested.

"No, sit down. It's bad, but I think we should talk. First, Irene tells me the semiannual insurance payment for your project comes due on June first. It's eighteen hundred and twenty-five dollars. That will bring your balance way down."

"If that's all, we'll just have to tighten our belts another notch until the beginning of July," Wrightson answered. The dean's expression remained grave.

"But that's not all, is it?"

"No. I feel like Cassandra every time you come in here."

"And I feel like the Trojan army. Go on."

"I received a letter on Saturday from HEW. It said that, with cancer on the increase and with all the publicity it's been getting and the public response, they've decided to channel a bigger percentage of their research funds that way."

"Let me guess. It's coming out of neurology's pocket."

"Part of it at least. Your funding is cut in half as of July first."

Wrightson banged his fist on the arm of the chair. "Robert, I am so damned frustrated. Millions of tax dollars floating around and not enough to send a little my way? Did you know the Army got more than a hundred thousand dollars to find out that frisbees with flares attached will not help us win nighttime battles?"

"I know. I mean, I didn't know that, but I understand what you're saying."

Wrightson made a sweeping gesture of dismissal with one hand. "Well, screw the U.S. government. Have you heard anything from the private foundations? Lilly? Merck?"

"Lilly's not interested. That's the last of my bad news. I haven't heard from Merck."

"Great! Eight replies in and all negative. Should I be sanguine about the two unanswered requests? Gosh, gee, I guess baseball player diseases are out of fashion this year. If the Pittsburgh Steelers' front four came down with some rare nerve disease we'd be back in business quicker than you could say 'Hut One, Hut Two.' "

Franklin had swiveled his chair, offering Wrightson his profile. He stared unblinking at the campus through panes of glass badly in need of washing. "It doesn't help to get bitter, Marc. I guess all you can do is shut down for a while until you find some more support. Maybe you can convince the zoo to hold your collection so you can save the insurance cost."

Wrightson stood up. "Not necessary, Robert. I'm too close to some very important answers to shut down just now, and I may not be as destitute as I seem."

The dean turned his chair back toward the center of the room and eyed Wrightson curiously. "Did you have any luck at that Florida serpentarium?"

"Yes. As a matter of fact, I had some very good luck. The first luck in weeks. Is there anything else you wanted to discuss?"

"No." The dean's look changed to perplexion.

Wrightson smiled. "Good? Because I've got to make a long-distance call to Florida."

10

FRITZ THANNER stood timidly on the swimming pool's fourth step, mustering the courage to take the final, chilly plunge, when the patio phone rang. Grateful for the temporary reprieve, Thanner climbed out of the pool and dripped his way across the concrete to the white wrought-iron furniture. The phone had stopped jangling. Thanner picked it up and said, "I've got it, Martha."

"Mr. Thanner, it's me," said the male voice on the other end. "Warren Crowley." Thanner pictured the red face and the ever-present silvered sunglasses. "I finally got it: the name of Miller's agent in San Diego!" His voice carried the unmistakable accent of excitement. "It's Dr. Marc Wrightson."

"Very good, Mr. Crowley. Have you transcribed the conversation?"

"Yeah. I've got it in front of me. Shall I read it?"

"Yes. Go ahead."

"This Wrightson evidently called Miller on one of the park's public lines, but you'll understand when I read it. Here goes:

Wrightson picks up the phone: Dr. Wrightson.

Miller: Hello Marc. Scott Miller. Sorry I was so long in getting back to you. I was in the middle of a demonstration when you called. I waited until coming back to the house to call you. I want you to use the residence number to contact me.

Wrightson: I tried before, but there was no answer. I understand that we need to talk in generalities.

Miller: Yes. Have you come to a decision?

Wrightson: I have. I think it's a fair offer, mutually beneficial to both our interests.

Miller: As do I. I'm very pleased.

Wrightson: I must be sure of two conditions, however.

Miller: Name them.

Wrightson: I want you to put two items in the mail as soon as possible. First, a check for half the discussed sum of my retainer, made out to the San Diego Neurological Research Fund. That's in care of the San Diego National Bank on Western Boulevard.

Miller: I've got it.

Wrightson: Second, a written guarantee of eight ounces of Australian and Asian venoms per month, including Tiger and cobra, for a period of one year, also as discussed. With your signature.

Miller: They'll be in the mail this afternoon.

Wrightson: There won't be any problem in storing the package. I have a number of vacant cases here on campus. Also, I've already called my friend with the Pearson. I told him I've got a sailing buddy visiting me soon. He's agreed to lend me his boat for the nineteenth.

Miller: Very good. I'll have to call you back to let you know when your buddy will be flying out. Should I use this phone number?

Wrightson: No. Call me at home. I'm usually there between five and seven at night or six to seven in the morning. Do you have the number?

Miller: Yes, I do. You included it in your first correspondence. I guess that covers everything for the moment. Marc, I believe you've made a wise and beneficial decision.

Wrightson: Time will tell, Scott. Goodbye, then.

Miller: Goodbye.

That's the whole dialogue, Mr. Thanner. I'll send you a copy."

"No, Mr. Crowley. Bring it here with you. Your work at that end is done. I want to meet with you as soon as possible to discuss the rest of the operation. The sooner you get to San Diego and begin studying Dr. Wrightson the better."

"I agree. I've got enough information now to locate him with no trouble. In two days I'll know his brand of toothpaste and the color of his jockey shorts."

"First things first. You're going to be working with my snake expert, Nate Gordon. I want to brief you about him and outline just how I expect you two to work together. I'll have a room reserved for you at the Hyatt House, Peachtree Street."

"You know, that was a pretty weird conversation," Crowley remarked out of the blue.

"In what way?" Thanner asked.

"Well, first because it sounds like Miller's using a medical doctor, and, on top of that, a guy he hardly knows. Why would a doctor need Miller's money?"

"I believe he's a research doctor, and he needs Miller's snakes," Thanner began to explain.

"And also," Crowley plowed on, "this guy Wrightson just now agreed to bring the taipan in for

Miller. But Miller already had the snake diverted to San Diego—just as if he knew he'd get Wrightson's help all along."

"An interesting observation," Thanner said, becoming a bit impatient. "I have every confidence you'll have all the answers soon."

"That's right," Crowley replied cockily. "OK., I'll see if I can get up there tonight. Bye."

Thanner set down the phone. No doubt Crowley would be celebrating tonight. Tanner knew the man by this time and expected no more from him. Tomorrow was time enough to talk. Crowley was no Einstein but he was right about one thing: Miller must have been very sure of his judgment of character, his powers of persuasion, or both to have had the taipan sent to San Diego before having secured Wrightson's assistance. Thanner's estimation of Miller went up a score of notches. This was not a man to underestimate.

BOOK
TWO

11

THE TELEPHONE'S BUZZING echoed off the hardwood paneling in Scott Miller's Rotarium office. When he picked up the receiver, his secretary said, "You have a collect call from Miss Marengasau, Mr. Miller. I've already accepted the charges." Miller was pleased by the efficiency of the young woman who had started with him a month earlier.

"Thank you, Carol." The next moment Miller heard a high-pitched, hollow whistling on the line. "Hello, Ioka? Where are you?"

"At the San Diego airport." Ioka's voice came through clearly on a strong connection. Miller placed the background noise as that of jet engines warming up. "Marc was waiting for me when I arrived. He is here next to me."

"How was your trip?"

"Fine." There was a momentary pause. "Marc says to tell you everything is ready to go."

"Very good. Remember, I want you to call me at home as soon as you've taken care of the business."

"I will," promised the high, bell-like voice.

"Oh, Ioka," Miller added quickly. "I almost forgot. Tell Marc I've changed my mind since our last phone call. I want our guest fed at the lab." Miller said nothing more for an instant, sensing Ioka's discomfort in the brief silence. "We don't have any idea how long our *guest* has gone without eating, but it's certainly been at least twelve days. I think he should have something before he goes on the plane. However, if you and Marc think it's impossible, forget it." Miller could hear faintly the conversation between Ioka and the neurologist. A few seconds later Ioka said, "Marc thinks it may be possible. He has a large place where we can open the box if it's not too big."

"Good. Just make sure you bring the temperature up to at least 82° first, Ioka."

"Yes. I will."

"Well, have a good time. Don't worry about how much you spend. I'll see you when you get back from your vacation."

"Goodbye, Scott," he heard her say, then found himself listening to the steady hum of the disconnection. Miller smiled with anticipation. Without conscious direction, still intent on the taipan, he picked up a small piece of artwork he used as a paperweight. It was a sleek, modernistic snake, molded from brass and coated with chrome. The head, a blunt arrowhead shape, had no eyes, nostrils or mouth. The body, about fifteen inches long, curved gently in reverse ess undulations, tapering gracefully to its tail. The statue was perfectly smooth, devoid of the suggestion of scales. Miller, at last aware of the object in his hands, held it closer for examination. His face was reflected in the snake, badly distorted.

Miller's secretary knocked discreetly, waited a second, then entered. "Your four o'clock appointment is here. Mrs. Berkeley and Mr. Schmidt from the telephone company. I offered them coffee."

"Good. Show them in, Carol," Miller said. He replaced the metal snake and rose to greet the two strangers as they entered the office. "Good afternoon, Mrs. Berkeley, Mr. Schmidt. Please make yourselves comfortable." Miller noted the conservative, classical cut of their business dress. Both carried briefcases. "I hope you're not going to tell me we're already behind in paying our phone bill," he quipped. "We've been open less than two weeks."

The woman made a half-hearted attempt at a smile and said, "No, this has nothing to do with billing, Mr. Miller. I'm from our Security Bureau, and Mr. Schmidt is a member of our legal department. We're here to see if you can help us clear up a problem that has recently come to our attention. Two days ago one of our installers was adding a coin booth line on a delayed work order and found a monitoring device spliced into one of your existing lines."

The news caught Miller by surprise. He had already noted that both were studying his face carefully, and he allowed his reaction to show, to assure them that he was not responsible. "Monitoring device? You mean a wiretap?"

"Basically, yes," Schmidt replied.

"On our business phones," Miller said. Berkeley shook her head.

"No. You've got three systems here, Mr. Miller. The public phones, the Dimension 100 for your business, and the two private lines running from your residence, which, I understand, is on the park property."

"Yes. That's right."

"The monitoring device is on these residence

lines." She pushed a report across Miller's desk. He recognized the number of his study phone typed onto the paper in three places. His jaw and neck muscles tensed, stretching taut the skin lying above them. His eyelids narrowed. "This is quite upsetting to me, Mrs. Berkeley," he responded, his voice dropping nearly an octave. The phone representatives exchanged furtive glances. Each had sensed the electric discharge of the man's anger. "I certainly had no knowledge of the device until this very minute."

"We're concerned also, Mr. Miller," the woman hastened to assure him. "We checked our files and found no record of an authorization for a monitoring system."

Schmidt added, "We've also contacted the state and federal judicial offices. They've issued no warrant or license for such a unit."

Miller stood abruptly. The representatives' heads followed his gleaming black eyes upward like tracing radar. "Would you excuse me for just a minute, please? I'd like to do some internal checking before we continue."

"Certainly," the woman said. Miller rushed out of the office, through his secretary's alcove, and out into the curving hallway. His mind worked furiously. Someone wanted to know about his personal business badly enough to install a wiretap and to have it monitored. That meant a determined and potentially dangerous adversary. A half a dozen of his dealings might have elicited such action, but Miller's entire focus centered on the importation of the taipan—partly because this was the very day of its arrival, but also because he had had vague premonitions of disaster for almost two weeks, accompanied by his recurring nightmare. His thoughts narrowed on the reporter with the mirrored sunglasses. Something the surly man had said had stuck in Miller's mind. When Miller had remarked that a surprise creature would be revealed in the empty pit in a few weeks, Carouthers had said something like, "I'll be listening for news of your surprise." Listening for, not watching for or looking for. The phrase had seemed ill-chosen, coming from a man who supposedly made his living with the printed word. Now, with the revelation of the wiretap, the phrase made perfect sense.

Miller checked his headlong rush at a door marked "Public Relations." He pushed open the door with vigor and stepped quickly into the office, nearly colliding with Lilla Sue Davis, who had pulled the sleeves of a sweater over her shoulders and was about to knot them together.

"Oh, hi, Scott," she said. "Did you want something? I was just getting ready to leave."

"Can you stay for another ten minutes?" Miller asked. "I've got an emergency."

"Sure. What's the problem?"

"Do you remember the last group of reporters we took through the park before opening day? It was on a Wednesday, I believe."

"Vaguely. Why?"

"One of them wore mirrored aviator's sunglasses and carried a camera. He strayed away near the end of the tour and refused to rejoin the group."

"Yes. I think I remember him."

"He called himself Carouthers. Said he was from the *Charlottesville Herald*. I want you to check on him. I think he's a spy. My private phone's being tapped, and he may be the one who's doing it."

"No kidding!"

"As soon as you get any information, come to my

office. I'll be waiting."

"I'll do my best, Scott," Lilla Sue said brightly as she picked up the telephone.

Miller hurried back to his office and found the phone company representatives still seated but with their briefcases yawning open. "Sorry for the interruption," he apologized. "I'm looking for an answer through my own channels. Is there anything I can do personally to help?"

"Yes, there is," Schmidt said. "First, you can agree to leave the monitor device on your phone line."

"That's fine with me."

"Next, I have two documents we'd like you to sign. The first states that you had no previous knowledge of the monitoring device, and the second gives the police and our security agents the right to conduct an investigation on your property."

Miller took the two papers. "I don't see a problem with either of these. However, I'll have to consult my lawyers before I sign them."

"We understand," Schmidt said, closing his briefcase. Miller waited for the lawyer to look up before he said, to both, "Why can't you just trace the line of the device to its source?"

Berkeley answered this time. "Because this particular device has no wires, Mr. Miller. It relays your calls on a radio signal which can be picked up within a one-mile radius. It's a rather sophisticated instrument, once used widely by government investigatory agencies. That's why we had originally suspected an unauthorized government surveillance."

"Is there a realistic possibility of locating the receiving unit?" Miller asked.

"I think we have a good chance. Your local community here is not too crowded. We'll check motels and rental units first. Do you have any idea who might want to monitor your calls?''

"I have so many diverse business interests, I wouldn't know where to begin. I'm afraid I can't think of anyone at the moment.''

Berkeley looked at Schmidt, and the two stood together. The woman held out her hand and said, ''You let us know if anyone comes to mind.''

Miller took Schmidt's hand also. "I certainly will." He ushered them out of his office and through the alcove, adding, "I appreciate your coming today. And I'll have those documents signed and ready to be picked up tomorrow.'' Miller watched the two disappear around the gentle curve of the hall, then returned to his office, deep in thought. If the wiretap was placed by someone after his taipan, trouble was imminent. From the conversations of the past two weeks, the listener would be able to glean all the data of the snake's arrival. Ioka and Wrightson might be in danger at that moment. If whoever was responsible for the tap was not interested in intercepting the taipan in California, he might try to take it at the Florida airport or in his park soon after it arrived. Then again, even if the wiretapper had no interest in the taipan, but was apprehended for an entirely different reason, he could spill his guts about the snake in an attempt to swap the information for a lesser sentence. Whatever happened, there was suddenly a very real chance that Miller would lose the taipan. He tried to pursue the possibility that the wiretap might have nothing to do with the snake, but his deepest instincts told him otherwise. He looked at the mirrored chrome surface of the snake paperweight and thought of the man who called himself Carouthers. His fingers tensed around the statue. Miller's world had suddenly been thrown into chaos and he felt totally helpless to restore its order. He cursed himself for allowing someone else to bring in his taipan.

Lilla Sue entered the office. Her eyes went wide. "Brother!" she exclaimed. "I guess you didn't want that anymore, huh?" Her eyes were fixed on Miller's huge hands. He looked down. Unconsciously, he had transferred his frustration to his immensely powerful fingers. The statue was now bent in a U-shape. At the sharp crease the chrome had begun to peel. Miller set the statue down without comment.

"Well, you were right," Lila Sue said, overbrightly, a reaction to Miller's black mood. "There's no such reporter as Carouthers. Not in Charlottesville anyway. First I called the city in Virginia. They have no newspaper called the *Herald*. Then I checked an atlas. Believe it or not, that's the only Charlottesville in the world. There are two *Charlotte*villes. One's in New York. I called information. Also no *Herald*. The other's in Tobago, so I let it go."

"Thanks, Lilla Sue," Miller said softly. His eyes unfocused in thought.

"Is there anything else I can do?" she offered.

"Yes," he said, suddenly galvanized. "I want you to call the airport and book me on the first available flight to San Diego. Whatever will get me there the fastest. Ask to speak to George Cartmell. Tell him you're calling for me."

Lilla Sue stepped into the secretary's alcove and picked up the phone. Miller took a small address book from his pocket and flipped to the back. While he searched for Wrightson's home phone number he heard the PR agent say, "Mr. George Cartmell, please."

Miller found the number, picked up his receiver, and dialed.

"Hello, Mr. Cartmell? This is Lilla Sue Davis. I'm calling for my boss, Scott Miller."

Wrightson's phone began to ring.

"He's fine. I'd like to book him on the very first available flight to San Diego."

Miller counted the rings. When he reached eight he hung up quickly and dialed Wrightson's laboratory number.

"Yes, Mr. Cartmell, that sounds great. Wait just a second while I write that down."

Miller let the phone ring nine times before he set down the receiver.

"Thank you very much," Lilla Sue concluded. She ducked her head into Miller's office. "There's a direct flight leaving in two hours and fifteen minutes. It works out the same as a connection flight." She put on an apologetic smile. "It's the best he could do." She handed Miller the information.

"That'll be fine," he answered. "I'll need the time to get myself packed." He looked around briefly, then noticed the two documents the phone company people had left. "Carol, would you come in here?" he called. The secretary shouldered her way past Lilla Sue roughly, obviously annoyed that Miller had asked the other woman to arrange for the flight. Miller said, "I'm putting Miss Davis in charge of the offices for a few days. If anyone asks, I was called away on a family emergency."

The secretary's mouth dropped open. Her cheeks took on a flush of embarrassment and surprise. Not only had Miller slighted her by denying her any responsibility, but he had done it with an insensitive brusqueness she had never seen in him. Miller bent over his desk to sign the papers, too preoccupied to notice the feathers he was ruffling. "Here, Carol," he said, thrusting the documents into the secretary's hand. "Have my attorneys check these. If they see no problems, release them to the phone company officials. They've discovered a wiretap on my private phone. You two are the only persons who know about this, so I don't expect any wild rumors to start." From his tone of voice and his look, both women knew he meant business.

"I'd like you to drive me to the airport, Lilla Sue, so I can brief you on the next few days' business," Miller said, collecting papers into a folder, them moving into the alcove.

"But . . ." Lilla Sue stammered, then stopped herself. She was about to remind him that she was in a hurry to leave when she remembered the twisted statue. "Yes, sure," she said instead.

Miller looked over his shoulder as he rushed out the doorway. "Well, come on! Let's hurry."

12

"HOW'S SCOTT?" Wrightson asked as Ioka hung up the phone.

"He sounds fine," she replied, stepping out of the way to let another traveler use the booth.

"Good. All right now, we can either drive directly to the marina and get an early start, or we can stop by my place and let you change. It's only a forty-minute detour."

Ioka wore a matching blue jacket and skirt and a ruffled white blouse. "That's not necessary," she answered, stepping onto the escalator. "I would rather start early and change on the boat."

Wrightson turned her toward the luggage pickup area. "You look a little tired. You've probably been working too hard."

"Yes, I have," she agreed. "After we finish with the taipan I can relax."

"By that I hope you don't mean just sitting," Wrightson exclaimed, "because I've got our itinerary all planned." They found Ioka's luggage and walked out to the parking lot. Wrightson owned a green Ford station wagon, the typical machine of a long-time bachelor and nature-lover. It looked as if it had never experienced a waxing. The wheelwells were caked with layers of dried mud. Clumps of dead weeds hung from the rear bumper. When Wrightson dropped the tailgate, the owner's profession was even more evident. Ioka saw a heavy-duty flashlight, a rolled-up sleeping bag, a dirty woolen sweater, piles of newspapers and scientific journals, a camera tripod, a snake snaring stick, an army raincoat, and a white capture bag. More items, unrecognizable, poked out from under the piles. Atop the confusion sat a woven wicker basket, covered by a red and white checkered cloth.

"What is in this, Marc?" Ioka asked, reaching in for it.

"Ah-ah. That's a surprise," Wrightson said as he dropped the luggage in her way and gave her wrist a light slap. "Now, if you will step into my limousine, I'll chauffeur you to the shores of the blue Pacific."

Wrightson drove out of the airport and nosed the car right at a stop sign. "The marina is close. We go down Harbor Drive, make a right on Nimitz, a right on Sunset Cliffs, and *voilá*, we're there! I'll show you the city tomorrow, after we pack Miller's precious snake onto that cargo plane." Ioka nodded, looking out her window.

"So did you have a good flight?" Wrightson asked after a silence.

"Yes." She said no more.

"Good weather all the way?"

"Um-hm."

"And how have the crowds been at the park this week?"

"Good."

Wrightson sighed. He was undeniably attracted to the woman, but he knew so little about her. He hoped she was just tired, as she had said, and not one of those hot-and-cold running women, the kind with mercurial shifts of temperament. What had touched her off this time, he wondered. Mention of the snake, of Miller, or both? He was tempted to ask. Instead, he rapped his knuckles very lightly against Ioka's head and said, "Hello. Are you still in there?"

Ioka turned to him and seemed to blush. "Yes. I'm sorry, Marc. I have some things on my mind, but really I am pleased to be here." She inhaled deeply, leaning partway out her window. "I can smell the ocean. It will be so good to be on a sailboat once more." They drove and spoke of the city, the weather, and other innocuous subjects.

"This is Mission Bay. Over there is the famous Sea World Park," Wrightson announced, pointing first straight ahead, then to his right as they drove over the floodway of the San Diego River. "Now, if I can only figure out how to get off this concrete maze and over in that direction." While he maneuvered the station wagon, Ioka looked past his handsome profile to the west, where boats of every size, shape, and description were moving out of the bay entrance channel and into the sparkling ocean.

Wrightson entered a yacht basin and parked. He reached behind his seat and dragged forth a heavy insulating blanket and a long, tightly rolled map.

"You take this map, and whatever luggage you need, and I'll take this blanket and the mysterious basket," Wrightson directed. They walked out to the sailboat, and, while Ioka went below to change, Wrightson unrolled the map and set to studying it. Engrossed in computations, he did not look up when he heard Ioka emerge.

"O.K., we're right here behind Point Medanos. We'll sail out past these lights, and follow the coastline until we reach Point La Jolla. Then we'll tack northwest on a bearing of 320° to La Jolla Canyon, right here. Now, I'm trying to figure which of these two lines indicates a measured nautical mile. Is it this one here or the one up here in ..." As Wrightson's eyes shifted to the top of the map, he saw two, bare fawn-colored thighs. His delighted eyes swept upward, past an abbreviated pair of white shorts, along a tiny, well-toned belly, lingered at a revealing bikini halter, then stopped at the woman's beautiful, make-up-free face.

"When you make changes, Ioka, you really make changes," Wrightson observed, nodding his head with appreciation.

She looked down at herself with a bit of alarm and asked, artlessly, "Is too much of me showing?"

"Oh, no! No indeed!" Wrightson assured her. "No, the girls around here wear much, much less in the summer."

"I thought today I could begin my tan," she explained, sitting at his side in the cockpit. "Now, show me the mile markings, and we will see how far we must go today."

Together, they plotted their course, taking into account the strength and direction of the wind at that moment. Then they removed the sail covers, and the young scientist stowed them below and fired up the engines while Ioka readied the sails to take wind. While the engine warmed, Wrightson pulled up the fenders and cast off the lines, fore and aft.

Ioka put the engine in reverse and goosed the throttle, smiling with pleasure as the wind whipped into her hair and carried it off her shoulders in wild, swirling waves.

The sailboat slipped back into the aisle stern first. Ioka took the engine out of gear and guided the tiller so that the boat's nose came slowly parallel with the length of the aisle. Then, when the boat had come at right angles with the channel, she jammed the shift into forward and set it out into the deeper waters, the prop chugging up a bubbling wake.

Wrightson watched the woman. She was definitely at home sitting at the helm of a sailboat. The boat plowed along, past Point Medanos and out beyond the jetty lights. Seagulls rode the invisible ocean of air currents above them, crying their plaintive sounds.

Once into blue water, Ioka headed the boat directly into the wind, motor still chugging, deep and throaty. Wrightson bent to the winch and hoisted the mainsail. Then he lifted the jib, letting it fall off to port. As he did, Ioka secured it, then cut the engine. The boat, heeling slightly under the force of the near-silent wind, swept forward into the waves, heading north. Wrightson stood and listened. With the engine cut, all he heard were natural sounds: the cry of the gulls, the wash of the waves, the gentle sough of the wind. As they sailed into deeper water, Wrightson made his way to the cockpit along the tilted deck. He was happy that once again his life was going so well.

o   o   o

The afternoon wind had all but disappeared, leaving behind the still, heavy air that hangs between the changes of landward and seaward breezes. The sailboat sat on a glassy sea, rocking gently on the crests and troughs of the widely spaced waves. Wrightson peeked up from the hatchway entrance. Ioka was furling the mainsail.

"We don't need to start the engine again," he said, watching her work. "The loran system has us triangulated right on the button." He handed up a light-blue windbreaker. "Here's your jacket. Without the sun it's too cool for what you're wearing." Ioka finished her work and put on the windbreaker. Wrightson appeared again, carrying a bulky bundle.

"Sea anchor," he explained. The sea anchor, shaped like a huge airport windsock, was dropped overboard, secured by a set of lines. If the boat picked up a current and began to drift, the anchors would tilt and inflate, and the water within the bag would drag against the current. That done, they set the running lights.

"O.K., skipper, we're set for the wait," Wrightson said, rubbing his hands dry. He looked at his watch. "More than two hours early. Damn good sailing, lady!" He moved closer to Ioka, and they looked out west across the ocean. The sun had just extinguished itself in the grey-blue distance, leaving behind red-orange fingers of light. Behind them, night reclaimed the land and the ocean to the east, washing imperceptibly from deep blue to blue-violet and into indigo, where the stars at last overpowered the failing daylight. On the horizon to the southeast, the sky shone a few shades brighter. There, above the glimmer, the full moon rose in supernal majesty, as if it had patiently awaited the sinking of the sun before establishing its rule over the heavens. Silence cloaked the sailboat.

"We sail well together, don't we?" Wrightson prompted.

Ioka looked at him with a placid smile. "Yes, we do."

"That's only because you're a very competent captain," he observed.

"Competent? Does that mean good?" Ioka asked,

the length of her arm pressed comfortably into his side.

"It means extra good," he assured her, then said, "It's curious, but after all this sailing, you look more rested than when we began."

She nodded. "When I sail my body is busy, but my mind is free to think of other things, happy things." She looked west into the twilight and her expression became pensive. It looked as if she would momentarily drift into a deep reverie, so Wrightson said, "I think it's time to open the mystery basket!" He disappeared into the cabin and reappeared a minute later, pointing to one of the cushioned benches. "Sit right there!" he commanded as he reached under the red and white cloth and fumbled blindly. With a triumphant look, he whisked out a green wine bottle.

"Liebfraumilch! The nectar of the gods. Well, the Teutonic gods, anyway." He felt around again and withdrew a corkscrew.

"Do you have wine glasses, too, in your mystery basket?" Ioka asked. Wrightson snapped his fingers.

"Damn! I knew I'd forget something. Isn't it amazing how you can plan and plan, and one little slip-up ruins your entire scheme?"

"I will drink from the bottle if you will," Ioka volunteered.

"That's what I like: a woman who's game," he remarked, watching Ioka wrestle the cork out of the bottle. "Wait! I have another surprise!" He reached once more under the cloth. With a theatrical flourish he produced three tangerines.

"Ta-da!" Tambourines, just for you." Ioka's laughter rang into the blanketing stillness of the night. "And that's not all, my dear. I've been practicing for the past few days." He tossed one tangerine in the air, then two, holding the third in the corner of his right hand. "And now if you please, three!" He tossed the third fruit and stretched under to catch the first as it dropped. His initial pass was a success, but soon all three tangerines were rolling wildly around the cockpit deck.

"Oh, shit!" Wrightson said, half-seriously, as he scrambled after them. "All those hours of practice shot to hell."

"You are very thoughtful, Marc, to do this for me," Ioka said quietly.

"Oh, no. I'm just an incurable romantic and a born fool," he replied, belittling his act. He sat next to her, bounced one of the fruits off his bicep, and caught it with the same hand as it popped up. He let the fruit fall into her open hand. "Do you want me to peel it for you? You must be hungry."

"No." Her voice was extremely soft. Her warm breath touched his cheek. Wrightson looked into her beautiful eyes. Unhurriedly he reached up with both hands to her face. His fingertips explored her cool, smooth skin. He leaned in and pressed his lips to hers. Ioka responded, pressing back firmly. His fingers slid forward and became enveloped within her wealth of silky hair. This time he was certain she would not pull away. His right hand drifted down the curve of her shoulder, gently insinuating itself over the yielding flesh inside her halter. Her lips parted, and she exhaled languidly.

"Marc," she sighed as the tangerine rolled from her limp hand and plunged into the ocean.

"Let's go below," he said, taking the woman by the hands. She followed without a word.

◦   ◦   ◦

Warren Crowley turned the car into the marina drive and was surprised to find the parking space he had left a half-hour earlier still vacant. The place was slightly elevated so that he and Gordon were able to overlook part of the mouth of the marina inlet. As Crowley backed in he noticed the shadowy form of Nate Gordon still propped against a palm tree where he had left him. Crowley turned off the engine, leaned his head toward the passenger window opening and called out, "Hey, Nate!"

The black man turned and recognized the face of his accomplice. Slowly he picked himself up from the grass, and sauntered toward the car. Behind him the lights of the marina winked on.

"Get in the car, Nate," Crowley said as Gordon approached. "People are gonna get curious with you sittin' there by the hour." Silently, Gordon climbed in. Crowley pulled a large white bag out of Gordon's way. "I know you said you weren't hungry, but I figured you might be by the time I got back," Crowley said. He opened the paper bag and offered a package wrapped in gold foil. "It's chicken."

Gordon shook his head. "I ain't hungry."

"Not even for chicken?" Crowley asked, skeptically. Gordon turned his head toward the marina. Crowley shoved the package back in the bag. He dug the packets of mustard and catsup and took out another package wrapped in paper. "Suit yourself. It'll be there." He unwrapped the paper, revealing an overloaded cheeseburger. Immediately, lettuce and onion spilled out of the sides of the bun. Crowley scooped the pieces up and stuffed them in his mouth. "I tell you one thing. I ain't goin' out there again until the traffic dies down. It's a fuckin' jungle on those freeways. Doesn't anybody ever stay home any more?" He squirted the contents of the packets onto the grilled meat.

"People wasn't made to be squeezed together," Gordon pronounced without looking away from the marina.

"Exactly," Crowley agreed, biting deeply into the burger. With his other hand he reached into the bag and grabbed a fistful of fries. "So, what did you do while I was gone?"

"Just sat under that tree."

Crowley shook his head as he chewed. "I don't see how you can sit still hour after hour. Me, I gotta have action. That's why I've gotta get outta this surveillance racket. It drives me buggy, just sittin' around." He took another bite, then glanced at his wristwatch. "Speakin' of sittin', I figure we got at least another four hours here. Why-the-fuck did they have to go out in a sailboat?" He wiped the back of his hand across his lips and turned to the black man. "Huh?" Crowley received no reply. "Yeah, but wait till they get the snake into that lab and leave. We'll be in and out of there quicker than you can say Jack . . . Rabbit." Tiring of the one-way conversation, Crowley poked Gordon's arm sharply three times. "Hey, man, hand me that book on the seat behind you!" As he took it from Gordon's hand he twisted it around to display the cover. "Have you seen this? *Small Arms of the World*. Eleventh Edition. Great book."

Crowley reached toward the instrument panel and switched on the car's dome light. He flipped open the book. Gordon looked at him. With night all around them and only the feeble courtesy light shining down, Crowley still wore his sunglasses.

"Look at this one here," Crowley said with moderate excitement. He poked Gordon again in the arm to insure his attention. "Smith and Wesson Mark 22, Mod. Brutal looking handgun, huh? Back in Viet Nam we called it the Hush-puppy 'cause we used it to kill the gook's sentry dogs. Did I tell you I was in 'Nam?"

Gordon nodded his head wearily.

"Yeah, I thought I did. Two years. With Electronic Countermeasures, ECM. Part of the Ground Ranger Division. See, I was in a special six-man team, outfitted with electronic jamming equipment. We used to sneak behind enemy lines and jam their frequencies. Sometimes we'd come across one of their little one-man outposts. The gooks would set up a radio post overlooking the main trails and roads. We'd sneak up in the darkness and kill with our bare hands. One shot in the throat and goodbye gook." Crowley demonstrated, swinging the slightly curved heel of his hand to within inches of Gordon's throat. Taken by surprise, Gordon blinked and rocked back in the seat. He gave Crowley a withering, warning stare, but the white man had his face buried once more in the book, flipping pages.

A minute later, Crowley laughed heartily, looked up and went on, "One time we caught a gook listener who didn't take us serious. So we wires his balls to his own radio. About twenty seconds later a message came over. The jolt knocked him cold. When he came to we told him a friend had called, and we'd reversed the charges." The tale brought tears of laughter to Crowley's eyes as he continued to leaf through the thick weapons catalogue.

"All these guns are beauties, but I don't need anything more than what I got," Crowley bragged. "Right back there in that briefcase. A Walther PPK with a sound suppressor, fitted special for me. You ought to hear it in action, Nate. Pff, pff, pff!" Crowley accentuated each sound by drilling his forefinger forcefully into Gordon's side. On the third sound, Gordon pivoted in his seat and his hand shot out in a blur and planted in Crowley's chest, the fingers digging in like cougar's claws. Crowley's skin was drawn off his ribs and his breath whistled out in surprise as Gordon palmed his chest as easily as an athlete might palm a basketball.

"Stop pokin' me, Mr. Crowley, you understand? First, I don't like workin' with people. Then, I don't like listenin' to people. But mostly, I don't like people touchin' me." Gordon lips drew back from his teeth in a snarl. He looked at Crowley's hands, wrapped around his thick wrist, straining to relieve the viselike grip. Gordon let go.

Crowley dropped back against his door, eyeing the black man with astonishment. "Hey, man, be cool. Take it easy. I didn't mean nothin'." He rubbed his aching chest. "Jesus, you're strong! I know how you feel, man. Like they told us in 'Nam, everybody takes a while to adjust to stress. I know this snatch is a big deal for you." Crowley had completely misread Gordon. The black man turned his face once more toward the marina. "You just let me do the worryin'," Crowley babbled on. "Nothin's gonna go wrong." He pushed his sunglasses back up his nose. "I think you're just hungry. Why don't you eat some chicken?"

*   *   *

Wrightson lay with his hands tucked under his neck, staring up through the open forepeak hatch at a score of starlit specks. Ioka lay quietly, having fitted herself to the contours of his side. She had thrown her left thigh slightly over his, her left arm stretched across his chest. Her hand molded to the curve of his right shoulder, kneading the deltoid muscle. Their commingled scents permeated the narrow confines of the cabin. Wrightson had never experienced such an overwhelming crescendo of passions or such a numbing, explosive release.

His eyebrows furrowed. He had had enough experience with women to know that these moments after the initial lovemaking were the most difficult to pass. Instead of speaking, Wrightson lifted Ioka's hand and kissed it. She pressed her lips to his shoulder.

"I'd better check the time," he said, lifting her arm gently off his chest and stretching over for his watch. "9:30!" he exclaimed. "The trawler should be here in half an hour. I'll go above and light the mast lantern." He pulled himself down the length of the bed and reached for his pants. As he scudded his feet into his sneakers, he stole a peek back at the woman. She had drawn the sheet to her chin, but when he looked at her, she smiled warmly, easing the awkward moment.

Once on deck, Wrightson checked the mast lantern, then switched it on. He followed its cutting beam, peering into the cone of space it carved into the darkness. Not a single answering light shone out of the gloom. A fresh breeze, cool and landward, gusted across his face. He grabbed the cloth-covered basket and went below.

Ioka had put on her halter and shorts, but she lay sprawled across the bed with a look that dared Wrightson to remove them again.

"Ah, good!" she exclaimed when she spied the basket. "I'm hungry now. Starving."

"Let's spread the cloth over the sheets," Wrightson suggested as he sat. "I don't want to have to buy the owner new ones." After smoothing out the cloth, Ioka yanked the cork from the wine bottle and downed a hearty swig.

"Cheese, bread, and plenty of fruit," Wrightson announced. As Ioka sampled the fare, he said, "So, lady, what plans do you have for your future?"

She tore off a hunk of sourdough bread. "I want to go to college and study medicine. I think I would like to be a veterinarian."

"That's commendable, but it takes a lot of years. Not that you're exactly ancient, but you should have started already."

"No," Ioka said. "First I must earn enough money to pay for two years of school."

Wrightson was perplexed and his face showed it. "I don't understand. I thought Scott took care of you. Why won't he pay for your schooling?"

"Because I will not ask him to. I cannot take anything more from Scott. He has been very good to me, but I must make my own life."

Wrightson took a gulp of wine for courage. "Do you . . . sleep with Scott?"

Ioka looked as if she would not answer for a while, then said, "No. I take care of him, cook for him, go places when he needs a woman by his side. I am a friend. His only true friend."

"Yeah, well, that doesn't surprise me," Wrightson declared. "First of all he's spent most of his life chasing around the world after adventure. Which tends to preclude lasting relationships. Secondly, in my humble opinion, he treats people like mountains, like things to be conquered, obstacles in his way to some private objective. I get the feeling that he's unwilling to share a lot of his inner self. I wonder if even you know the man completely."

"I know him," Ioka countered with confidence. "I know what a good friend he is. I also know that two persons are needed to make one friendship, but everyone is so afraid of Scott's powers that they will not even consider such a thought."

"You talk like fearing the man is nonsense," Wrightson observed. "But don't you fear him yourself?"

Ioka lowered her eyes. "Yes. At times I fear him. Not for what he does to me, but for what he is doing to himself."

"Maybe I'm being very unfair," Wrightson admitted after an awkward silence. "Please, tell me more about him so I can understand what you mean."

Ioka sat back against the bowed wall of the hull as if the explanation would be a long one. "I was almost sixteen when I first met Scott. I had returned to my father's boat because it was summer vacation from school. Scott was living there. My father had lost a great amount of money to him in a poker game, more than he could afford to lose. Scott knew this and asked to board on my father's boat. In a while they became very close friends. At night they would go ashore to drink and gamble or to visit the street women. After I came home, Scott bought a sailboat twice as big as my father's. My father was very proud and did not want such charity, but Scott said we needed more room since he had made up his mind to stay in Mālaysia to become my father's partner in snake hunting. My father always had wanted a son, and he treated Scott like one, very pleased by Scott's intelligence and his bravery. He is the bravest man I ever met. He would tell us stories about his racing car crash or the time when he nearly was killed trying to rescue mountain climbers. But he never told these stories like . . ."

Searching for the right word, Ioka puffed out her chest.

"Bragging?" Wrightson suggested.

"Yes. Bragging."

"He talks often of danger and death, doesn't he," Wrightson said, more an observation than a question.

"Yes. But he seems to have no fear of death."

"And yet he does fear something," Wrightson insisted.

Ioka paused a moment to consider his statement, then said, "I think maybe two things. One is loneliness. My father and I decided that a man who must seek adventure after adventure and woman after woman does so to fill his loneliness. When we became his family, that fear disappeared. My father gave him the gift of all his knowledge of hunting snakes, and Scott was thankful and learned well." Wrightson remembered Miller's words on snakes and death at the party. Then he heard Ioka's voice catch. "In little time my father came to trust Scott completely. Then, as I feared he would, he began his foolish talk of the demons of Naraka-pintu."

"Is that where this giant taipan comes from?"

"Yes. No one lives on the island. The people who live near it say it is the opening to the world of the dead. Giant snakes keep all living people away. But they are not real snakes. They are evil spirits, monsters who live on the souls of their victims. My father laughed at these stories and told everyone that he would not be afraid to catch such a snake. He . . . bragged that two brave men such as himself and Scott could catch even the devil himself if he took the form of a snake and crawled upon his belly. Scott liked the story. Every time they got drunk, that is all they talked of. They waited until I had returned to school.

I did not even know they had gone to Naraka-pintu until Scott came to my school to take me away. He told me that he and my father had hired two helpers and sailed to that island. The helpers would not go off the beach, so my father and Scott went into the jungle alone."

She looked forlornly at the checkered cloth. "Such foolish men. Scott said my father looked for fresh water at dawn and got lost. Then he heard him calling for help, and when he found my father he was nearly dead from horrible bites. Scott saw the taipan, and tried to follow it and kill it, but it disappeared into the heavy jungle. They buried my father at sea. Scott feels that he is responsible for my father's death. That is why he has cared for me like a daughter."

"A daughter, huh," Wrightson said, skeptically, as he gazed at Ioka's face and body. "And in all these years, he's never tried to make love to you?"

Ioka shook her head vigorously. "Since my father was killed, Scott has not slept with any woman."

"Impotent?" Wrightson asked, astounded.

"What is this word?"

"Never mind," he said quickly, then exhaled. "Brother, that must have been one fearsome snake!"

"But it's *not* a snake, Marc. It's a monster. My father and Scott did not understand that the stories are true. This thing he must have in his park is a demon who has chosen a snake's body to live on earth."

Wrightson would have scoffed at that part of Ioka's superstitious heritage that led her to believe such drivel, except that she looked so genuinely terrified.

"So, why hasn't Miller gone back in all this time to capture one of these snakes himself?"

"He cannot. As my father was dying he made Scott promise that he would take care of me and never again hunt the taipan." Her hand worked the curves of the wine bottle nervously. "But Scott thinks of nothing but that creature. Somehow, it is his second fear, greater by far than his fear of loneliness. Not of the snake itself, but something to do with it. He will not talk of the taipan for days, but always he comes back to it. And he has terrible dreams. The first year after my father's death he had them every night. This year only sometimes, until the last two weeks. Now they come often again. If he was so afraid of this creature, why does he want to have it?" She shook her head gravely. "I do not understand his thoughts. I think maybe he believes he can be done with his dreams only if he can face the taipan in his Rotarium."

Wrightson nodded to himself. He could appreciate the catharsis that a public milking might bring to Miller. For such a proud and brave man, failure to save his only friend in his time of mortal need, whether or not that was at all possible, would undoubtedly constitute the greatest imaginable shame. As a millionaire, Miller's only burden was his responsibility to Ioka. It seemed entirely plausible that he would devote his full energy, time, and resources to rid himself of imagined guilt by first creating a perfect setting, a world of incredibly deadly snakes, then by crowning the taipan king of that world, and finally by bringing it into the Rotarium and personally draining the poison that had taken his friend's life. Still, such a grand obsession over an accident not Miller's fault seemed to Wrightson more than a few steps over the line of sanity. He pushed the thoughts into a corner of his brain for future contemplation.

"Your life's been pretty rough, living with Miller's obsession, hasn't it?" Wrightson asked.

Ioka pointed the neck of the wine bottle at him in a gesture of exasperation. "You must not think Scott is an evil man! People must only fear him if they keep him from getting what he wants. I warned you not to work for him, but you had to have venoms for your research. I worried for you because you seemed so innocent. But now I think you, *also,* are a man of strong will. I am no longer afraid for you. You will have nothing to fear from Scott, so long as you get the taipan safely to him."

"You mean *we* will have nothing to fear, so long as *we* get the taipan safely to him," Wrightson corrected. "And if we don't?"

Ioka's eyes went dark. Her answer was a slow, solemn shake of her head. "Once I have gotten the taipan to Scott, I owe him no more. This will make me free."

The noise of an airhorn blared through the night.

"That must be the *Snowbird,*" Wrightson said, rising from the bed. "Let's be done with this as quickly as possible." He went sternward and fired up the engine.

The trawler, heavily laden, rode low in the inky waters, about two hundred feet to port and three hundred feet off the bow. Ioka maneuvered the sailboat alongside the trawler's rust-rough hull. As Wrightson dropped the fenders and readied the lines, he scanned the *Snowbird*'s glowing deck. Half a dozen hands stood at the rail, curious but destined never to be enlightened.

The two boats lightly collided. Wrightson tossed the lines up. A rope ladder was lowered, and he and Ioka climbed aboard. Waiting for them was the captain of the *Snowbird,* Lennart Sjomann. Except for his pea jacket and knitted yellow and black cap, he didn't seem at all the stereotype of the old sea-dog Wrightson had imagined. Instead, Sjomann was young, almost boyish in appearance, the owner of a broad smile and a tangle of white-blond hair which poked out from around the cap. He smoked no pipe, had no full-blown beard, no deep-creased wrinkles. Wrightson felt cheated, somehow.

"Hallo! I like punctuality," Sjomann exclaimed, offering his hand. His accent conjured up images of Norwegian fiords and Viking dragonboats. Sjomann turned to the woman.

"Ev'nin', Ioka," he said with force.

"Hello, Lennart." In explanation, she turned to Wrightson and said, "Scott uses Captain Sjomann's ship for many jobs. We met three years ago in Stockholm."

"Tick as tieves we are," Sjomann agreed, crossing two of his fingers and chuckling. He gave Wrightson an appraising glance, then pointed toward the bow. "Your cargo waits you dere. I want to be rid of it as soon as possible. Bad luck, dat ting. First time in all my years at sea I ever lose a sailor overboard."

"What?" Ioka said breathlessly, blanching.

Sjomann nodded. "Machinist's mate fell overboard two days out of port. Middle of the night with a sea as calm as dis. Now, I'm not a superstitious man, but . . ." His voice trailed off ominously.

Wrightson looked at Ioka's wide-eyed expression, but he refused to be pulled into the story emotionally. "Give the man the money, Ioka." She drew a thick envelope from her windbreaker.

"Two tousand?" Sjomann asked with studied indifference.

"Why don't you count it," Ioka replied coolly.

Sjomann laughed. "You tink I don't trust you? Miller's woman?" He studied Ioka's handsome companion for a reaction. Wrightson stared back, his face set. Sjomann laughed again and pushed the envelope deep into his pocket. "Listen, I am sorry I haf no time to talk but we must be at Long Beach by morning, as if we never haf stopped here."

"We can understand your fears," Wrightson said, liking the man less and less in spite of his broad smile. Perhaps, he decided, because of it.

"And if you haf any trouble bringing dat crate in, I never saw eider of you. Understand?" As he pronounced the warning, all trace of boyishness vanished from his face. Wrightson sized up the captain as precisely the sort of ruthless yet competent man Miller would employ. Without giving an answer, Ioka steered Wrightson back toward the rope ladder. From over his shoulder Wrightson heard Sjomann say, "If I were you, I drop dat crate in da sea."

"Don't look at him!" Ioka said firmly as she guided him over the rail to the ladder.

"Wait!" Sjomann cried out with a mocking voice. "Give me annuder two tousand and I do it for you!" His raucous laughter rolled across the waves. "You can understand my fears?" he bellowed. "What about your fears?"

A hoist swung over the rail of the trawler, bearing a rectangular shape in its net. As it was lowered to the sailboat, Wrightson studied it. The bamboo crate looked solid enough, but hardly the kind of box to contain an evil spirit. He smiled to himself. He and Ioka lifted the crate off the limp net to allow the hoist to swing clear. Once they set it on the cockpit deck it sat without movement or sound, which, Wrightson admitted to himself, made it all the more unnerving.

The *Snowbird*'s crew cast off the lines, and Ioka steered away. The trawler's engines came to life. The yellow and black cap appeared at the rail, a dark figure below it.

"Hey, good luck!" Sjomann yelled. "I got a feeling you need it!"

The trawler steamed rapidly into the darkness. Soon only its running lights were visible. Wrightson stowed the crate below deck, but a corner of it could be seen from the cockpit.

"Please throw your blanket over it, Marc." Ioka said, her eyes purposely avoiding the galley.

"Aren't you afraid the taipan will suffocate?" he asked.

Ioka turned her gaze toward the stars. "Maybe the captain is right. Perhaps we should drop it into the sea."

Wrightson walked down the steps and picked up the blanket. "Are you thinking about the man who fell overboard? Forget it. Sjomann desires you. I read it plainly in his eyes. He probably knows you're a bit superstitious, and he's not above trying to scare you with a phony story to get back at your coolness toward him."

"Sjomann told no story," Ioka replied firmly. "A man drowned, and that had nothing to do with superstition. You know, Marc, because you are a scientist you look down on everything you cannot explain with a formula."

Wrightson looked up sharply, surprised by the rebuke. "Oh, come on, Ioka. You're an intelligent, well-educated woman. You should be ashamed of yourself even suggesting that this thing is more than a snake."

He dropped the blanket over the crate.

"There is good and evil all around us, Marc. It has nothing to do with the education of a person's senses. If you listen to your heart, you will know that what lies in that box is evil. Scott has upset nature by taking the taipan from its island."

Wrightson laughed explosively. "Of all the snake stories I've heard this one about the taipan living on . . . soul food!" He covered his mouth as his laughter ended in a coughing spasm. Regaining his control Marcus apologized. "I'm sorry, Ioka, but I just can't take this discussion seriously."

Ioka eyed Wrightson with cool anger. "I see I am only a superstitious native girl to you, Dr. Wrightson. Perhaps you have more respect for William Shakespeare. He said, 'There are more things in heaven and earth, Horatio, than are dreamt of in your philosophy.'"

For a few seconds Wrightson sat dumbstruck. Then he asked, "How much did Miller pay to get this crate here?"

"Sixteen thousand dollars, so far," she answered.

"That's what I thought. I'm afraid that both science and superstition shall have to bow to economics. If I want my venoms, I've got to keep that thing safe, be it snake or demon. And I will. Now, let's forget the talk of murder and get it on that plane with all due haste, O.K.? I'll raise the sails; you get us into the wind."

13

BY THE time Ioka and Wrightson headed the nose
of the sailboat past the Mission Bay jetty and into
the marina itself, it was after two A.M. The city lights
had thinned out considerably. Once docked, they
gathered their belongings and took them to
Wrightson's station wagon. Then they returned for
the blanket-draped crate.

"I can't get over how much lighter this is than I
expected," Wrightson remarked. "I thought a
nineteen-foot snake would weigh at least forty
pounds. No noise or shaking. It must still be sedated
by the night breeze." Ioka was silent. Beads of perspiration shimmered on her forehead, despite the
cool air. Halfway to the car they met a fisherman
lugging poles and tackle down to his boat.

"Looks like I'm early and you're late," the friend-
ly stranger observed. "Whatchya got there, Davy
Jones' locker?"

Wrightson laughed, forcing it harder than necessary. "Nope. Nothing that interesting."

"Something you caught?"

"Something that caught us," Wrightson answered as he hurried Ioka toward the car.

The biology extension campus lay about five miles due east of Mission Bay, where the city's suburbs thinned into forest and mountainside. While he drove down U.S. 8, Wrightson blew off verbal steam, making wry observations on predawn fishermen, on people who wax curious only about things one wishes to hide, and anything else that basically avoided the subject of snakes. On the surface, he and Ioka had smoothed over their argument about the taipan almost immediately. In reality, he felt the tension all the while they tacked back to the marina. By the time he turned into the lot nearest the biology building and parked, he had resigned himself to Ioka's mood, confident it would disappear when she saw the taipan leave the runway in the cargo plane the next day.

"How are we with the time?" asked Ioka as she stared over her shoulder at the bamboo crate.

"Fine. Half past two." Wrightson got out of the car, walked to the back, and dropped the tailgate.

Ioka joined him. As she lifted her end of the blanketed box, she asked, "Won't you meet the cleaning people or the university police?"

"If we do, let me do the talking. They're used to me coming and going at all hours. It's called the bachelor professor syndrome. The night janitor doesn't come in until three, which gives us about fifteen minutes leeway."

Moving swiftly but with caution, they crossed the dark, damp-slick lawns and arrived at a set of steps which led down to the basement level of the building. Wrightson pulled out a key as they struggled to maneuver the crate down the stairs, around the tight turn, and through the door. They continued up a short hallway and to the right, until Wrightson pointed to a door with his free hand.

"This is it. The mad scientist's laboratory," he murmured under his breath, not sure Ioka would understand or appreciate his remark. He unlocked the door and turned on the fluorescent lights. The lab was as still as a photograph. Tables, snake cases, shelves were crammed to overflowing. All the paraphernalia of scientific investigation were as he had left them that morning when he had prepared the lab to receive its fearsome guest. They carried the crate into the room and over to the outside wall, setting it on the floor.

Wrightson said, "This is the case I told you about. It's got a very accurate temperature regulation unit." The case, about three feet wide, four feet long, and three high, sat on top of a large metal air-conditioning unit. The cover of the case, fashioned from wood and thick, smoked glass, was beveled at about 60° to perpendicular. Wrightson untwisted the four safety latches and lifted the cover. "It's now at room temperature. What should we raise it to?"

"Set it for 82 degrees. Tomorrow morning, when it has digested the mouse, we can lower it to 68." She looked around the lab. "Where do you keep your mice?"

Wrightson pointed across the room with one hand while the other fished into his pocket and pulled out his key ring. "Unlock that door with this key, then look to the right." While Ioka entered the adjoining room, Wrightson lifted the crate and placed it inside the case. "It fits, but just barely," he noted with relief.

"Is this one all right?" Ioka held a wriggling white mouse in her hand.

"Sure. Lock the door and bring it over." He looked down at the bamboo lid and the leather straps that encircled it. "Now, this evening's jackpot question is 'How do we get the mouse in to the snake?' "

"We cannot," Ioka declared as she looked around the lab. "We must let the snake out to the mouse."

"I was afraid you might suggest that." Wrightson leaned against the corner of the case. "What are you looking for?"

"Can you get me some string?"

"String? No problem." He stepped to his assistant's work table, found a ball of twine, and held it up. "This O.K.?"

"Yes, fine. Give me about ten feet." As Wrightson took the twine in both hands, then stretched his arms wide twice, measuring off a double span, she said, "First I will knot the string around part of the lid. We can push the string through one of the air holes in the top of the case, then pull on it to lift the lid off the crate." Wrightson sliced the twine with a gleaming scapel and handed it to Ioka.

"Hold the mouse," Ioka instructed. She reached into the case to tie the twine around one of the crate's strap loops. She fed a double strand upward through the air hole and pulled it around a nearby water pipe. "Now, place the mouse inside!" Wrightson dumped the tiny ball of fur in the case. It stayed, unmoving, in the space between the crate and the case wall. Ioka undid the leather straps, then secured the glass-faced cover to the front of the case. She took the twine in her hand and said, "You watch to see if the box opens."

Wrightson peered through the dark glass. As she pulled on the twine, the lid of the crate slowly lifted. "Very ingenious," he remarked. "You pass mechanical aptitude with flying colors." Ioka smiled wanly. Wrightson checked her securing knot and found two half-hitches, expertly tied. "Before we try to lock the snake back inside its crate tomorrow, we'll lower the temperature to sixty, all right? I want it extra torpid, just for safety."

"Will no one come in here before then?" Ioka asked.

"No. We're just finishing up the semester, and the others who use this lab are on vacation. We also do our own cleaning here, so it's perfectly safe from the janitor. Don't you want to wait and see this devil face to face?" he asked, looking into the glass at the space between the lid and the crate's sides.

"No!" Ioka said emphatically. "Please, just throw the blanket over the case! That will warm it more quickly."

"I wanted to show you that it's only another snake," he remarked without risking eye contact. He checked the tightness of the cover latches, then arranged the insulating blanket over the entire case. "How many hours until the plane arrives?"

Wrightson looked at his watch. "It will be here in less than twelve hours. Did you turn off the lights in the other room?"

"Yes." Ioka had folded her arms over her chest and was rubbing her hands against her exposed flesh.

"Cold?" he asked.

"Nervous," she replied. Wrightson threw his arm

around her and led her to the door. "Just a few more hours, Ioka. Let's go to my place and get some sleep," he said soothingly, as he turned out the lights and locked the door.

      °   °   °

"It's about fuckin' time," Crowley grunted as the figures of the man and woman climbed from the biology building's basement steps. A ring of red light shone on Crowley's eyelid and brow through the sight of the infrared Starlight snooperscope he held. "I thought they were gonna spend the night in there." He refocused the scope on the station wagon and waited for Wrightson and Ioka to clear the hedges and trees that softened the lines of the building.

"Hallelujah!" Crowley hooted. "They're empty-handed. In ten minutes that snake is ours." Crowley and Gordon sat in their rented car under the low branches of a shade tree, tucked between two other cars parked on the street. Just beyond the sidewalk next to them lay a strip of grass, then the biology parking lot and finally the biology building itself. The campus was deserted; the only car in the lot was Wrightson's station wagon.

"That's it, assholes, get in your car and go home," Crowley directed softly. "Tomorrow, when you come back for your little basket, it's gonna be gone."

"Duck your head," Gordon commanded. "They're gonna drive right by us."

Wrightson started his car and drove it slowly from the lot. Only after he had reached the street and passed Crowley and Gordon did he turn on his lights.

"Bye-bye," Crowley said gleefully as he slid back

up in the seat and looked in the rear-view mirror at the waning taillights. He reached into the rear seat, opened his briefcase, and pulled out the Walther PPK pistol.

"Whatcha doin'?" Gordon asked.

"Bringing my insurance," Crowley replied. "I'm not about to get caught."

Gordon raised his finger menacingly. "You take that with you, Crowley, I don't go in. An' if I don't go in, Mr. Thanner won't buy that snake. You remember what he said about me bein' in charge?"

"And you remember what I think about that bullshit? I don't go into any job without protection."

Gordon gave him a cunning smile. "Didn't you say you was trained to use your hands as weapons?"

Crowley coughed nervously. "Uh, yeah."

"Then you *got* your protection." He held one of his massive fists in front of Crowley's face. "I used this plenty of times, an' I never got caught once. Somebody gets in my way tonight, I knock him cold. You bring that gun, you'll maybe kill somebody. An' no snake's worth that."

Crowley stared at the familiar fist. His chest still smarted, physical evidence of what the black man could do unarmed.

"All right. No gun. But don't try to change my plan for getting the snake. We're gonna do it just like . . ." Crowley paused at the sound of the high-torqued engine as it rumbled up the street. Both men ducked down as the headlight beams swept into their car. The engine's whine diminished. When Crowley and Gordon looked up, they saw a red MG convertible pull into the biology lot and park.

"What the fuck is this?" Crowley said, confused

by the quickness of the incident. The driver of the MG shut off the engine and killed the lights. Crowley grabbed his Starlight scope and trained it on the little car. "Ah, Jesus Christ. A couple of college kids." The owner of the MG had pulled it into the lot so that it faced Crowley and Gordon, not fifty feet away. Crowley rotated his focusing ring. "Can you believe it? They picked this lot to neck in."

"Beep the horn," Gordon suggested. "They'll get scared and leave."

"I won't have to," Crowley informed him. "I been here three different nights. A cop car will roll into that lot between two fifty-five and ten after three. We just have to sit tight and wait. Man, look at that little girl! What a face. Great mouth. Bet those lips will feel good around his cock. Shit, he's a fast worker. He's got his hand on her left tit already, massaging it around." Crowley shrugged and returned the instrument to his eye. "Punk kid. Still in college an' he's driving an MG. Fuckin' permissive parents. I never got any of that shit when I was his age. Now he's got her sweater up. Jesus, she ain't wearin' a bra. Look at that sweet nipple! He's puttin' his mouth down on it now. I can't see his hands. I'll bet he's fingerin' her snatch, too. An' I'll bet she didn't have panties on neither."

"Hey, man, if you got to watch, do it," Gordon said with disgust. "But don't announce it like a football game."

Crowley kept his eye glued to the scope. "Yeah. All right. I was kinda steamin' myself up anyway. I tell you, she's a fuckin' piece. If this was some deserted road, I'd go over there and beat the shit out of him and then fuck the shit out of her."

"Better get down now," Gordon warned. "Here comes your cop car."

The couple had apparently also noticed the police car. A few seconds later the MG's engine came to life. Crowley stole a look over the rim of his door. "I love it! The cops didn't even stop. They're following the kid's car. Let's go!"

Gordon and Crowley skulked around the perimeter of the lot, weaving in and out of the carefully landscaped plants, until they drew parallel with the basement stairs. Crowley squatted behind a bush, and Gordon dropped to one knee, checking the campus behind them.

Crowley pointed to one of the casement windows that lined the building at grass level. "That's the window there. Like I said, the doors have burglar alarms, but there's nothing on the windows. I can shut off the alarms once we're inside." As if from thin air, Crowley produced a flat wedge of metal, slightly indented on the curved end. "I'll go first. Give me ten seconds to open the window." He held up the tool. "Instead of peddlin' useless shit like history and philosophy, they ought to teach kids practical things like these: 'Survival in Modern Society 101.'" He laughed, then was gone, running across the open lawn to the building. Gordon counted to ten, then followed. By the time he arrived at Crowley's side, the window hung open. "After you," Crowley offered, with a dramatic sweep of his arm.

Gordon backed through the narrow opening. Once his bottom half had passed through the frame, he kicked around in the darkness, feeling for a foothold. A few feet below the window, his shoe touched upon a soft surface. Tentatively, he tested its ability to support his weight. He found that a solid surface lay just under the soft one. Gordon eased himself in the rest of the way and jumped down to the floor. The room was extremely dark. He decided to stand still and let his eyes accustom themselves. Crowley climbed in and landed on the blanket. Then, using his momentum, he hopped down the rest of the way in one deft motion. The blanket slipped off the case.

Gordon reached into his back pocket and brought out a small flashlight. He thumbed the switch and trained the beam on the crumpled blanket. "Didn't the woman have this under her arm?"

"Yeah. I think so. Listen, don't touch anything else before you put on your gloves." Crowley himself had just finished slipping on a pair of disposable plastic gardening gloves. He scooped the blanket from the floor and threw it on top of the case, covering the twine and the length of water pipe Ioka had used as a tie-off point.

Gordon played the light around the room. "There's a lot of snake cases in here."

"It's not going to be in a case," Crowley declared positively. "It's still in its basket. The last time Miller called Wrightson, which was two days ago, he said specifically not to open the crate the taipan arrived in."

Gordon took a few steps into the room. "Well, I don't see that box nowhere. Maybe it's in the next room. We saw the light go on in that window for a little while."

Crowley prodded Gordon lightly with his hand. "Check it out!" Gordon sidled cautiously between a row of tables, picking his path with the light. Crowley, left with only the faint shaft of window light, stepped to the middle of the room, as far from the dark, enclosing shapes as possible. He had needed this job badly, and so he had never mentioned to Thanner or Gordon that he suffered from an insane fear of snakes. Cocky as he was, Crowley knew he could not pull the job off without Gordon's help, because the thought of even touching a *box* with a snake inside it made his flesh crawl.

"It's locked," Gordon called across the shadows in a forceful whisper.

"Then let's finish checking this room before we break in." As Crowley and Gordon peered under the tables, a series of noises came through the door from the hallway.

"Someone's in the building," Gordon said. The sounds coming from another part of the building echoed blatantly off the plaster walls. To Gordon it sounded like a metal garbage can was being dragged along the stone floor. The person who was doing the dragging was alternately whistling and humming one of the latest disco melodies.

"Don't sweat it," Crowley assured his partner. "It's the janitor. He's emptying the garbage cans from the bathrooms. I cased the whole layout. He's down three doors and around the corner. He'll go out back to the garbage bin without coming anywhere near here." The sound of metal scraping stone stopped.

"Sounds like he's raking leaves," Gordon whispered.

"He's putting the trash in a plastic bag. He should be going out any second. Then he'll start upstairs." Crowley was right. In less than a minute the syncopated whistling faded to nothingness.

Crowley's eyes chanced upon the glass-covered

case. "Hey, Nate, what about this thing?" he suggested. "It's big enough to hold that basket."

"Yeah," Gordon agreed. "Maybe they wanted to hide it." He turned his light on the case cover, but the heavily smoked glass surface threw back a blinding glare. "Some other snake could be in there, but I can't see nothin'."

Crowley put his hands on two of the latches. "No. This must be it. That's why we found the blanket on top. Let me undo these, and then I'll lift the cover. Just in case it's another snake, you stand back a couple of feet and shine the light in." Gordon took a position directly in front of the case, holding the light steady, as Crowley undid the last two latches. "Ready?" he whispered. Gordon nodded. Crowley pulled quickly back and to the left. As fast as he lifted the cover, something behind it shot out of the case into the room. Crowley was barely aware of the lunging black shadow, one shade darker than its surroundings. The form flashed across four feet of open space, heading directly for Gordon. The big man threw his arm up to ward off the attack, causing the flashlight's beam to flare wildly across the ceiling. Gordon's face, caught in the shaft of light coming through the casement window, was a mask of frozen horror. The next instant, the black shadow fastened itself to Gordon's neck, at the place where it joined his shoulder.

"Je-sus Christ!" Crowley screamed. Gordon dropped the flashlight, yet there was still enough light for Crowley to see the hideous head of the taipan, its fangs buried deep in Gordon's neck. The black man twisted down and to the left, batting at the snake. The taipan relinquished its hold. The sparse light caught one of the gleaming fangs and reflected its shape to Crowley's bulging eyes. Crowley's muscles convulsed spasmodically, drawing the glass cover up close to his body like a shield.

The taipan launched itself out of the case again, stretching an unbelievable five feet. Gordon fell backward to the floor to avoid the attack. The snake's head glided into space and held itself steady on its slender neck, three feet above the floor, defying gravity. Crowley could have sworn the eyes were glowing red from some self-contained energy deep within the snake. Its jaws dropped open. Rows of teeth showed, barely visible beneath a sheath of white flesh.

Gordon continued to back away from the creature. He had clapped one hand involuntarily to his painful wound. His eyes remained riveted to the near-motionless head. He tried to stand, and did so with difficulty.

"Gordon," Crowley cried out in anguish. "Save me!"

Gordon looked dumbly in Crowley's direction. He was incapable of rational thought. He continued backing from the taipan, more slowly now, his knees wobbling and threatening to buckle. His hand found the doorknob. The taipan whipped its head back and forth and hissed wildly. Gordon twisted open the lock, leaning heavily on the knob.

"Don't leave me, Gordon!" Crowley shrieked, nearing total hysteria. He took a desperate step toward the door, the cover still clasped tightly to his chest. The taipan, catching the glint of the glass cover, swung its great head at Crowley. Another foot of its body flowed from the case. Crowley gasped and retreated until he found that he had backed himself into a cul de sac. He started to whimper. At the same time, Gordon had thrown open the door and pulled his weight around to the outside knob. Then his slow-motion movements ceased. Gordon's eyes rolled up into their sockets. He pitched forward through the doorway. His arms did not break his fall.

The janitor came around the corner with his broom raised just as Gordon toppled into the hall like a felled oak. "What'reya doin'?" the old man cried out. Gordon hit the floor full force. The janitor heard the sound of bone breaking. He winced and let his broom fall. He bent quickly and turned the man over. Gordon's eyelids were closed. His nose had been pushed flat and his front teeth had been knocked somewhere into his throat. Saliva dropped over his slack lips.

"Oh, my God!" the janitor moaned, catching his breath. He swung the door open to see what kind of accident had befallen the man. As the hall light illuminated the room, the janitor's eyes fell on the most terrifying sight he had ever witnessed. Something like a snake, but ten times larger, was hissing at a gleaming square of light in a dark corner of the room. When the hall's brightness fell on the snake, it swung its head toward the door and threw open its monstrous jaws, letting loose a raspy, demonic noise. The janitor gave a yelp and yanked the door shut with all his might. Gordon's corpse momentarily forgotten, he bolted down the hallway, screaming incoherently.

Crowley moaned as the door slammed shut. He had prayed that the voice might mean rescue. Now he was alone in the room with the monster, weaponless, cowering behind a pane of glass. He had slid down to his knees, tucked into a tight ball. The taipan, distracted by the sudden rush of light from the hallway, had apparently forgotten about Crowley. Now, with the door closed, the room was plunged into darkness, mitigated only by the glimmer of the walklamps outside the building. The snake raised itself to the level of the open window. Crowley held his breath, afraid to make the slightest sound. The taipan's head slithered through the open space, followed silently by foot after foot of body. It seemed a full minute before the last of the snake disappeared from the room.

Crowley rested his chin on the cover, completely drained, listening to the anticlimactic stillness. He was swimming in sweat. His hands shook as if palsied. With great effort he set the cover against a cabinet and stood up. His eyes never left the rectangular space of light. For all he knew, the snake might change its mind and return to the room. Crowley edged his way to the door and opened it. Outside, lying face up and quite obviously dead, was Gordon. Crowley's eyelids blinked furiously. As he took a step, his shoe caught on something solid. Panicked, he jumped out and slammed the lab door. He heard a thud inside the room, and then there was nothing but the sound of the walls amplifying his shallow, spasmodic breathing. Crowley stepped gingerly around the corpse. He looked down at his pants. A dark stain had spread across the crotch and down as far as his knees. Crowley gave Gordon's body one last look, then dashed for the nearest exit.

14

THE PHONE RANG ONCE, and Wrightson's hand reached out automatically. As both bachelor and popular professor, it was natural for him to receive calls from his nocturnal friends and students at all hours of the night.

"What," he murmured. The weight of sleep in his brain told him that he had been unconscious only a few minutes.

"Professor Wrightson?" a male voice asked.

"That's right."

"Campus police. We just got a call from Eddy Bosak, the janitor at Biology. He reports a snake loose in your laboratory." Wrightson sat up, alarm signals tripping rapidly in the base of his skull. "He also reports a man dead in front of the door. Dean Franklin . . ."

"Have you dispatched a car to the building?" Wrightson interrupted, his mind starting to calculate.

"Yes. We have."

"Call those officers and tell them not to go inside

the lab! There are a number of very poisonous snakes in there, and somebody may be seriously bitten."

"Hold on." The dispatcher clicked off. Wrightson shook Ioka. She moved restlessly, still asleep.

"Ioka, Ioka, get up! We've got big trouble."

"What is it?"

"Get dressed," he said urgently. "There's been an accident at my lab. I don't have the details, but it may . . ." Wrightson heard the line being re-engaged.

"Professor Wrightson?"

"I radioed, but the officers must have gone inside already. However, a second car is on the way. They may be able to halt them."

"I hope so," Wrightson breathed, almost a prayer.

"Dean Franklin wants you to meet him in front of your lab as soon as you can get there."

"I'm on my way." Wrightson dropped the receiver to its cradle and rushed to his closet.

"Is it the taipan?" Ioka asked. She had almost finished throwing on her clothes.

"Find the car keys! We'll talk on the way," he replied as he collapsed backward on the bed and yanked on a pair of denim jeans, both legs at once. He rammed his feet into a pair of loafers, the first shoes he found in the closet. He grabbed indiscriminately among his shirts. His hand fell on a light-blue, short-sleeved one. Pulling his arms through the sleeves, Wrightson tore out the front door without bothering to lock it. Ioka sat in the front seat of the station wagon, motionless but obviously quite agitated. Wrightson threw the shift lever into reverse and backed recklessly down the driveway. He shoved the selector into second before the car had reached the street, and it took off along the sidewalk for a moment, bounced over the curb and onto the asphalt.

"Sorry," he said, teeth clenched, as he removed the arm he had thrown protectively across Ioka's chest, "but if we don't get to the lab in five minutes, there won't be much chance for us. The custodian said he saw a snake in my lab and a dead man lying in front of the door. I hope it's not one of my colleagues." Ioka gasped. "No," Wrightson corrected himself. "The janitor would know all of them. It doesn't make any sense."

"It is the taipan," Ioka announced fatalistically. "No case could hold such a demon."

"Get a grip on yourself!" Wrightson said angrily. "If we want to save our skins you'll have to remain calm. There may be a way around this, but not if you charge in there confessing that we smuggled in an evil spirit. Let's just flow with the situation. Maybe another snake got loose. I have a dozen specimens in that room."

"How many of your snakes could kill a person in the time it takes to reach the lab door?" Ioka asked, eyes closed, head lolling back.

"You're right," Wrightson admitted, flooring the gas pedal. "It sounds pretty grim. Even so, if the cops stay out of the lab like I told them, we still have a chance. First, we check the guy's body to make sure he was bitten. If he was, and the taipan did it, we'll know before we enter the lab. The marks will be big, right?"

Ioka's eyes remained closed. "Yes, if it bit the man in naked flesh there would be a number of wounds and tearing."

"O.K. If we enter the lab alone, we can either capture or kill the taipan, hide it, and take out a coral snake I have in there. We'll call in the cops, show them the coral snake, and put it back into its case."

"You and I cannot capture it," Ioka said flatly. "If we go into that room, it will kill us, too."

* * *

"You guys go first!" Eddy Bosak pushed Patrolmen Valasquez and Corrigan in front of him as he neared the biology building's basement stairwell.

Patrolman Corrigan grinned. "Ah, come on, Eddy. How big can it be? Most snakes aren't longer than your arm." He jogged down the stairs.

"Maybe not, Mike," Eddy replied, bringing up the rear, "but what I seen was three times that long, and it wasn't half out of its box." They rounded the corner. Nate Gordon's body lay as the janitor had left it, twisted on its right side. The patrolmen bent to check for pulse at the heart and wrist.

"He's gone," Velasquez announced. "We can take our time with the ambulance."

Corrigan looked up. The janitor had flattened himself against the opposite wall, eyes like tiny moons. "Whatsa matter, Eddy? Afraid of a corpse?"

The janitor pronounced: "I'm not afraid of nothin' dead. It's what's alive on the other side of that door's got me shakin'." Corrigan chuckled. "Go ahead and laugh, Corrigan," Bosak snorted in reply. " 'Cause I'm gonna get the *last* laugh when you open that door. It's got a body thicker'n my arm, a head like a football, orange eyes, and teeth like this." He dangled the fore and middle fingers of his right hand for the patrolmen to contemplate.

Corrigan took another look at the corpse. Something horrible had happened to the man, whether or not it was the work of a gigantic serpent. "O.K., then, Eddy, just stand back." He withdrew his service revolver from its holster and unclipped a flashlight from his belt. "There may be somebody else still in there who needs first aid, Nardo," he said to his partner. "You open the door halfway, and I'll check."

Velasquez turned the doorknob cautiously. Once the door was open a crack, he nudged his foot along the bottom and shoved. The door swung in with considerable effort, and a long, dark shape swooped down into the open doorway. Corrigan twitched with fright. His revolver went off, blowing a large chunk of wood out of the top of the falling coat rack. The long rack hit Gordon's body and rolled off, a green scarf fluttering down after. All three men jumped back. The gun's blasting report boomed sharply in the halls.

"Son-of-a-bitch, Corrigan!" Velasquez shouted, one leg high in the air as he danced away from the door.

"How did I know it wasn't a snake?" Corrigan shouted back.

"Corrigan? Velasquez? You guys O.K.?" a voice called from the top of the stairs.

"Yeah. We're O.K.," Velasquez said, eyeing his partner with disgust. "Now you're gonna spend three hours filling out a firearms discharge report, you shithead." Two more uniformed campus patrolmen came around the corner, escorting a harried-looking gentleman, dressed in a grey, sharkskin suit and a green and brown plaid flannel pajama top. He had slippers on his feet.

"Dean Franklin," Velasquez said, with proper deference.

"Who fired that shot?" Franklin demanded.

Corrigan's sheepish expression spoke for itself, but the patrolman defended his action. "We had to open the lab door to see if anyone was inside. Mr. Bosak said that a large snake was loose in there, so I drew my revolver."

"A *giant* snake," Bosak corrected, then retreated to his wall.

Corrigan gave the janitor a withering look. "When Patrolman Velasquez opened the door, this, uh, coat tree fell out and, uh, I thought, uh . . . it was the snake."

"Nice shot," the dean said with acerbity. "Weren't you instructed not to enter that room?"

"No," Corrigan said. His look of surprise assured Franklin of his honesty. Franklin, however, was not about to lose his momentum.

"Well, you just missed the order. Now, pull that coat tree out and shut the door! While we're standing here arguing, the snake could crawl out and bite us all, for God's sake!" He looked at the corpse with a tremor of revulsion. "Who is he?"

Corrigan and Velasquez looked at each other. Velasquez came to his partner's rescue. "We just got here. We haven't had time . . ."

"To do anything but shoot a coat tree," Franklin sighed. "All right, check him now." While the two patrolmen went through Gordon's pockets the dean mentally bemoaned the second-rate quality of his college's campus police. He turned to the other officers for sympathy. "The semester would have been over in a few more days. I was hoping to coast the rest of the way."

"He's got no identification. His pockets are clean," Velasquez said.

"Thank God he's too old to be a student," Franklin said. He turned to the second team of patrolmen. "You might as well call University Hospital, then notify the city police." The officers nodded and left. Franklin hitched up his beltless trousers. He nodded toward the corpse. "Probably after the lab equipment. Damn it, Wrightson, where are you? I had a feeling this project was going to cause trouble." His lips disappeared as he tensed the muscles in his jaw.

As the patrolmen's footsteps diminished, another set of sounds replaced them. Franklin looked up. Wrightson and an unknown woman came into view. Wrightson held a snake-catching device, Pilstrom tongs, in his hand. "Professor Wrightson, we have an extremely serious matter on our hands," Franklin said without going through the normal amenities of greeting. "This man is dead, and I believe that one of your lab specimens may have killed him."

"Has anyone been inside the lab?" Wrightson asked, puffing lightly from a recent sprint.

"No. But the janitor here saw the man fall through the door." Franklin faced the janitor. "Isn't that what you reported over the telephone?" Bosak nodded. "You said you also saw a big snake crawling around loose in there, didn't you?"

"Not big. *Giant!*" Bosak repeated. "And it wasn't crawlin'. It was kinda slidin' out of a big box."

The janitor's forceful description caused a tight knot in Wrightson's stomach. He glanced at Ioka, who was ghostly pale, staring at the corpse, oblivious to the dialogue. "If the man was attacked, he ought to have bite wounds," Wrightson stated. "Have you found any?"

Corrigan shifted nervously from one foot to the other. "Uh, we didn't have a chance to check yet."

"Is it all right if I do?" Wrightson asked.

"Go ahead," the dean replied. Wrightson handed the Pilstrom tongs to Ioka. While he bent down next to the corpse, Dean Franklin gave Ioka the once-over. She was dressed in shorts, halter top and windbreaker. Franklin had often wondered about Wrightson's bachelor life. Now, looking at the beautiful woman, he developed a definite opinion. Ioka did not notice his stare. Her eyes were fixed on Wrightson's hands.

Wrightson grimaced at Gordon's battered face. He ignored the broken nose and teeth. He also saw no point in checking the extremities. The flow of venom would have been too slow from those points. If the man had been bitten inside the lab and then died literally outside the door, the venom must have been injected into a major vein or artery, one leading directly into the brain or heart. As he closely examined the victim's head and neck, his hand chanced upon a few unraveled strands of material in the neck of the corpse's lightweight pullover. He drew the collar away. At the base of the throat, where the neck joined the shoulder, he saw two jagged sets of tears. Bleeding had been minimal. Wrightson looked up at Ioka. She bit her lower lip and nodded almost imperceptibly.

Wrightson exhaled. "Yes. He was bitten."

The dean leaned over to examine the bites. "I thought there would be two little puncture marks," he said. "What kind of snake would do this?"

"I have a number of snakes in my lab capable of causing such a wound," Wrightson lied. "I'll have to go in there and find out which one it is." He paused

for a second, staring at the corpse's bare right forearm, exposed where the sleeve had been pulled up.
Then he stood. He turned to Corrigan. "Could I borrow your flashlight?" The patrolman unclipped it and
handed it over. Wrightson gave Ioka a quick glance.
"Now, would everyone please stand well back from
the door? I'm going to open it." They all obliged him
immediately. He shone the flashlight beam through
the narrow opening and, seeing no movements,
reached his free hand in, feeling for the light switch.
His heart slammed against his ribs as he reflected on
how quickly the man had died from the taipan's bites.

"I'm glad it's him and not me," Bosak whispered to
his patrolmen friends.

Wrightson signalled for silence. No sound came
from inside the lab. He handed the flashlight back
without turning his head and slipped the door open a
few more inches. His attention went immediately to
the large case directly across from the door. The cover
had been removed, the blanket pushed up in a lump.
Inside, Wrightson could see the raised lid of the bamboo crate, but there was no sign of the snake. Then he
spotted the open window. His heart quickened its
beat, pumping blood into his head with such dizzying
force that he could hear it rushing through his ears.
His eyes examined the entire room, found nothing,
then swept back for a second look. Cluttered as the
room was, there were very few places where a
nineteen-foot snake could hide. He slipped through
the door, holding it half-closed, then gestured for Ioka
to approach. She pushed the tongs through first and
entered. Wrightson eased the door shut, grabbed
Ioka's arm, and led her to the open case. "It's not in
here! Nowhere!"

"Where could it have gone?" she asked, searching warily, unconvinced that the snake had vanished.

"Through there." Wrightson nodded to the window.

"Oh, God!" Ioka gasped loudly, forgetting the men outside.

Wrightson clapped his hand over her mouth. "We have to get out of here as soon as possible and find it. Do what we planned in the car!" He took the tongs and moved swiftly to another case. He unfastened the cover, opened it, and thrust in the tongs. He pressed the trigger and withdrew a beautifully mark d coral snake which wriggled angrily in the grasp of the rubber-tipped pincers. Meanwhile, Ioka had pushed the blanket aside and had untied the twine from the water pipe. She reached into the case to grasp the crate, but paused. "Marc!" she whispered urgently, and held up the dead mouse. The taipan had not eaten. He looked at her pale face, then signalled for her to drop the rodent inside the crate. She did so, then closed the lid and pulled the bamboo box out of the case.

"Stow the blanket inside it and push it under that table!" Wrightson whispered as he passed her on the way to the door. When she had finished, he threw open the door, smiled, and said, "We've got it!" He held the squirming coral snake in the general direction of the four men.

"Be careful with that!" Franklin said sharply as he backed up a few steps. The patrolmen, too, retreated. Eddy Bosak, however, stormed forward from his wall and said, with great indignation, "That's not the snake!"

Wrightson blanched, then fought to compose himself. "It must be. I just found it on the floor in that corner. I'll show you." He backed into the room.

"I'm telling you that's not the snake!" Bosak said firmly. Corrigan gave him a half-amused look. "That's not even a quarter as big as what I saw. What I saw was a monster. Eyes like . . ." He continued to babble as Wrightson guided the dean and the officers to the supposed place of capture, deep in the farthest corner of the room.

"You can see the cover over there on the floor. The man must have thought he'd find something valuable inside the case. He probably put his head in to see and was stuck. I'm sure he had no idea we keep snakes in the lab."

"Can you put the snake back in now?" Franklin asked, unable to take his eyes from the serpent. Wrightson dropped it inside and secured the cover.

"I don't care *what* the professor says. That's not the thing I saw," Bosak insisted, growing more agitated by the moment. "Now, who are you going to believe?"

Franklin turned to Corrigan with an exasperated look. "I think all this has been a terrible strain on Mr. . . ."

"Bosak," Corrigan and Velasquez prompted in chorus.

"Yes," Franklin replied, undaunted. "Why don't one of you take him home, and we'll call him in for the investigation tomorrow."

"Or maybe you think I was so scared my eyes played tricks on me," Bosak continued in a higher-pitched voice, "Well, they didn't do no such thing. I ain't exaggeratin'. It must have been twenty-five feet. Maybe thirty!"

"Tomorrow, Mr. Bosak," the dean said in a patronizing voice. "You can tell us tomorrow when we're all much calmer." Corrigan led the janitor away, berating him for making such a vociferous fool of himself. Bosak would not be cowed, however, and his indignant protests echoed down the halls for another minute.

"All right," the dean said, with a relieved tone of finality as he rubbed his eyes wearily. "The whole incident looks fairly self-evident. The thief came in through the window, started looking for something of value in the lab and was bitten. There's his flashlight. He had no identification on him, so he was probably a professional. That ought to make the publicity a little less damning for the university." He sighed soulfully. "Why didn't you tell me the snakes you kept were so deadly?" he asked Wrightson.

Wrightson shook his head. "He was just unlucky. If he'd been bitten on the hand, he'd probably still be alive."

Franklin said, "I'm going straight up to my office. I'll have to call the president and half a dozen other authorities." He looked at the patrolmen. "Let me know when the city police arrive. And, Marc, go home and make yourself presentable. This project is yours. I think you're the most qualified to explain the presence of deadly snakes on university property. I'll cover for you until you get back."

Wrightson nodded, picked up the capture tongs, and gestured for Ioka. As they walked through the door, Franklin sighed with relief, "At least it didn't happen in the middle of the semester. Those goddamn radicals on the school newspaper would have had a field day with this. With my luck, they can still run a special edition.''

15

"WHAT DO we do now?" Ioka asked, hurrying after Wrightson, taking three steps for every two of his, searching the dimly lit campus.

"We catch or kill the damn thing," he answered, eyes fixed straight ahead, flashing with anger. He turned off the path into the biology parking lot and headed for his car.

"Wait, wait," she said, grabbing him by the arm. "We cannot. Not two of us. Didn't you see what it did to that man?"

Wrightson gripped her tightly around her shoulders. His eyes narrowed. "Yes, I saw. And I was frightened half to death. But we really don't have a choice, Ioka. We brought the taipan in, and we're at least partly responsible for that man's death. If, by some major miracle, the coronor buys my story about the coral snake bite, we may get away with this. But if we let the taipan escape, there's going to be a few bodies I'll never be able to explain." He took her hand and pulled her along behind his lanky strides. "Feel the air! It must be down around 70°. Two hundred feet out of the lab and that monster undoubtedly began to feel the difference. Then its one drive had to be finding a warm place. The nearest warm place." His free hand waved in front of him in a sweeping general direction. "You see those dark objects over there? They're houses." Wrightson had reached his station wagon and unlocked the tailgate. He pulled out a capture bag and a flashlight and set them on the roof. "It's gonna crawl in the first open window it finds. Then under a couch, a bed, or up inside a baby's crib. If you feel badly about that man, wait'll the taipan kills an entire family. Here, slip off your windbreaker and put this on!" Wrightson handed the woman a grimy vinyl raincoat, four sizes too large. He rummaged through the piles of blankets, rags, and newspapers until he found himself a plaid woolen jacket. He froze in place. "Oh Lord! What if the nearest warm place is right back through that window!"

They ran to the side of the building. The paths there were well lit. If the snake were somewhere on the lawns they would have seen it. It was not in sight. Wrightson halted Ioka at the walkway. "You keep a lookout for police." He pointed to the street where a campus patrol car's flasher threw beams of red light across the lawns and shrubbery. "We're supposed to have left by now." Wrightson took a few steps toward the window. He found footprints pressed into the dew-covered grass. Edging along the building, next to the open window, he heard the dean delivering a tirade on campus research projects.

"Look!" Ioka called out softly. Playing the flashlight beam around the area, she had chanced upon faint, sinuous impressions in the grass, the dew shaken from the blades. "It moved that way." She pointed the beam into a clump of bushes.

"Let me wipe out the marks before we follow," Wrightson said. All we need is for some smart cop to walk by and recognize a snake's trail." He quickly obliterated the path, which they picked up on the other side of the greenery. The path led almost directly to a large greenhouse, the closest structure to the biology building. It's facade shimmered in the feeble, artificial light like a magnificent Victorian ghost, its transparent walls rising straight up some twenty feet, then curving up and inward into an enormous horizontal bow shape. Wrightson pointed to the structure. "There's our best bet. That greenhouse stored heat all day and is still releasing it. The taipan may have curled up against a wall to wait for daylight." Bushes crowded against the greenhouse, planted thickly to help retain the naturally generated warmth. Wrightson got down on his knees and peered into the shadows.

"Please stay in the light," Ioka pleaded, trying to anticipate his movements with the flashlight beam. "If it even scratches you, you will be dead in five minutes."

"Five minutes, ten minutes. Who counts when you're having a great time?" he muttered, edging under the evergreen needles.

"What?" she asked.

"Forget it. Let me have the flashlight." He grabbed the handle and slid the circle of light up the glass wall.

"Oh, shit!"

"What is it?"

"I think the snake may be inside the greenhouse. The lowest pane here has a hole in it, big enough for our friend." Wrightson shone the light through the hole, revealing a patch of the lush interior. "I don't see any blood, but it's a pretty smooth break. It could have slid through unharmed."

"What do we do now?"

"You look all around the greenhouse, carefully, for other marks in the grass. I'll stay here." He handed her the flashlight. "With my recent luck, it's still outside, under the next bush."

Ioka returned a few minutes later. Her grim expression told the story. Wrightson stood and brushed the dirt from his knees. "O.K., we try the greenhouse."

The side door had a simple lock. Wrightson shoved with all his might. On the third heave a section of the jamb gave way with a splintering crack, catapulting Wrightson into the greenhouse.

Inside, the domed roof acted like a parabolic reflector, magnifying the faintest sound. Moisture that had condensed and collected on the cool upper panes plummeted down among the plants with sharp, clocklike ticks. Exaggerated also were the odors, as if the plants were competing for honors of most pungent, most fragrant, most pervading. In a far corner, ultraviolet lights cast their eerie glow on a large white table.

Wrightson turned to Ioka, who had followed him in and shut the door. "Let's just stand still and listen for a minute."

Space was obviously at a premium, creating a very singular jungle. Wrightson, no tyro at botany, marveled at the proliferation of exotic shapes and colorations. Huge ferns and palms rooted in floor tubs pushed their branches to the limits of the roof. Smaller plants stood erect in serried ranks of multisized tuscan clay pots, like brightly colored platoons of uniformed infantry. Near the door lay a formidable pile of peat moss, a large pitchfork buried deep in its black center.

"We'll never see it in this light," Wrightson quickly concluded. "We'll have to take a chance someone will notice." He eased toward a pair of light switches on a support beam and flicked on a row of bulbs. The illumination was dim and widely spaced, not intended for night work. Wrightson put on his jacket. "I want you to have the tongs, Ioka. You've had much more experience with them than I have. If we find it, I'll distract it with anything not nailed down. Right now I could care less if Miller gets his precious snake slightly damaged."

Wrightson moved forward in a crouch, checking underneath the tables at every fourth step. The areas in shadow far exceeded those in light. If anything, the few bulbs, strung out like the lights in a Christmas tree lot, had emphasized the deepness of some shadows.

"These plants are too close," Ioka warned, her voice quivering with fear. "If it is here, then we are the hunted ones, not the hunters."

"But how can we miss seeing it?" Wrightson asked. "It's nineteen feet long." He paused. "If we don't see it, surely we'll hear it." Ioka looked unconvinced.

Wrightson duck-walked into the center of the greenhouse without incident, turning a corner to face another row of tables. He straightened up to ease his muscles. Through his weary mind flashed the memory of the Rotarium arena and the gigantic King cobra. He remembered his thoughts then—how he could not have been bought, blackmailed, or cajoled into that arena. Yet now he stood, searching for a bigger, more aggressive, more poisonous snake in a setting close to its natural habitat, armed with nothing but a capture bag and a flashlight. Gone were the advantages of the white walls, the sloping floor, and the mechanically cooled air. His stomach muscles knotted involuntarily, forcing out his breath in an ironic imitation of a laugh. Ioka moved closer to him.

"What's this?" Wrightson said suddenly as his eyes fell upon a red cylinder fastened to a support beam. "A fire extinguisher."

"So?" Ioka said, not impressed.

"You know what these things have in them?" Wrightson countered. "Liquid carbon dioxide, the same as dry ice." He unhooked the extinguisher and hefted its weight in his hands, pulling the nozzle from its retaining clasp. "You just turn this baby upside down, and you've got one damned good way to freeze a cold-blooded killer."

"Listen!" Ioka cocked her head. Faintly but unmistakably, hissing sibilated through the greenhouse. "It's here!" she whispered. Their eyes met, then searched the grey-green shadows desperately. Now every drip-spattered leaf merited attention. The snake was everywhere and nowhere.

"At least it's not loose outside," Wrightson offered as cheerfully as he could. He assessed their position. "This was not a good idea, coming in to the middle. We should have kept one of the walls to our back." He pointed to a cleared space at the bright end of a row of tables. "Let's move over there slowly. You watch the left side; I'll take the right."

They inched forward, Wrightson in the lead. He resumed his habit of four steps, then bend, four steps, bend. "Nineteen fucking feet, and I can't see it," he said to himself, no longer able to maintain the silence. He bent over one more time.

"Get down!" Ioka yelled as she planted her foot on his protruding rear end, kicked forward, and sent Wrightson sprawling along the floor. He rolled over, still clutching the extinguisher. As he righted himself he caught a glimpse of Ioka skimming the floor backward on hands and feet like a crab, still clutching the capture pole. He followed her eyes up to the tree branch that overhung the path. Hanging three feet above his head was the taipan. Until that moment he was certain that nothing could surpass the giant monster he had conjured up in his fertile imagination. The taipan's physical proportions, in fact, were no more awesome than his mental image. But Wrightson was totally unprepared for the aura of evil that emanated from the beast, touching him even across the distance that separated them.

The taipan's head dangled from a strong branch, anchored by three coils of shiny black flesh. Its jaws stretched wide, displaying its fearsome fangs. Its powerful hisses echoed off the glass walls. Wrightson flattened himself to the floor, then, following Ioka's lead, crabwalked quickly out of reach.

Discovered, the snake was not about to be caught in the tree. It uncoiled itself from the branch and deftly dropped to one of the tables, working its way swiftly among the maze of pots. Wrightson jumped up and whacked at the disappearing tail with the bottom of the extinguisher. A clay pot shattered. The snake hesitated; then its great head reared up from the plants, and it turned to face its attacker.

Wrightson let loose a cloud of white vapor which enveloped the snake and fogged the clear coverings of its eyes. Bewildered, the taipan reared back. Wrightson squeezed off another burst of gas, this time longer. He felt the numbing, welcome cold on his fingertips. Plants withered before his eyes. His vision became obscured by the growing fog.

"It's working!" he shouted triumphantly.

"Get back!" Ioka screamed as she came up off the floor.

Wrightson obeyed instantly, rocking back as far as he could, until the small of his back pressed hard against the opposite table. The taipan lunged out of the gases, stretching to the full length of its striking range. Wrightson felt the rush of air. The yawning mouth, fang-filled, loomed in front of his eyes. Then, two inches from Wrightson's face, the head snapped back. The snake had misjudged the distance, confused by the cold fog.

Ioka picked up a spade and sent it crashing into a pot next to the taipan's head. Other pots tipped over, rolling in tight arcs to the table's edge, plummeting to the concrete, exploding with the crack of pottery and the thud of dirt, as the taipan lashed its tail in a frenzy, shifting its attention to Ioka.

Wrightson, totally shaken by the narrow brush with death, jammed his thumb on the extinguisher lever with maniacal energy. No longer did he think of capturing the beast. All his efforts were concentrated on getting himself and Ioka out of the greenhouse alive. "Jump over the table!" he yelled. Ioka obeyed, decapitating a dozen delicate blooms as she made an athletic vault. She stopped and stretched back for the tongs. The taipan slid easily across the gap between the tables in determined pursuit of the woman, but apparently slowed by the cold gases.

"Leave it, leave it!" Wrightson shouted, but Ioka yanked the tongs loose from the clutter and debris, and made a mad dash for the door.

Fog carpeted the greenhouse floor, tumbling off the tables like bulky balls of cotton. The extinguisher was rapidly losing pressure. Wrightson could see only small sections of the snake. He had lost sight of its head in the swirling vapors. Not waiting another moment, he raised the canister over his head and hurled it into the middle of the fog. Then he, too, raced for the door.

As he dashed through the threshold, Ioka slammed the door and leaned her weight against it. "The broken glass!" Wrightson yelled as he ran by, not sacrificing any momentum. He crawled under the bushes, ignoring the branches that whipped across his face and arms. Finding the hole, he pulled off his jacket and stuffed it in. For good measure he rolled a large stone against the jacket.

Gasping from the effort, Wrightson crawled out from the line of bushes, staggered to a tree, and collapsed against its trunk. Ioka followed and threw herself down on the opposite side. Wrightson hung his head with nervous exhaustion. He felt for Ioka's hand and found it clammy and trembling. "Are you all right?"

"Yes." She drew in a long breath. "It was sliding off the branch toward you. If you had stood up, you would have been killed."

"I'm sorry, Ioka. I was wrong. Maybe it's not the devil or a supernatural spirit, but it's also not a natural snake. The creature is evil. I felt it down to my bones."

"Yes."

"I mean, I've handled and seen a lot of deadly snakes, but no matter how frightening they were, there was never any question in my mind that they were snakes. I guess if anything in this world is a demon, that taipan is it."

Wrightson stood slowly. "You walk around the greenhouse and make sure it doesn't escape. I'm getting the police."

16

THE TELEPHONE rang for the twelfth time. Miller slammed down the receiver and looked at the clock in the San Diego airport terminal. 3:42 A.M. He opened his address book again, then shut it. He would only be wasting more precious time in calling the laboratory. If there was no answer at Wrightson's house, Ioka and Wrightson were either at the lab or on their way to it. He had to get there as soon as possible. Miller looked angrily at the plane that had brought him to San Diego just minutes before. He grabbed his suitcase and ran across the terminal lobby, cursing airplanes and everyone who had anything to do with them, from the design engineers right down to the maintenance men. An attendant in the Orlando terminal had kept assuring him the delay would be temporary, first a half hour, then an extra half hour, until Miller had missed the only other connections leaving Orlando for San Diego that evening. All he could do was stand helplessly before the departure lounge windows while the minutes ticked by, stare at the idle flying machine, and will it to readiness.

Miller rushed through the automatic doors to the first cab in the taxi stand line. As he threw himself into the rear seat, he asked hurriedly, "Do you know where the Biology Extension of the University of California—San Diego is?"

The cab driver pushed his cap back and straightened up in the seat. "Sure." He started the engine.

"How long to get there?"

"It's clear across town. But at this hour? Fifteen, sixteen minutes."

"I'm in a hurry. Make it in ten, and there's an extra fifty dollars in it for you."

The cabbie smiled. "You just made a dull night special, mister. Check your watch!" The Checker shot away from the curb, tires squealing.

The cab rolled up the street to the extension campus at moderate speed, preceded by a city police car, lights swirling on its roof.

"What's going on?" the cabbie wondered aloud.

"I don't know," Miller replied. "Stop here!" the squad car pulled into the parking lot between two other police vehicles. Two officers got out and walked toward the building ablaze with light.

"You don't have to tell me, mister," the cabbie said sadly as he pulled the Checker to the curb. "I knew I'd lost the bet as soon as I had to slow down for that cop car."

"You would have won," Miller said, handing the driver a ten and a fifty.

"Hey, thanks, buddy. Real sporting. Looks like trouble up there. You want me to wait for you?"

Miller looked at the campus, quiet and deserted in spite of the one lighted building and the police

activity. "Yes, wait. Drive down to the end of the
street and kill your lights and engine. If I don't
show up in ten minutes, take off."

"Gotcha," the cabbie said, and steered his machine into a u-turn. Miller walked past the police
cars. Only one civilian car, a battered station wagon, sat in the lot. Miller looked inside it and recognized Ioka's windbreaker. He took a few tentative
steps toward the building, then paused to assess the
situation. While he stood thinking, a man loped out
of the shadows into the glow of the walklamps,
heading toward the lighted building. Miller turned
to hide, then recognized the figure.

"Marc!" he called softly. Wrightson continued to
stride purposefully forward. Miller ran to intercept
him. "Marc!"

Wrightson turned. His head snapped back with
surprise. He stopped dead. "What the hell are you
doing here?"

"What's happened to my snake?" Miller asked.

Wrightson answered by balling his hand into a
fist and cocking his arm. "You bastard," he swore as
he threw a roundhouse punch at Miller's head.
Miller reached out and caught the punch in mid-
flight as an ordinary man might stop a child's. His
huge hand closed around Wrightson's, then, with a
swift, continuous motion, whipped the man's backward into a hammerlock.

"You crazy bastard!" Wrightson continued, flailing at Miller with his free arm. "What's happened
to your snake? Nothing. It's in the best of health. It
almost killed me a few minutes ago, and it did kill
someone else, but your goddamn snake is just
great!"

"Calm down!" Miller commanded. He choked

off Wrightson's struggles by applying more pressure, then marching him roughly into the nearby shadows. Wrightson started to speak, but Miller pressed his free hand over Wrightson's mouth. "Listen to me. I just flew across the country to help you, and I'm in no mood to be attacked. Yesterday afternoon, I was told by representatives from the phone company that my private phone was being monitored. I put together a few isolated incidents that had been bothering me and came to the conclusion that someone was after the taipan. I tried to call you immediately, but you must have gone straight from the airport to the boat basin. Am I right?" Wrightson nodded. "My only alternative was to hop on a plane. That was the best I could do. Now, what's happened here?" Miller lifted his hand.

"You can let me go," Wrightson said calmly. Miller released the hold. "Yes, someone was after your snake. The taipan killed him in the lab. He must have come in through the window right after we left."

"What did he look like?"

"About your size. Black."

"Black?" Miller repeated, clearly surprised.

"Yes. And he was a professional handler. I didn't tell anyone, including Ioka, but I noticed a number of old snake wounds on his right forearm when I examined him. Speaking of Ioka, aren't you interested in how she's doing?"

"Of course," Miller answered sharply. "How is she?"

"Other than the fact that she's about to have a nervous breakdown, she's fine. She just saved my life. The taipan escaped out the lab window after it attacked the man. It crawled into the greenhouse over there. We tried to catch it, but it was too much for us. We've got it locked in. Ioka's watching to see that it doesn't get out again. I was just on my way to get the police." Wrightson turned to go.

"Hold on," Miller said urgently, grabbing Wrightson by the shirtsleeve. "I need you to answer a few more questions. Did you notice anything strange happen around you before you got the snake here?"

"No. Well, one of the *Snowbird*'s crewmen died at sea."

"What?"

"Nothing to do with the snake. He fell overboard."

"How about at the boat basin? Was anyone there when you unloaded the snake?"

"Only a fisherman going out early."

"What did he look like?"

"Like a fisherman. Middle-aged. Bald. Chubby."

"How about on the way here?"

"I didn't notice anyone. I wasn't expecting to be tailed," Wrightson said with exasperation. "What are you driving at?"

"Then you brought the snake into the lab and fed it," Miller pressed.

"Right." Wrightson explained how they opened the crate with the twine.

"But how did you untie the bag inside?"

"What bag?" Wrightson asked.

"Tasaki wouldn't ship a snake in a rough wooden crate without other protection. There had to be straw or some packing softener in the crate, and a loose bag."

"There was cloth on the bottom of the crate. It

might have been a bag. But I saw no string or wire. We certainly didn't untie it."

"When you opened the lid, did you actually see the taipan?"

"No. Ioka wanted to leave right away. Maybe the black man untied the bag."

"Maybe," Miller agreed. Wrightson briefly retold all the events from the time he and Ioka were called to the lab up to sealing the taipan in the greenhouse. "That's it," he concluded. "I decided there's no way the coroner's gonna buy my coral snake story. First, he'll spot the old snake bite wounds on the dead man's arm. Then he'll call in a herpetologist, who'll take one look at the guy's throat and phone the police. Two minutes later every cop in this city will be looking for me. You know how small a coral snake's head is. It's lucky to get its mouth around a man's thumb much less his neck. You should have seen those tears. I've gotta tell the police the truth before they come looking for me."

"We're not as bad off as you think," Miller countered. "At least no one's trying to steal the snake anymore," he lied, thinking of the phony reporter. "I've got a plan. Even if you decide to tell the police, the taipan has to be captured as soon as possible. Don't you agree?"

Wrightson eyed Miller with suspicion.

"Marc, every second it's not in a capture bag, it may escape. Are you sure that greenhouse is totally secure?"

"No, I'm not."

"Then, first things first. We've got to capture it *now*."

"All right," Wrightson conceded. "Let's go." They sprinted to the greenhouse. Ioka was patrolling the glass walls, the flashlight in one hand, the capture pole in the other. She stared at Miller in complete disbelief.

"Scott!" she gasped.

Miller wrapped his arms around her and held her tightly. "I found out a few hours ago that there might be trouble," he explained, "so I flew out immediately. Are you all right?"

"Yes."

"Good!" he exclaimed before she could say anything else. "Give me the pole. I'm going in after the taipan."

Ioka looked at Wrightson, who stood awkwardly by the embracing couple. Wrightson threw up his hands and shrugged. "Don't, Scott!" she pleaded. "Call the police. Let them put gas in there."

Miller shook his head. "I don't need any help. I can catch it." He had a look of absolute confidence. Ioka stood silent for a moment, looking into the black eyes. "I will help you."

Wrightson stepped forward. "Damn if you will! That thing almost killed you once. If he wants to die, let him, but don't throw away your life, Ioka."

Miller, oblivious to the argument, started toward the broken door alone, clutching the capture pole like a battle standard. Ioka said, "Marc, you don't understand what this snake means to him. I must help him this one, last time. I must." She dropped her head, sensing Wrightson's anger, then hastened after Miller.

Wrightson kicked a tree hard, then followed. "All right. You win. I'll help, if you promise to let him do the capturing. And stay far from that beast!"

Miller threw open the door. He turned to Ioka and Wrightson. "Since we only have one capture pole, it's folly for you two to go in alongside me. Stay well behind and watch my flanks." He studied the greenhouse with professional eyes. Wrightson followed his example. After his recent encounter he looked at the place with a different perspective. The beauty of the structure and its contents seemed now a colossal irony, like a cathedral usurped by the Devil.

Miller stepped into one of the aisles. As Wrightson had done, every few paces he lowered his head and checked under the tables. Wrightson followed a half dozen steps behind, surveying the incredible destruction he, Ioka, and the snake had effected in a matter of seconds. Entire sections of table top had been swiped clear, and below, in the aisles, dirt, pot shards, and uprooted plants littered the floor.

Miller dropped to one knee. "Give me that flashlight," he said. It passed from Ioka to Wrightson to Miller. A second later Miller said, "It's escaped. Look!" Under the middle row of tables, a long delta of silt flowed into the mouth of an open drainage pipe. In the silt were imprinted the unmistakable ess marks, leading directly into the pipe.

All three looked in impotent silence.

"Oh, Lord!" Wrightson said wearily. "An uncovered drain never occurred to me."

Miller looked at the greenhouse's north wall, where the pipe headed. He jumped up and ran for the door. "Come with me, Marc! Ioka, stay here!" Without a word, Wrightson followed Miller into the night.

The greenhouse sat atop a grassy hill. A hundred feet beyond the building's north wall the hill sloped down steeply to a dry ravine. Miller slowed his progress and signalled for Wrightson to do the same. "Don't stomp the ground! It'll feel the vibrations." Miller walked to the edge of the ravine and shone the flashlight along the lip. "Here's the outlet," he said. The open pipe jutted from the embankment a foot below the grass. "Now we've got it. This pipe is precisely the kind of place a snake would hole up in—warm, dark, and quiet. It won't be so cheery in a minute, though." He turned to Wrightson. "I saw a gardening hose attached to a spigot in the greenhouse. Tell Ioka to push it into the pipe and turn the water on full! Then come back here with the capture bag!"

Wrightson dutifully retraced his steps to the greenhouse and found Ioka leaning forlornly against the door. As he neared her, he said, "Scott feels certain it's still in the pipe."

"What do you think?" she asked.

"I think he'd better be right or this nightmare is going to wreck my entire life." He walked into the greenhouse and glanced around, hands on hips.

"What are you looking for?"

"A hose. Scott said he saw one in here."

"Yes. It's over there behind that table."

"He wants to flush it out with water." Wrightson picked up the hose by its brass nozzle and dragged it to the mouth of the pipe. The hose's shiny, green, cylindrical length resembled a snake's body even down to the texture of the reinforced rubber, like diamond-shaped scales. Wrightson found himself passionately wishing his life had taken some other major turn two years earlier when he first began investigating snake venoms. "I'm going to bring the capture bag down to Scott now. You turn the water on it in a minute then start feeding the hose into the pipe. You've got at least fifty feet there. Maybe you can push it out." He held his hand up and crossed his fingers. Ioka nodded solemnly, then moved to the faucet connection.

When Wrightson reached the ravine he found Miller standing directly above the drainage pipe, capture pole ready. The flashlight lay on the ground, its dimming amber beam aimed at the pipe end.

"What do you want me to do?" Wrightson asked.

Miller stared at the young scientist for a moment. "You hold the bag, Marc."

The water began gurgling from the pipe, first at a trickle, then rapidly in a miniature flood. "There's no way it can stay in there with all that cold water," Miller declared. Leaves and twigs rode the chocolate-colored stream into the ravine. The parched earth sucked up the water immediately. As the two men watched the torrent, the silt-choked waters began to take on a crystal clarity. Wrightson said, "Ioka must have shoved the hose halfway down the hill by now." Miller made no response. Only when he picked up the flashlight and began to swing its feeble beam up and down the ravine did Miller indicate to Wrightson that he had admitted defeat.

Wrightson sighed. "You, of all people, should know that this is no ordinary snake." Unwilling to constrain his anger and frustration any longer, he said, "Taipan three, humans nothing." Miller gave him his impassive, hollow-souled stare. "O.K., enough screwing around," Wrightson said decisively. "I'm going to do what I should have done fifteen minutes ago—get the police."

Miller sneered. "And what can they do? Police are trained to hunt men, not snakes. You could send a hundred policemen tramping through this undergrowth with no success. Most of them could be fifteen feet from a motionless, dark-brown snake and never see it. And, Marcus, you and I know that taipan. It might be motionless when it wants to be, but if a cop gets within fifteen feet of it, it will certainly attack. Before they got it, one or two of them would be killed." Wrightson's facial expression told Miller he had pressed the right psychological button. "Look, I know two herpetologists at the San Diego Zoo. I'm sure they can call on half a dozen qualified amateurs to assist. That's all we'll need."

"But the police *must* be told about the taipan, if only to protect the people living in the area," Wrightson insisted.

"No question," Miller agreed.

"Anyway, I have to clear the air for my own sake. Lying's done me absolutely no good, and I'm finished with it," Wrightson asserted.

"There's no more need to lie. All you have to do is bend the truth a tiny bit," Miller suggested, setting down the pole.

Wrightson crossed his arms. "Let's hear it. And don't forget I've got to convince the dean as well as the police."

Miller held out his hand, as if the explanation would momentarily materialize in his upraised palm. "Why can't this work? Three weeks ago a bamboo basket was left at your house. It had a note on it that said something like: 'Dr. Wrightson. This is a giant taipan. I bought it illegally. I'm an amateur snake collector. I thought it would be a great addition to my collection. It proved too big, too violent, and too delicate for me to keep. I heard about your research with snake venoms and thought you could use it. Signed, Anonymous.'"

Miller watched Wrightson's face. It was blank but attentive. "Now, you were afraid to bring the taipan to your lab since it was illegal, and you had no idea where it had come from or how Anonymous had gotten his hands on it. You especially didn't want to involve your assistants. You made a few discreet inquiries, read the newspapers to see if such a snake had been stolen from a local zoo or collection, and turned up nothing. Meanwhile, the taipan proved too much for you to handle at home without a proper case. Mention its need for special temperature and pressure environment. You wanted the snake's venoms but needed someone else to care for it. That's when you read of my new park and my interest in rare, deadly snakes. You contacted me, secure in the knowledge that my park was 2,500 miles away, and no one would link the taipan with you or your research. I wrote back, extremely interested. You visited me, and we struck a deal where I would display and care for the taipan, and, in return, you would get its venom and the venom of a number of other snakes. The last part is so close to the truth, it's not even a lie. And, of course, I'll back you up to the last syllable. Supply documentation of our correspondence and your visit—corroborate everything you use to embellish the story."

Wrightson rubbed the back of his neck, made a full turn, and faced Miller. "Your plans always sound so fucking simple. If it was as simple and foolproof as you promised me back in Florida, why are we in this mess?"

Miller reached out in a gesture of supplication.

"Come on, Marc. Be reasonable. I had no idea someone was after the snake."

"I know," Wrightson replied. "I'm just trying to make a point. You're so sure your plans will work out, you don't allow for unforeseen problems. For example, you've been holding that pit in front of your park empty for a lot longer than, say, the sixteen days since you received my first letter. Shouldn't I tell the police I got the taipan about a month ago and wrote you soon after?"

"Yes, of course," Miller agreed with alacrity, sensing that Wrightson, despite his anger, was willing to buy the plan. "That does ring truer."

Wrightson saw Ioka coming down the hill. He shook his head to indicate their failure. She did not look surprised. He turned back to Miller and nodded sharply. "All right. It's close enough to the truth to make sense. And it protects Ioka. No use burning her for this."

Miller, elated by the new victory, continued his prompting. "You say you brought it to the lab for better care. The semester was ending, and your assistants had gone. I flew out last night to pick up the snake, but the black guy broke in and upset everything."

"I might as well point out the wounds on his arms."

"Definitely. Tell the police you suspect he may have been a professional snake handler. I'd like them to pursue that line of thinking. Maybe they'll find out who it is that wants my snake."

Ioka came within hearing range. Miller said, "I'd better coordinate our story. I'll tell Ioka. You go make it official."

"Aren't you coming with me?" Wrightson asked.

"No. We'll search the immediate area for a while." Miller studied the first traces of daylight separating the horizon from the sky. "At least we've got a little false dawn to see by."

"Man, you are just *determined* to die, aren't you?" Wrightson observed with an incredulous expression on his face. Miller ignored the remark.

"If we don't see anything in a few minutes, I'll come up and call my friends. Meanwhile, you tell the police I'm down here looking. And tell them my plan for the taipan's capture."

Wrightson nodded, too weary to raise further objections. "I'll be in the dean's office. He has to be told, and I'm sure there are plenty of high-ranking policemen there by now." Wrightson studied the aura of power and confidence that Miller exuded. He wondered if even Miller knew how much was mask and how much real. He knew that he would never again give the man his complete trust. "Any last-second 'facts' you forgot, coach?" he said sarcastically.

"No," Miller said.

Wrightson turned his back on the man. "You let him lead the way, Ioka," he said as he climbed the hill. "It's his snake."

o   o   o

Wrightson found the dean's office open, with every light aglow. Strangely, he hadn't seen a policeman since he'd entered the building. He was positive he'd run into an army of blue uniforms, most of them surrounding and beleaguering Dean Franklin, but he was wrong. He crossed through the outer office, thinking of the best way to drop his terrifying news. For a moment he thought Franklin's private office, too, was empty. Then he saw the dean standing at the window, hands clasped behind the small of his back, staring blindly at the campus. Franklin was evidently deep in thought, out of contact with his surroundings. Wrightson said, "Uh, Robert . . ."

Franklin turned slowly and gave Wrightson a quizzical look. "Marc, what happened to you? I thought you'd gone home to change. You look like you got caught in a mud-slinging contest."

Wrightson glanced down at himself. In all the confused action he had forgotten about his clothing. His jeans and shirt were filthy with dirt and caked mud, as were his hands. "It's a long story," he said.

"Here, take a few tissues," Franklin offered. "What the hell *did* happen to you? You've even got some blood on your face."

Wrightson took the tissues and daubed at his scratches, then brushed futilely at the mud stains. "If you think I look bad, wait 'til you see the greenhouse."

"What do you mean?"

Wrightson gestured to the dean's chair. "Every time you give me bad news, Robert, you always ask me to sit first. I think it's my turn to make that suggestion."

"All right. I'm sitting."

Wrightson looked the dean in the eye and said, "I lied about that coral snake in the lab. It didn't bite that man."

"What?"

"The snake I showed you and the others wasn't the one that killed him."

"But why did you lie?"

"Because the killer snake is loose. It escaped out the window."

"Oh, my God!"

"I wanted to get outside as quickly as possible to catch the snake."

"But I don't understand why you had to lie to do that." Wrightson was about to respond when Franklin asked, "Did you catch it?"

Wrightson shook his head. "I trailed it to the greenhouse and tried to catch it, but it escaped again."

"I want this from the beginning and in detail," Franklin demanded.

Wrightson sat and told the story from the time when he displayed the coral snake to the time he discovered the taipan was not inside the pipe. Then, parroting Miller's explanation almost verbatim, he told how he had allegedly gotten the taipan and intended to get rid of it. He closed with Miller's plan for its recapture. "Miller is down near the greenhouse right now, trying to find the taipan."

"You've been using this word, 'taipan,' for the past few minutes," the dean said. "I have no idea what kind of snake it is, other than obviously extremely deadly."

"It's from Southeast Asia. About twenty feet long." As Wrightson had expected, Franklin's eyes bulged with surprise. "Very dark brown, nearly black. It's fast and unbelievably vicious. It's nothing less than a monster."

Franklin had heard enough. He half-stood and leaned across his desk, looking down on Wrightson. His skin color darkened rapidly from pink to crimson. "This changes the whole situation. Five minutes ago I was worrying about the accidental murder of a burglar. Now you tell me the thing that bit him is a twenty-foot illegal snake, and it's escaped off campus!

Jesus Christ, Marc, it's one thing when someone breaks into our research lab and gets himself killed. It's another when some *Thing* breaks out and threatens the lives of innocent people." Franklin paced back and forth from the window to his desk. "A whole new situation." He thrust an accusing finger at Wrightson. "I backed your project all the way, even though I was always worried someone might get hurt. You know, I've had constant pressure from inside the university and out to halt your project. People are frankly scared shitless of snakes. But I've always upheld the role of the functional university, and I ran interference for you any number of times. You asked me to use my influence to get you new funding, and I agreed. Maybe I wasn't too successful, but goddammit, Marc, at least I was always honest with you!" His voice had become strident. Veins throbbed visibly on his neck. "And I thought you were being honest with me."

Wrightson, chastised by the statement and genuinely embarrassed, said nothing in his defense.

Franklin asked, "When you first got to the lab and saw that the taipan had escaped, why couldn't you have taken me aside and confided in me?"

"Because the second you knew exactly what was loose, you would have called out the riot squad."

"You're damned right! That's what we need here— a S.W.A.T. team to hunt that snake!"

"No, we don't. That's the reason I went out to try to capture it. I know what to expect. I know where it will hide, how it would attack. You send a hundred inexperienced policemen out tromping these hills and one or two may get bitten. The only safe way to catch it is to use professional snake people."

"You explained all that. But it will take time to get

enough professionals together. In the meantime, someone has to be called in to protect the community and the campus."

"Scott Miller will be here in a minute to call people. The taipan should be inactive until the sun rises. It's outdoors in the cool air now, not in the lab or the greenhouse."

"It's almost dawn already," Franklin warned, glancing out the window. "The only reason I haven't picked up the telephone to call the riot squad is because a Lieutenant Novack from Homicide is downstairs in your lab right now. I'm waiting for him to come back here at any moment." Franklin paused to regain his composure. Methodically, he tucked his pajama tops into his pants. "In the meantime, Dr. Wrightson, let me fill you in on your future at this institution. As of this moment, you have none. Forget about teaching and tenure. Forget, also, about your research project. I think you might save us both a great deal of further embarrassment by tendering your resignation. The sooner the university is able to divorce you from its faculty, the sooner it'll recover. God forbid your snake should kill any townspeople. I'm not even going to think about that." Franklin's words picked up momentum from sentence to sentence. "We're on opposite sides of the fence now, Marcus. You put us there by storing that snake in your lab and then later by lying in front of all those witnesses. Now, you do whatever you have to do to protect yourself; my duty from this moment on will be to myself and the university. If I have to flay you alive, I won't hesitate. Where's the inventory of every snake in your lab I've been asking you for the past week?"

Wrightson looked dumbly at the dean. "What inventory? You never asked me for . . ." His jaw dropped. "Oh, no, Robert! That's totally unfair. You wouldn't do that to me."

Franklin banged his fist on the desk. "Don't you tell me what's unfair! Anyone else, but not you!" He took a deep breath to continue, then looked up to the outer office and stopped short. Wrightson turned and saw a tall, thin man walking slowly toward them. The man wore a loose-fitting grey suit and a solid blue tie. His head and the suit were mismatched. The head properly belonged to a second-rate hockey pro. He had his hair cut short in military style. It was thick and straight, like brush bristles, steel-grey at the temples. As he came toward them, Wrightson tried to decide if the man was stoop-shouldered or if he had just shoved his hand especially deep into his pocket.

"Am I interrupting anything?" the man asked with the insouciant tone that indicated he didn't give a damn if he had.

"Nothing important, Lieutenant," Franklin said. "Lieutenant Novack, meet Dr. Wrightson."

"Lieutenant Novack." Wrightson offered his hand.

"So you're the snake doctor," Novack said without moving to accept Wrightson's hand. "You ready to make your statement?"

"Dr. Wrightson has much more to tell you, Lieutenant," Franklin said. "Why don't you sit down?"

This time Wrightson began the fabrication with the taipan's arrival at his house. As he explained his visit to Miller's park and the deal they had made to provide Wrightson with venoms, Novack's expression was one of mild interest. To Wrightson's relief, the detective made no interruptions, letting the scientist tell his tale the way he wanted. For Franklin's benefit, Wrightson emphasized the desperate situation of his near-fund-less research and the taipan's potential importance toward a medical breakthrough. Novack appeared manifestly unimpressed. As Wrightson related the taipan's escape, however, the detective's expression hardened. He flipped open a spiral pad and began taking notes. Wrightson freely admitted lying about the coral snake. Novack's lips curled into a half-smile, yet he still withheld verbal comment.

Franklin, literally on the edge of his chair, broke in as Wrightson began the greenhouse segment. "To make a long story short, it escaped from there, too. It's loose somewhere in the area, and it's got to be caught before it kills again!"

Novack gave Wrightson a disgusted look, then reached for the phone. He dialed quickly, shaking his head. "This is Novack. Get every available unit up to the university's extension campus. We've got a deadly snake loose here." As he listened he stuffed the pad back into his breast pocket. "No, of course that doesn't have a code number. Broadcast it as a 'general assistance report.' And no sirens. I don't want to wake up the neighborhood. Yeah. Thanks."

As soon as Novack hung up, Wrightson said, "Miller, the man who came from Florida, is out searching for the snake right now. He thinks it would be best to use only professionals to hunt it."

"Yes," Franklin interjected. "No point in having a hundred inexperienced policemen tramping over the hills. They wouldn't know how to look for a snake, and one or two of them might get killed."

"That's true," Novack agreed. "I sure-as-hell don't want to hunt for it." He waved his arm toward the door. "O.K., you, Doctor. Let's go. I want to talk to this snake hunter right away." Wrightson stood without comment.

The telephone rang. Franklin picked it up. "Hello, Dean Franklin." He listened. "You're from which newspaper? Wait a moment." He cupped his hand over the mouthpiece and said to Novack, "It's a reporter already. What do I tell him?"

Novack took the phone. "Who's this? Dutton, this is Novack. Yeah, *that* Novack. The body's on its way to University Hospital. Nothing big. No, you can't. Because I'm talkin' to him right now. Get back to him later. Don't give me that deadline crap. Get your lazy butt over to the University. That's where you'll get the answers. Right, bye." As he handed Franklin the phone he said, "They know nothing about this taipan, of course. Let's try to keep it that way until we catch it. As soon as they get wind of the story, they'll be up here in a flash, bringing the whole neighborhood outdoors. If anybody else calls, tell them you're preparing a statement."

Franklin nodded, relieved to have someone experienced in such matters telling him what to do.

"C'mon, Doc," Novack said, as one might when commanding a lap dog. He stepped out of the office, hand thrust once more in his pocket. Wrightson listened to the cadence of the detective's cleats, reverberating in the hallway.

"You college people are a goddamn pain in the ass," Novack declared suddenly, not looking at Wrightson. "You know that? San Diego's got to be one of the biggest military towns in the country, but we don't get half as much trouble from enlisted men as we do from all you high-minded pacifists. Oh, an occasional drunken brawl or a knifing maybe, but it's always simple. It happens, Bang!, and it's done. Not with you ivory-tower boys, though. One week it's a demonstration for the poor down-trodden migrant workers. I still haven't figured how holding up traffic downtown for two hours is helping the plight of wetbacks."

They left the building and walked briskly along the sidewalk toward the greenhouse. Novack continued. "The next week it's the community's turn. They find out some professors are growing deadly bacteria for the Army or making mutant monsters with DNA. Then *they* hold up traffic, demonstrating against the university. Or some mongoloid dictator, fifty thousand miles away, is liquidating his people, and it's a spontaneous rally with posters and paper littering the streets. Mind you, not one person's saved in the mongoloid's country, but you can bet your ass twenty store windows get broken in San Diego. Now which way?"

Wrightson pointed toward the greenhouse, barely visible among the trees, and took the lead. His pace quickened in an effort to outdistance Novack's diatribe.

"Nuclear power plants. Nuclear bombs. Black Panthers. Red China. Left Wing. Right Wing. Chicken Wing. Man, that's what I hate the most—the belligerent faggots." Novack stole a glance at Wrightson's handsome features. "Hookers at frat parties. Jumpers every exam period. ODs, DOAs, SLA, PLO. Or the worst of the bunch—Phds. And, lo and behold, Doc, now it's your turn. You couldn't do research with flowers or sea water, could you? Nope. You have to use twenty-foot poisonous snakes. Man, this is the weirdest one yet."

Under other circumstances, Wrightson would have shot holes in Novack's blatant prejudices with a few well-aimed words, but he had learned from sitting in front of Franklin that it was wiser to hold his tongue.

Once Novack left the walkway and ventured into the shrubbery, he was obliged to say, "Stay away from the bushes and shadows! The snake could be anywhere."

Wrightson's warning caused Novack to hop instantly to the side. Grunting his annoyance, he chose a path across the middle of the lawns. "Suppose you tell me something about this man Miller's qualifications."

Wrightson, glad the tirade had ended, said, "He's quite powerful and successful. Very intelligent." He was about to mention Miller's educational background but thought better of it. He wanted at least one of their trio to be seen well in Novack's eyes. "He's built his own serpentarium and stocked it with snakes he caught all over the world," Wrightson exaggerated. "You couldn't hope to find anyone better qualified or more willing to chase this taipan."

"That must be him now," Novack observed, looking at Miller and Ioka trudging slowly up the hill. "Nice-looking broad. Yours or his?"

Wrightson ignored the question. His attention fastened on the capture bag in Ioka's hand. It hung flat and empty.

"He sure is big enough," Novack said with apparent awe.

"Did you find a trail?" Wrightson called out.

"No, nothing," Miller called back, shouldering the capture pole, his eyes trained on the stranger.

"That's bad," Novack said.

Wrightson stepped between the men and said, "Scott Miller, this is Lietenant Novack of San Diego Homicide. Miller took one leggy stride forward and extended his hand. "Call me Scott." Novack gritted his teeth as he felt his bones compress painfully together under the pressure of Miller's handshake. He stood as if frozen for a moment, caught in the hypnotic stare of Miller's caliginous eyes. Miller released the spell with his winning smile. "I'm glad you're here, Lieutenant. We really need your help." Novack was about to fashion a take-charge reply when Miller added. "I don't think Dr. Wrightson understood the ferocity or cunning of the snake he was given. I hope he won't be judged too harshly for a snap error in thinking when he tried to capture the taipan without skilled help. After all, he's a scientist, not a professional hunter like the two of us." Miller shrugged his shoulders. "College professors are removed from reality. What can you expect?"

Novack nodded vigorously. "Brother, have you said a mouthful!" Wrightson, standing at Novack's back, rolled his eyeballs heavenward. He glanced at Ioka. She shook her head slightly.

Miller said, "Lieutenant Novack, I know nothing of this terrain. I'm relying on you to coordinate this operation. While I'm assembling the hunters, you'll have to patrol the populated areas and keep the people out of the woods."

"I'm working on it already. There should be a dozen men here shortly."

"Splendid! It's heartening to know I'm working with a man of competence. I need to make some phone calls to get volunteer hunters up here," Miller said, thrusting his hand into his pocket and regulating his gait to Novack's.

Novack said, "That makes more sense than a hundred cops tramping over hill and dale. Knowing some of those guys like I do, one or two are bound to get bitten."

"Absolutely," Miller agreed, putting a hand lightly on Novack's shoulder. Wrightson had been completely forgotten by the two as they walked up the hill like a pair of old school chums. Wrightson stopped short. For the moment another man had become the object of Miller's magical charms. From his personal experience and now as a dispassionate third person, he was able to watch, close up, the swift, effortless manipulation of Miller's persuasive will. With great remorse he remembered Ioka's warning on the night of the party. He looked at the woman, climbing the hill silently behind her benefactor. He was certain she knew more than she would admit about the psychological source that fueled his obsession. Wrightson hurried up the hill after her.

17

"PALISADE CELLS, parenchyma cells, intercellular spaces, xylem, and phloem. That's the mesophyll," Alyson DeWindt recited, peeking at the cross-sectional drawing of a leaf in her biology book as she filled the tea kettle. "Right!" she exclaimed, quite pleased with herself. She set the kettle on the ancient range and turned on the gas. Next, she reached up to the kitchen window sill and flipped on the radio. Immediately, the relentless chord progressions of a rock song, accompanied by a cacophonous collection of percussion instruments, filled the house. Alyson and two other coeds, Courtney Mann and Cherie Glover, shared the aging dwelling that sat two blocks from the university extension campus.

As her slender body gyrated happily with the music, Alyson took an egg from the refrigerator and set it next to the skillet.

"What time is it, Alyson?" Courtney asked, standing in the living room, which more or less flowed directly into the kitchen-dining area. Courtney was wrapped in a terry-cloth bathrobe and was rubbing one eye drowsily.

"Seven after seven," Alyson sang out blithely, grinding one hip against the counter, her eyes squeezed shut.

"How about being a little considerate for just once in your life and turn off that damned radio?" Courtney suggested with exasperation. "I was up 'til two studying for my anatomy exam."

"Why couldn't you have gone to bed at eleven and gotten up early to study like I'm doing?" Alyson replied, reaching into the refrigerator for the butter.

"Because my exam isn't until one o'clock. And besides, you snot, I don't run my life according to your schedule." She turned abruptly and stormed back to her room, slamming the door.

"Touchy, touchy!" Alyson murmured as she turned down the radio. As she flipped the book's pages to the next diagram, Cherie scuffed her way sleepily across the living room toward the bathroom. She peeked into the kitchen and said, "Aly, do me a favor and feed Bast. I'm in a rush. I've just got to shampoo my hair, and it takes half a day to dry it."

Alyson looked at her housemate. Cherie wore an abbreviated nightie that barely covered her crotch. She held out her long, bleach-blonde hair for Alyson's examination. Her oversized breasts showed plainly through the nightgown's diaphanous material.

"God, Cherie, you're such a shameless exhibitionist!" Alyson said to the curvaceous coed.

"If you've got it, flaunt it," Cherie replied, a rather cruel remark in view of the fact that Alyson was nearly flat-chested. "Please feed the cat. Where is she?"

Alyson pushed her thumb in the direction of the back door.

"Thank you," Cherie said in a flippant tone, not waiting for an answer.

Alyson scowled. "When are all these petty, little favors gonna end?"

Cherie executed a pirouette as she turned from the kitchen. "As soon as I finish typing your term paper." She disappeared into the bathroom.

Alyson sighed and reached under the sink for the cat food. She set it on the counter and took the cat's dish from the draining rack. Shaking the remaining water from its corners, she walked to the kitchen's screen door and called out, "Bast! Here, Bast!" She banged the dish against the door jamb. "Psss, psss, psss, psss! Here, Bast!" The six-month-old cat, still really half-kitten, had ostensibly been named for the Egyptian cat goddess, Bast or Bastet. In reality, her name was Bastard. She was a good-natured but rather homely calico, the runt of an unexpected litter that no one but Cherie would take.

Alyson opened the screen door and stepped outside. She looked past the small patch of unmowed lawn to the rambling garden in which Bast loved to play. The garden was lovingly tended by an elderly Italian gentleman who had lived in the house until his wife died. He had since moved to town, but came back often to work in the yard.

"What a beautiful day!" Alyson exclaimed to herself as she looked out at the early morning sun and drew in a breath of fresh air. "It's gonna be a hot one. Bast!" She banged the dish again, then walked down the back steps and peered into the garden, looking for some movement among the grapevines, Italian green bean trellises, and the young tomato plants. Seeing nothing, she gazed back beyond the garden, to the ravine that bordered the property. In that particular spot the ravine broadened and became more level. Alyson still saw no sign of the cat. She turned around and looked at the three sagging steps, the brown paint badly peeling, exposing the grey wood beneath. She stooped to see if the cat was hiding.

A hissing noise from inside the house rapidly changed to a shrill whistle. "The tea kettle!" Alyson said. "Bast! Oh, stay out here, you goddamn cat!" She threw up her hands in disgust and rushed into the kitchen, leaving the screen door open.

Bast had been tracking the progress of a tomato worm as it inched its way up a pole. The cat's ears stood straight forward. Her eyes glowed with interest. Not even the calls from the house could divert her attention. As the worm reached eye level, Bast struck out a paw and swatted the insect to the ground. The worm rolled into a green ball. The cat stepped around it for a fresh perspective. As she raised her head, she saw something far more worthy of her attention. Instantly, every hair on the cat's body stood on end. Her tail flattened and beat the ground; her back arched high. Six feet away, winding through the labyrinth of plants and trellises, was an enormous brown-black snake. Bast had never seen such a creature before, but she knew instinctively that it was a mortal enemy. The cat drew back, hissing as she retreated. The taipan, knowing it had been spotted, unhinged its jaws and let loose its own sibilant sounds. Bast gave ground, growling throatily. The snake lifted its head and drew up its body, preparing to strike. It lunged forward with swift, deadly accuracy, but the cat was no longer in the same place. Anticipating the attack, she had agilely leapt behind a tomato plant. As the snake reared back, Bast turned and raced for the safety of the house in great, bounding strides. The snake pursued.

Alyson had just set her teacup on the table and was returning to the range to crack the egg into the skillet when Bast tore through the kitchen and into the living room. She was growling loudly, and her fur was puffed out wildly from her neck to the tip of her tail. Alyson took one look at the cat and burst into laughter. In a quick series of leaps, Bast jumped from the floor to the couch to the end table, and thence to the top of the bookcase. Alyson picked up Bast's dish and banged it against the counter. "Come get your breakfast, you nutty cat."

As she stepped from the counter, Alyson heard a raspy hiss from the open door. She spun around. Slithering purposefully through the doorway was an enormous monster, so long that she could not see its tail. It forked tongue darted in and out. The horrible head glided under the table, moving toward the living room. Alyson dropped the dish, shrieked with all her might, and collapsed in a dead faint.

The taipan continued into the house, intent on following the cat's scent. Inside the bathroom the sound of running water suddenly stopped. "Alyson, what's the matter?" Cherie called.

The taipan's head and neck slid into the living room. Bast growled fiercely, searching in vain for higher terrain.

"Alyson?" Courtney yelled as she rushed into the hall, tugging at her bathrobe. She stepped into the living room just as Cherie threw open the bathroom door. The sudden movement distracted Courtney for an instant. When she swung her head again toward the kitchen, she caught the shape of a dark, hoselike

mass on the floor, framed between the wall and the
easy chair. She tried to check her headlong motion,
but before she could stop, part of the shape rose rapidly and lunged at her. She threw herself backward and
fell heavily on the floor, her right arm extended to
break her fall, her left thrust upward for balance. The
taipan compensated for the moving target and buried
its fangs in the soft folds of the outstretched sleeve.
The needle-sharp teeth ripped into the terry-cloth's
looped pile and caught. Infuriated, the taipan
snapped and chewed viciously, working its saliva and
venom into the fabric. Courtney looked up at Cherie,
who stood in the bathroom doorway, clutching a towel
in front of her. Courtney pleaded with her eyes for
rescue from the living nightmare, but Cherie was
equally frozen with fear and incapable of action. Both
girls had been struck dumb, their terror and revulsion
dammed up inside them. The only noises to be heard
were the growling of the cat and the frenzied lashing
of the taipan's tail. Courtney's instinct took over. It
told her she must get free of the robe to save herself.
Gasping for breath, she sat up and began to shrug the
material from her shoulders. The taipan, seeking to
gain a hold for leverage, threw a coil around the girl's
feet. She kicked relentlessly at its cool flesh, forcing
the coil to unwind. Courtney's left arm was useless to
her. The taipan was caught in the fabric just above the
elbow. If she used the arm in any way, it would bring
the fearsome reptilian head nearer to her face. By rolling on her side, she succeeded in working the robe
down as far as her shoulder-blades. The quick maneuver, however, shook the taipan's head free. Almost
without recoil, it launched itself at the nape of her
neck, stitching bite wounds across the top of her back
like a living sewing machine. Courtney rolled over

and over, moving back into the hallway. At last she screamed, protesting the fiery pain that flamed across her back. The taipan slid forward in pursuit.

"No!" Cherie bellowed with indignant rage. Without conscious thought, she squeezed the towel she held into a ball and threw it as hard as she could at the snake. The towel fluttered part-way open and landed short, grazing the snake lightly in its middle. It drew back, allowing Courtney to crawl into her room. Cherie heard the door's lock being thrown.

The taipan's head swung around. Cherie ducked backward, out of sight. Somewhere she had heard that although a snake's eyesight was poor, supposedly it could smell and feel vibrations quite well. To be safe, she stayed motionless where she was, pressed tightly against the door to the shower stall. A second later it dawned on her that she would be much safer if the bathroom door were closed. A back-scrubbing brush lay on top of the toilet. She grabbed it and reached across the sink to the door. She guided the brush head under the inside knob and pushed slowly, reasoning that a subtle movement might not attract the snake. She was wrong. Before the door was halfway shut, the taipan's head shot through the remaining space, striking the brush handle. Cherie screamed and dropped the brush. The snake's head and neck filled the opening. Its eyes glistened with rage; its mouth yawned open.

Cherie jumped into the shower stall and slammed the door. She pressed back into the tiny cubicle, as far away from the plexiglass as possible. The room was eerily silent. Except for her heavy, labored breaths and the steady drip of the showerhead, amplified by the tight space, there would have been no sound at all. Shivering uncontrollably from fear and the water

evaporating off her totally nude body, Cherie fixed
her gaze on the shower door. Through the translucent
glass she saw the thin, dark shadow sliding across the
floor. The distorted figure drew itself up a few feet,
swinging to and fro before the shower door. "Go
away! Get out!" she screamed at the top of her lungs.
The creature refused to oblige her. It pushed its head
up another foot, testing the air constantly with its
tongue. Cherie looked around the stall for a weapon.
All she found was a tube of shampoo and a half-used
bar of soap.

The taipan hissed. "Shut up!" she yelled back with
desperate bravado. The hissing continued. To drown
out the horrible sound, she turned on the shower. A
sudden inspiration made her set it as hot as she could
stand. The taipan slid upward along the glass.

The shower door's upper edge measured six feet
from the floor. Between the door and the shower
frame, which was secured to the ceiling, lay eight
inches of open space. Cherie watched the taipan's
shadow rising inexorably. It would soon clear the
door. Get out!" she screamed, over and over, giving
into hysteria. Slowly she sank to the floor, huddled
in a fetal position, with her arms crossed over her
breasts. Her tears mixed with the shower spray. Her
eyes fixed themselves on the opening above the
door. Steam had begun to pour over the edge and
into the rest of the bathroom. The tip of the taipan's
head appeared in the space. Cherie quaked
anguishly. The taipan paused. The steam annoyed
and confused it. It looked down at the animal cowering on the other side of the barrier and hissed
with vexation. Cherie screamed, "Help me! Help
me!" over and over, as fast as she could replenish
her lungs.

Alyson moaned and shook her head. Cherie's persistent cries had forced her back to consciousness. When she had fainted, she had collapsed against the counter like a rag doll, sliding into a sitting position. She looked up and gasped. The tail end of the snake, almost as long as Alyson herself, still lay in the kitchen. Its undulated form curved into the bathroom, where Cherie was obviously trapped.

Alyson stood slowly, pulling herself up by the counter. In the sink she found a steak knife, unwashed from the previous night's supper. She picked it up and clutched it above her shoulder with an overhand grasp. Armed, she gained the courage to move. The telephone sat on a serving stand on the opposite side of the dining table. Without taking her eyes from the snake, she edged cautiously toward the phone, step by step.

Suddenly, the snake's tail moved. Alyson jumped back involuntarily and collided with a chair, losing her grip on the weapon. It spun across the floor as she and the chair went over together. The snake's body reacted immediately, drawing in upon itself, consolidating its length. Alyson scrambled to her feet and reached for the telephone. The taipan's head appeared from the bathroom doorway. It looked straight at her. She dropped the receiver and retreated along the wall toward the back door. The taipan lowered its head to the floor and tensed to attack. "Cherie, Courtney!" Alyson yelled. "I'm gonna get help. Don't move!" The taipan made a determined rush toward the girl. Alyson threw herself at the open doorway, clearing the steps with a great leap. She stumbled, caught herself in mid-stride, then ran as fast as she could toward the nearest house.

18

WARREN CROWLEY pushed a cigarette between his lips and started to light it, then remembered he had one burning in the ashtray. As he stuck the fresh one back in the pack and stretched toward the ashtray, he noted that his hand had not yet stopped trembling. He sucked in a lungful of smoke and sighed with grateful relief, eyes squeezed shut. He unwrapped the towel from around his waist and used it to massage his hair, still damp from the shower.

On the floor at the foot of the bed lay the trousers he had worn the night before, zipper up. Crowley stared at the large stain mark, running from crotch to knee. The smell of stale urine insulted his nostrils. He gave the trousers a vicious kick. They landed across the room, in front of the drapes.

The morning light had intensified considerably since Crowley had gone into the bathroom to take his shower. He switched off the bedside lamp, crossed to the dresser and closet, and put on a completely new outfit. He grabbed his cigarettes and sunglasses and started for the door. Halfway out, he stopped, then turned back into the hotel room. He picked up his attache case and set it on the bed. Inside, packed in foam rubber, lay his Walther PPK. He checked the bullet clip, rammed it into the gun, and threw a shell into the firing chamber. Wrapped around the cool familiar metal, his hand did not shake quite so much. For the first time in hours, Crowley smiled.

The hotel had its own coffee shop. Crowley entered it and sat at the counter. He set the attache case on the formica surface, just to his right. He looked around. The shop was almost empty.

"What'll it be?" asked the middle-aged, black waitress, looking at her twin reflection in his mirrored sunglasses.

"Just a cup of coffee and a doughnut," Crowley murmured. He found a discarded morning newspaper stuck between the sugar holder and the ketchup, pulled it out and began to read. His eyes shifted back and forth down a column, then drifted off.

"Mind if I move your briefcase?" the waitress asked as she whipped a dishrag along the counter.

"Don't," Crowley muttered.

The waitress put her hand on the case to set it on the floor. Crowley's arm lashed out.

"I said, Don't!"

She drew back her hand and looked at the man with mild surprise. Sunglasses hid his eyes, but she read tension clearly enough in the bulging jaw and neck muscles and in the set of his lips.

"Sorry, mister. I thought you said, 'Don't mind,'" she remarked, controlling her irritation.

As she passed by, Crowley reached out and touched her arm with a crumpled dollar. "Hey, give me change, willya?"

Sullenly, the waitress reached into her pocket and counted out a dollar's change from her tips. She slapped it to the counter. The man twitched and whipped his head around, reacting to the sharp noise. The movement caused his sunglasses to slide halfway down the bridge of his nose, exposing his dilated, maniacal pupils. She stepped backward with alarm, then rushed into the kitchen.

Crowley picked up his briefcase and crossed to the telephone booth. He closed his eyes, trying to dredge the ten digit phone number from his memory. He pulled a pencil from his pocket and scribbled the number on a corner of the phone directory. He dropped in a coin. He dialed for the operator and gave her the number.

"A person-to-person collect call to Atlanta, Georgia. To Mr. Fritz Thanner. My name is Warren Crowley." Crowley listened impatiently as the message was relayed to Thanner's maid, as Thanner was called to the phone and as the message was given again and accepted.

"Did you get it, Mr. Crowley?"

"No." Crowley took a breath. "We didn't. And Gordon's dead."

"What?" Thanner said with a rush of breath.

"It wasn't my fault," Crowley blurted.

"Where are you?"

"Don't worry. I'm in a public phone booth. It wasn't my fault!" Crowley began to run his words together in an effort to tell his whole story at once. "The snake was supposed to stay in its crate. Miller made a special point to tell Wrightson that the day before it arrived. But the asshole disobeyed orders and let it out. It was loose inside this big case. We couldn't tell because the case had a dark cover on it." The words came easily, since Crowley had rehearsed his defense a dozen times.

"You mean Gordon was bitten to death?"

"Yeah. Everything was going perfect, but the snake jumped out of that case like one of those jack-in-the-boxes when Gordon opened it. He didn't have a chance. I never saw anything so terrifying in my life. And it was gigantic."

"Did both of you get out of the building?"

"No. Gordon died in about a minute. The thing bit him right in the neck. I couldn't . . ."

"Get on a plane right now, Mr. Crowley."

"Wait! You gotta understand there was nothin' I could do. The fuckin' monster almost killed me, too. You had to put Gordon in charge, right? He made me leave my gun in the car. It almost killed me, too. I could have blasted it to shit."

"But you left the snake and Gordon there and ran."

"No, the snake crawled out the window. I tried to help Gordon, but he was already dead. I want to wait until somebody captures it, and then I'll get it for sure."

Thanner's voice came over the wires, ultra-calm. "Don't even consider that, Mr. Crowley. The job was bungled, so just get on a plane. I'll . . ."

"I didn't bungle, goddammit!" Crowley shouted into the mouthpiece.

"I didn't say you did," Thanner coolly assured him.

"Listen, Thanner, I don't fuck up jobs! I'm a professional. It was Wrightson and Gordon who bungled their jobs."

"Crowley, you listen to *me*. I'm ordering you to get out of San Diego."

"Bullshit! You're paying me to get that snake, and I'm gonna do it!"

"Crowley."

"I don't fuck up jobs," Crowley shouted. He slammed down the receiver. He wiped his sleeve across his sweating brow, then rested his forehead on his quivering hand. "I'm gonna get that snake. I don't fuck up," he said softly.

19

THE DARK walnut paneling within Dean Franklin's office had begun to warm, absorbing the rays of morning sun that poured through the windows in brilliant rectangular shafts. Miller lifted his hand from the wall and reached across the dean's desk for a pen. His other hand held the telephone receiver to his ear.

"O.K., may I have that number again, please?" Miller scribbled on the back of a used envelope.

Wrightson shifted wearily in his chair. He stifled a yawn until most of the contaminating haze from Franklin's cigar drifted lazily out an open window. Then he opened his mouth and let the air rush into his lungs. His shoulder and neck muscles quivered with exhaustion. He was not the type of person who could function efficiently for twenty-four or thirty-six hours straight. His body refused to take IOU's for sleep. He looked across the room at Ioka, who sat in a near-catatonic state. Excess oils had matted her hair into irregular tangles, casting blue shadows across her pale complexion. Wrightson was sure he looked equally drained. "Want some coffee, Ioka?" he asked. When she failed to respond, he asked again. She blinked and came out of her private thoughts to shake her head. He offered her a weak smile, trying to refresh her sinking spirits, but she had retreated once more, behind her dark, hollow eyes. It was just as well. He himself felt utterly hopeless, and it no doubt read right through his phony smile. He crossed his arms and slumped down into the chair cushions, making himself as inconspicuous as possible.

Miller was hanging up the phone as Novack entered the office. The detective crossed to one of the windows. "Well, that makes eight police cars down there so far. In a few minutes, it'll be an even dozen. Another party rolls into full swing." He turned, looked at Wrightson, and said, "Thanks for the invitation, Doc." He pulled open the window and leaned forward into the sunlight. "Did you get ahold of any of those snake people?" he asked Miller.

"I just spoke to a security guard at the San Diego Zoo," Miller said. "He told me the regular staff come in at eight. I tried calling my friend at home, but he's probably on his way to work."

"So are a lot of people," Novack remarked, staring at the scene in the parking lot. He shook his head in disbelief. "Will you look at the heavy artillery coming out down there. They look like a bunch of Jap extras in a Godzilla movie."

Miller continued. "The herpetologist's name is Anastasio Zahkarov. An unusual name, but he's highly regarded. He'll get my message when he arrives and will call here. There's no point in my waiting around. I've got to get outside, even if it's by myself."

"All right," Novack agreed. "But help me with my

job. Two captains down there are arguing about how to divide the area into search sectors. They know about your plan, but they need to know exactly where you and the snake hunters will be so they won't overlap you."

"I'll need a map to tell you," Miller said.

"We have local topographic maps in the geology room," Franklin offered, pulling the chewed up panatella from his tight lips. He opened the top drawer of his desk, took out a master key, and handed it to Wrightson. "You know where they are. Bottom drawer of the map cabinet."

Wrightson went on the errand without comment, glad to have a temporary respite from Novack's accusing stares. He returned with a pile of pastel-colored contour maps, identified as "National City Zone."

Novack studied the map, tracing the sprawling residential areas to the south and the jumble of mountains and valleys to the north with his forefinger. "Do you really think you can catch it?" he asked Miller.

"Yes. I feel certain." Miller's pencil played across the tightly drawn contour lines. "Here we are on the extension campus. Here's the ravine where the snake disappeared. My guess is that it followed the ravine down toward Mission Ridge Road."

"Great!" Novack replied loudly. "Maybe somebody driving to work will run it over."

"No. You won't find it near traffic," Miller explained. "The road vibrations would keep it away. It would probably just crawl through one of the culverts under the road and continue following the gorge."

"East or west?" Novack asked, noting that Mission Ridge Road lay in a gorge that dipped toward the sea in one direction and climbed into the mountains in the other.

"I won't know until I get out there and actually see the terrain. Judging by the map, I'd say I should look on the north side of the road in the unpopulated area. You and your men should confine your search to the south and west where the residences are. For example, just a few blocks from here there's an elementary school."

"Red nine. Red nine." The emergency frequency on Novack's walkie-talkie crackled to life. The radio voice alerted: "All Mission quadrant units proceed to 212 High View Drive. Investigate a 407 in progress. Repeat. 407 in progress."

Everyone's attention riveted on the detective. He alone in the room knew the San Diego Police code number system.

"An animal attack two blocks from here," he said tensely. "Could be the snake." He snatched the top map and left on the run, followed closely by Miller.

*   *   *

The four streamed across the campus lawns like a runaway parade at full gallop, Novack in the lead, his unfurled map fluttering wildly in one hand and his walkie-talkie in the other; Miller thrusting the capture pole ahead of him like the guidon in a cavalry charge; Wrightson clutching the capture bag under one arm while he struggled to keep the extra maps rolled, and, lastly, Ioka, empty handed but struggling gamely to match the pace set by the three big men. Novack was literally maintaining a running conversation via his walkie-talkie.

"Goddammit!" he cursed between puffing breaths as Miller drew even with him. "They've confirmed it. It *was* the snake."

"Did it kill someone?" Miller asked.

Novack lowered his scarlet face and concentrated

on his route. "We'll soon find out." He depressed a button on the radio: "Mobile control, don't let anybody go in the house. I'm almost there."

They plunged down into the ravine and ran in the direction of the lights, the noises, and the motions. The center of activity was an L-shaped white ranch house of the most homely and innocuous quality down to the detail of clematis twining through trellises set between the flowerboxed windows. On either side of the house Novack and his retinue could see curiosity seekers already crowding the sidewalks. Next to the curb sat five police cars and an ambulance, red lights whirling. Cars on the street crept by, their drivers rubbernecking to catch a glance through the milling crowd.

Novack bore down on an isolated patrolman standing in the middle of the garden. "What the hell are you doing?" he demanded.

The burly chicano officer either recognized Novack or guessed his rank and authority by the brusque tone of voice. "Looking for the snake. The girls who were attacked don't know whether it's still in the house or if it crawled out."

Novack put his hands on both knees and doubled over momentarily to catch his breath. "Get out of there and tell the other men not to wade into heavy shrubbery!"

The officer gave the detective a defiant look. "I killed snakes before."

"Not snakes nineteen-feet-long, I'll bet," Novack said pointedly, watching the officer's jaw drop. "You heard right. Nineteen feet long, and one little scratch from its fangs will kill you. Spread the word to your fellow officers why don't you."

"See what I mean?" Miller said as the officer

stepped gingerly from the vegetable plants.

"You didn't need to tell me," Novack replied. As the officer walked toward the row of patrol cars, Novack shouted, "Where are the officers who first responded to the call?" The chicano pointed to two uniformed policemen standing at the side of the house. They were escorting a pair of young women into the hands of the ambulance crew. The blond-haired girl, bare-legged and bare-armed, looked waterlogged. As far as Novack could tell the rest of her might be bare underneath the blanket in which she'd been bundled. He crossed quickly to the officers. "Novack—Homicide," he announced. "You the first two here?"

"That's right," an intense, dark-eyed patrolman responded. "I'm Watts." He nodded toward his partner, a liquid-blue-eyed Nordic. "He's Schiller. You want to talk to the girls?"

"Let's hear what *you* got from them first," Novack suggested.

Watts said, "It's spotty. They're both in shock and kind of incoherent. We just talked the one in the blanket out through the bathroom window. Seems the skinny one left the back door open, and their cat came running in a while ago with a giant snake chasing after it. The skinny one fainted, and the big-chested one locked herself in the shower stall. When the skinny one came to, she ran to the neighbors and had them call the police. As far as she knows, the snake is still inside. There's also a third girl in there. They think she was bitten."

Miller looked at the small house, enwreathed with blooms. "I'm going inside, Lieutenant." He brushed past the patrolmen, capture tongs raised.

"Hold on!" Novack said forcefully. "I don't want

even you going in there alone. Watts, Schiller, back him up!"

The officers looked at Novack, then at each other, both wishing the detective had made the assignment a voluntary matter. Silently, without enthusiasm, they unstrapped their revolvers.

"Follow me in, but don't shoot unless I tell you," Miller warned. He headed for the back porch. "Not unless I tell you!" He worked his way swiftly through the kitchen into the living room. "We have to be quiet if we want to hear it," he said, a polite command. The officers were scudding forward apprehensively. As they lifted their feet Miller heard a plaintive mewing from the direction of the ceiling. He spotted the cat, still cowering atop the bookcase; Miller was certain the taipan was no longer in the house. If it had remained in the living room, sooner or later it would have slithered onto the couch, over the lampshade, and up the bookcase, either killing the cat or forcing it to jump down. "I don't think it's here anymore," he announced as he poked the capture tongs under the couch and chairs.

"How can you be so sure?" one of the patrolmen asked, unconvinced.

"Because it's almost twenty feet long," Miller answered. "Do you see it?" He knew that, if the slender taipan was so inclined, it could coil itself into a large sewing basket, but he refrained from informing the officers of that fact. They would only want to know why it wouldn't make that effort to escape detection and would insist that the house be given a thorough, time-consuming search. Then Miller would have to tell them about this particular snake. Even if it had decided to curl up somewhere, it would attack the in-

stant it smelled the pervading odors of three per-
spiring men.

Miller edged his way into the silent hallway. One
door was open. It led into a bedroom. He knelt and
peered under the bed and the dresser. He found dust,
nothing more. "Not here," he said to the officers who
crowded his heels.

"Where's the other girl?" Watts asked. "Hello!
We're police officers!"

"Miss!" Miller yelled. "It's all right now. The snake
has gone. Miss?" He tried the doorknob across the
hall and found it locked. "Can I break this in?" he
asked the patrolmen. Both shrugged noncommitally.
Miller took a step back and threw his shoulder into the
door. It burst open, hit the wall, and rebounded sharply. Miller caught the knob and held it.

They found the girl in a prayer position, kneeling
on the floor with her head and arms resting on the
mattress. The officers shuffled their feet nervously.
The back of her robe was splotched with blood. Miller
put his hand to her throat to check for a pulse. Standing directly above her, he could see the ugly succession of bite marks. From the back, she had looked
quite peaceful, but now Miller looked into the young
face, frozen in deathly horror. He reached down and
closed her eyelids. "You can get the medical people in
here," he said quietly. He waited until the patrolmen
had gone, then quit the bedroom and walked pensive-
ly out of the house.

Novack was standing by the back porch. "That's
two dead. So far," he declared.

Miller stared at the detective for a moment, then
said, "It must have crawled out when that girl ran for
help."

Novack looked bewildered. "Is it natural for a snake

to attack and flee so quickly?"

Miller nodded. "In the case of the laboratory and here I'd say it's perfectly natural. First of all, the taipan doesn't attack humans as a source of food. It simply attacks anything alive. Secondly, the snake certainly doesn't want to be confined."

"Just seems too damned smart for a snake," Novack mused aloud. "Well. at least it's bitten itself out for a few hours, used up all its venom," he added hopefully. "Right?"

"Nothing could be farther from the truth," Miller said gravely and pointed to the growing crowd, now swarming around a television news van that had just pulled up. "See all those people? If they would stand still, the taipan could go right down a line, inject each one with a fatal dose of venom, and have plenty left over to kill you and me. It manufactures venom pretty much like we do saliva—almost inexhaustibly."

"Holy Jesus!" Novack said tersely. "And look there. Now the little kids are going to school. Hey, Simmons!" he shouted to a distant plainclothesman. "Did you get those extra units over to the school?" The man nodded. "O.K., Scott, come up with me and show the brass which areas you and the snake hunters will be searching. Then I'll let you get started. When your help arrives, I'll show them the areas you want them to cover."

They started climbing the flagstone path to the sidewalk. "I'll want to take Dr. Wrightson and Miss Marengasau with me," Miller requested.

"Sure," Novack said, looking for the pair. He noticed that the television reporter had already cornered them and was gesturing for the film crew to hurry. "Jesus H. Christ," Novack said disgustedly. "The good doctor will have that news bitch's liberal heart bleeding for him by the second sentence. I gotta get over there and keep things in perspective." He pointed to a plainclothes policeman and handed Miller his map. "Talk to that guy there and tell him what we're up against," he said as he trotted toward Wrightson, Ioka, and the female reporter.

Miller looked around from his high vantage point. Far off, over the graded contours of San Diego, he could see silver glimmers of the grey Pacific Ocean. To his right rose the relatively young Mission Ridge mountain range. He had never stood there before and yet the picture was disquietingly familiar. He pulled the map open between his hands and oriented it to the land. He looked again at the mountains, this time with far greater interest. Then he affixed his beguiling smile and turned toward the man Novack had pointed out, extending his powerful arm.

"Hi, I'm Scott Miller."

20

THE EFFULGENT SUN BURNED down through the hillside's dappled shadows. Not even the brisk gusts of wind blowing up the ridge from the ocean could rid the air of its unusual humidity. Wrightson paused momentarily from his climb and wiped his sleeve across his face. He could not believe the sun would still be sitting so high in the sky. It seemed an eternity since he, Ioka, and Miller had walked through a culvert under Mission Ridge Road and begun their methodical but fruitless search. Wrightson looked at his watch. Its hands pointed to 1:45, proof they had been looking only five and a half hours. As he started climbing again, Ioka, half hidden among the trees, shouted down to him.

"Who were those people?"

"They said they were hiking, but they had long sticks and an empty knapsack," Wrightson called back. "I told them in gory detail just what kind of snake was loose out here, and they beat it back to the road. I think I changed their illusions about saving San Diego."

Miller appeared from behind a large tree, very close to Wrightson. "That couldn't have taken you half an hour," he remarked, his eyes still sweeping the ground.

"No, as a matter of fact it didn't," Wrightson responded, placing himself automatically, thirty feet to Miller's right, and falling back into the search routine. "I went down to the road to see if I could spot Zakharov or the other hunters."

"You know they're in the field," Miller said. He gestured to the walkie-talkie that hung from Wrightson's belt. "Every few minutes you hear them reporting in to Mobile Control."

"I know. Five hours of 'Have you seen it Blue Three?' 'Negative.' 'Have you seen it Blue Two?' 'Negative.' You marked off the maps and assigned the search sectors. Exactly where are the other teams?"

Miller impatiently unfolded his map and pointed to three separate locations. "Here, here, and here."

Wrightson took the map from Miller's hands. "My God! You've given us twice the search area you gave any of them. It must be a one and a half mile square. We'll never cover all of this alone."

"We could if you'd stop wandering off," Miller replied, taking the map back and refolding it.

Wrightson pointed a finger angrily. "Don't try that crap with me, Miller. The only reason I'm here is because Novack assigned me to you. If it were up to me, I'd be following that gorge near the road downhill. Don't think for a moment I'm happy to tag along behind you on your personal crusade."

"You want to find the snake and stop the killing, don't you?" Miller responded calmly, working his way toward a steep rockstrewn runoff, long dry from the six-week drought that had beset the area. "You could search that gorge until kingdom come and you'd never find it. It's going up into these hills, not down toward the city."

Wrightson was about to respond when the walkie-talkie came alive. "Mobile Control, this is Red Two. We have finished searching our area. No luck. Over."

"Red Two, hold on. Blue One, come in. Over."

Miller took the radio from Wrightson's belt. "This is Blue One. Over."

"Blue One, would you like some of Red Two to help search the blue area? We have an excess of officers in the red zone, and a few have volunteered to work with you snake people. Over."

"Negative, Mobile Control. Tell them to join with Red One and search the extension campus again. Over."

"We copy, you, Blue One. Out."

Miller handed the radio back. Wrightson said, "You'd do this all by yourself if they'd let you, wouldn't you?" Miller walked off without answering. Wrightson sat on a rock and watched the man doggedly searching the brush with no sign of flagging. Ioka, a little ahead, was still walking a zig-zag course, head lowered. She had not taken as much as a breather in almost six hours. Her shoulders slumped with fatigue. Once or twice a minute she reached behind her neck unconsciously and massaged it. Wrightson despised Miller for putting the woman through the added ordeal after she had already suffered so much that morning. It was true that Ioka had volunteered, but Miller must have known the gesture was from loyalty alone, that she was mortally afraid of the taipan and driving herself dangerously close to physical and mental collapse. The man had only to remove the blinders his obsession had placed around his perception and he would see. Ioka was giving every bit of energy she possessed, and Miller, who supposedly loved her like a daughter, was gladly taking it. Wrightson decided that perhaps it was Ioka who needed the perceptual blinders removed so she could see what Miller was doing to her. He made up his mind to force the reality of the situation upon the two.

Wrightson's thoughts were interrupted by Ioka's shout. "Marc! Come this way. Scott has found something!"

In spite of his pessimistic attitude, Wrightson found himself running to join the pair. Between the boulders, rocks, and pebbles of the dry runoff the mud silt lay as a smooth powder. A long, sinuous ess shape disclosed the unmistakable track of a large snake.

"So you were right after all," Wrightson admitted with a touch of admiration. "It's come through here."

To his surprise, Miller said, "Not necessarily. It could be the track of a large bullsnake. They're found in this area."

"Come off it," Wrightson said. "The track heads uphill, just as you predicted."

Miller shook his head. "Maybe you can tell that, Doctor, but I can't. The silt is too soft. It's caved in around the impression as the snake passed."

Wrightson plucked the walkie-talkie from his belt.

"What are you doing?" Miller demanded.

"I'm obeying your orders. You told the other teams to radio Mobile Control the instant they spotted the snake and not to attempt to capture it without a coordinated plan."

"That was meant for them, not us. We know what to expect."

Wrightson nodded. "Precisely. With my first-hand knowledge of that snake, I want a dozen more men up

here helping us." As he raised the device to his
mouth, Miller's right hand lashed out and slapped it
roughly away. It flew from Wrightson's hand and
bounced off a large rock, chipping off a corner of the
plastic body.

"Scott!" Ioka said with alarm.

Wrightson stood aghast. "Mister, you're completely *insane*. You really don't want that snake
caught if it means someone else is going to do it!
Don't you realize yet that the minute that taipan
crawled out the lab window, its recapture and destruction became a hundred times more urgent than
your personal vendetta?" He swept his arm up toward the mountain peaks. "Look at this terrain. Really look at it! It's not at all inconceivable that the
snake could elude us for days or weeks. I've been
reading up on taipans the past week. Did you know
this is their season for laying eggs? What if this one
is a pregnant female? This is a perfect habitat for it.
We've got to capture it immediately. The only way
you can capture it yourself is to follow a trailblaze of
corpses. Living things—not notches carved in trees.
That's not such a horrible prospect to you though, is
it?"

Miller drew his massive frame erect with anger.
"No, that's not true at all. Must I remind you over and
over that I knew nothing of the plan to steal the
snake? Those two deaths were not my fault."

"Not the first," Wrightson admitted. "Maybe not
the second either. But the next one, certainly. If you
don't let me call help up here, you're obstructing justice."

"I told you," Miller said, his voice low and edgy, no
longer trying to pacify the scientist. "I can't tell if this
is the taipan's track. I don't want to draw the other

searchers away from their sectors if I'm wrong."

"You're lying through your teeth," Wrightson said acidly. He caught Ioka's baleful expression out of the corner of his eye. She was standing far enough away to be physically out of the altercation, but near enough to hear every word. Her look reminded Wrightson of the warning she had pronounced on the sailboat—that one had only to fear Miller if one got in his way. That was exactly what Wrightson intended to do. The time was perfect for a grandstand play to bring Ioka to her senses. If he had to risk taking some physical punishment to accomplish it, he believed she was worth it.

"You're really demented," Wrightson began. "I wish you could be standing where I am, looking at yourself. I know your story about how Ioka's father died. How he went into the jungle alone for water and was ambushed by a taipan. How you charged to his rescue but too late. What melodrama! What unadulterated bullshit! You wouldn't be so obsessed about this snake if that were true. The truth is that you were the direct cause of her father's death. Face it, Miller, just once in your gloriously successful life you were a coward, and nothing you can do is going to erase that. You're trying to create some miraculous chance for atonement, but Ioka's father will still be dead, no matter what you do."

Miller took a step forward. The muscles in his face quivered with rage, yet he seemed unwilling to stop Wrightson's words. Wrightson held his ground, but inside his heart thumped wildly, looking at the man's incredible build. "You know what I think? I think the two of you tried to capture a giant taipan on that island. You and Marengasau had never seen anything like it and were caught off guard by its ferocity. I can understand that perfectly, now that I've faced one. I think you froze, maybe for only five seconds. But in that time the snake concentrated on Ioka's father. Without your help, he was overwhelmed."

Miller strode forward, bringing himself almost upon Wrightson. "It was not that way!" He looked imploringly at Ioka. "It wasn't!"

Wrightson retreated down the gully, not because of cowardice, but because he wanted to complete his version of the story for Ioka's sake before his mouth was mashed to an inarticulate pulp. "You want to know my biggest clue to your cowardice? When you told Ioka you couldn't go back to Naraka-pintu to capture a taipan yourself because of your promise to her dying father. You're so great at fabrication. Is that the best you could dream up? You couldn't return to the scene of your failure because you knew the next time the taipan would kill *you*. The only way you could hope to reclaim some degree . . ."

Miller dropped his capture pole and rushed down the hill with a furious burst of speed. Wrightson did not even contemplate retreat. He simply collapsed as a quarterback would when faced with a tremendous pass rush. Miller, however, would not let Wrightson reach the ground. He caught the smaller man by the shirt, dragged him off his feet, and shook him violently. "Shut up!" he yelled with terrible agony. "Shut up!" He lifted Wrightson to the level of his chest and threw him against the gully slopes. Wrightson landed hard and rolled into a ball, throwing his arms over his head.

"Scott, stop it!" Ioka screamed, running between the men and pushing her arms into Miller's broad chest. Miller looked at the woman, begging her with his black eyes not to believe Wrightson's story. Slowly he unballed his fists, picked up his capture pole, and walked silently up the stream bed.

"Now do you see the truth, Ioka?" Wrightson asked, getting up painfully. "Do you see how my words hit home! I know you've been lying to me, too. That nonsense you gave me about not knowing what troubled him so much about the snake. The snake isn't his enemy. He's his own enemy. You know he was responsible in some way for your father's death. Come with me. Let's get out of here."

Ioka sank down to a moss-covered stump that overhung the gully. "Everything you say is right, and that is just why I cannot."

Wrightson's eyes went wide with incredulity. "Not even now? After . . . You mean I took all that punishment for . . ."

The walkie-talkie, still lying within the jumble of rocks, came on. "Hello, Blue One. Blue One. Over." Wrightson recognized Novack's voice. He walked over to the radio, picked it up and pressed the talk button.

"This is Blue One. Wrightson speaking. Over."

"Wrightson, this is Novack. I need you to come in immediately. City Hall and Police Headquarters are swamped with panic calls. They want an explanation why the snake hasn't been caught yet. As long as you have to go downtown this afternoon to file your statement on the lab break-in, you might as well explain the capture plan to them. Over."

Wrightson looked at Ioka. "That son-of-a-bitch doesn't fool me. They want a scapegoat downtown, and he volunteered me." Ioka rose from the stump and touched his arm sympathetically. Wrightson depressed the button. "O.K., Novack. I'm coming in. Over."

"Good. I'll meet you at the biology parking lot and drive in with you. Out."

Wrightson put the walkie-talkie in Ioka's hand. "You give this to Miller and tell him you can't look anymore."

"No, Marc," she said softly but firmly. "Scott may have done what you said, but he did not kill my father. The taipan did. The truth of what happened does not matter. My father was to blame for his own death. He did not respect the legends, and he died for that. Scott still lives, and he can be saved. He believes if he can only capture this taipan he can return to his old person. If he believes this can happen, it shall. You think you know him, but you did not see him before my father died. He was loving and kind. He needs me to help him, not to blame him."

Wrightson threw up his hands in exasperation. "Ioka, you're as blind as he is. He needs help, but not the kind you want to give him. He needs a psychiatrist. Your constant presence is just a reminder to him of his debt to you and of his failure to save your father. Each time you give in to his obsession, your passive assent assures him that he's justified in pursuing this crazy quest. He's lost, and you will be, too, if you follow. I'm a man of reason. I can't allow myself the luxury of putting my fate in the hands of demons and spirits. But I will admit there may well be a balance in the world, and Miller has upset it by taking that snake from its island. They come halfway across the world from two different directions to meet here, and one or both of them is certain to die. You may, too, if you follow Miller."

Ioka sighed. "You are right, Marc. But I must try to help Scott anyway."

Wrightson pulled the capture bag from his belt and threw it to the ground. "Then damn you! Damn you, damn Miller, and damn the taipan!" He turned abruptly and started down the hill.

"Marc!" Ioka called without conviction, knowing she could say nothing that would bring him back.

"Damn me, too, for getting involved with snakes and medical research, or for ever trying to help anyone," Wrightson shouted as he walked. "*Me.* From now on I'm going to think about *me.* And I'm going to get out of this God-forsaken town as fast as I can."

                              * * *

Wrightson pulled into the driveway of the rented cottage, climbed out of the station wagon and slammed the door hard. He was tired and hungry, but not half so much as he was angry and embittered.

"I'm lucky I've still got my damned skin," he muttered to himself as he stalked into the cottage. The filing of his statement and the subsequent interrogation had been a demeaning ordeal, compounded with the rejection he had received from Ioka. As he had anticipated, both the police and the mayor's office thirsted for a scapegoat, and Wrightson seemed the clear choice. The first three times he told his story, he maintained a degree of professional politeness. Later, as interrogators came and went in a never-ending succession, always asking the same questions, posed so that he couldn't help but incriminate or humiliate himself, he began to lose his patience. He answered either monosyllabically or with pithy, nonprintable repartees, and his belligerent attitude convinced those in charge that he richly deserved their scorn and censure. Finally, a phone call to Dean Franklin from the mayor's office provided a face-saving deal. Wrightson would lose his job and his research project.

The bosses seemed satisfied to let him go without formal charge.

"Probably couldn't find a law to throw at me," Wrightson muttered as he walked into the kitchen. In rapid order he consumed the leftovers from the previous day's picnic: an apple, a wedge of cheese, a cluster of grapes, and half a bottle of wine. While he ate he threw dishes, pots, pans, detergents and other household goods into a pile of boxes he had been storing in a corner.

"I'm amazed they didn't tar and feather me and say 'Be out of our town by sundown,'" he went on dramatically. "Would God that were possible!" He crammed the boxes to overflowing with no semblance of order, then moved to the living room and began emptying bookshelves, working off his anger with a flurry of frenzied movements. "Just as well I'm an unknown, underpaid teacher. This way I can load every one of my meager possessions in my euphemism of a car and get the hell out of here in one trip. Sunup and I'm gone." As he spun by the television set he flicked it on. A game show was reaching its pseudo-exciting conclusion. Wrightson could tell because the stereotypical housewife from Central City, U.S.A. had just won a shiny, red Detroit compact and was jumping up and down ecstatically in the host's outstretched arms.

Wrightson carried the boxes out to the station wagon and dumped them in the rear. He left the tail gate down and walked back for another load. He attacked the hall closet next, pulling out all his coats and sweaters, then reaching into the back for the seldom-used paraphernalia. There was the umbrella he had needed all winter but couldn't find, a baseball bat with a hairline crack in it, an old snake capture pole, and a single action pump shotgun his brother-in-law had bought him three Christmases before and which had not come out of the case since. On the floor lay two unopened boxes of single O buckshot. He gathered up his finds, lugged them to the car, and stuck them wherever they would fit. The shotgun he buried beneath the old magazines and newspapers, fearful that it should be spotted if he stopped the car. He pulled out a few scientific journals, made a snap decision to fire them out, but found halfway to the garbage that he couldn't.

As Wrightson walked inside to finish clearing the living room, he saw that the six o'clock news had come on. The camera panned to the anchorman, wide of eye, clear of skin, and wavy of hair. He smiled plastically: "Good evening. Tonight, news of a giant snake panic in the city; a three-alarm fire sweeps a warehouse in La Jolla; and your property taxes may be going up. Again. All this in sixty seconds." Wrightson loaded one more box, then kicked off his shoes and walked into the bedroom for his running sneakers. As he sat to do the lacing, the reporter said, "Early this morning, a man as yet unidentified was bitten to death in a research laboratory on the UCSD extension campus. He had allegedly broken in to steal equipment and inadvertently opened a case containing a rare and very deadly giant Australian snake. The snake, which is reported to measure nearly twenty feet, is called a taipan." A photo of a normal taipan flashed on the rear projection screen behind the reporter. "Later this morning the same snake attacked and killed a university coed, Courtney Mann, who lived two blocks from the campus. The snake is still at large, having eluded an intensive police dragnet. Persons in the northeast sector of the city are cautioned to keep all doors and windows securely locked, to avoid areas of dense vegetation, and, if they see the snake, to avoid it and immediately call the police.

"Action News learned the snake had been smuggled into this country. It had been secretly accepted by a university professor doing neurological research which involved snake venoms." Wrightson saw his own harried face on the screen. The reporter, trying to smile and look grave at the same time, continued. "Dr. Marcus Wrightson appeared at city hall this afternoon and accepted full responsibility for storing the snake on university property. A three-alarm fire broke out in . . ."

Wrightson stretched out his foot and toed the television off. He picked himself up slowly from the couch and walked to the back porch.

The swollen sun was dropping rapidly toward the rim of the Pacific. Wrightson gave his senses to the heady sea breeze. A feeling of profound emptiness welled up from deep within him. He would miss the ocean, the cottage, his students, and, most of all, Ioka.

Wrightson had intended to run down the beach one last, nostalgic time, but he found he had no strength left. He decided there would be time enough for that in the late evening, after he rested for a while. He flopped down under the palms that studded the beachfront and watched the endless succession of waves lapping the sand. In less than a minute he was sound asleep.

21

THE PLEASURE dome, a large banquet and entertainment complex in downtown San Diego, had been booked solid. The garish neon-rimmed marquee in front of the parking lot announced TONIGHT/SUDDEN DEATH CONCERT/EEC CONFERENCE/SALKIN 50TH ANNIVERSARY/POA DINNER. Spray-painted lust vans filled with high-school and college students crept up and down the aisles of cars in search of empty spaces while more than a thousand other teenagers milled outside the doors of the Pleasure Dome's largest hall. The sound of two dozen portable radios blasting away at ear level intensified the noise from the youthful crowd. A fog of smoke drifted over the throng, pungent with the smell of marijuana. Someone started yelling "We want in" over and over until gradually the majority of the crowd picked it up, shaking their fists above their heads good-naturedly, bouncing with the rhythm of the chant. The four policemen who stood between the young people and the building looked completely bored. The crowd soon tired of the chant. They shifted its rhythmic pattern to the name of the group they had come to experience, Sudden Death, warming up their vocal cords in anticipation of a night of screaming.

One of the double doors opened. A phalanx of teenagers immediately pressed forward. The police closed in around the door. A man stepped through, waving his arms. He shouted, "Get back! Stand back! We'll open up in five minutes." The crowd groaned and booed with vigor. "Get back, please," the man continued. "All tickets for tonight's performance have been sold." The booing increased. He shouted, as loudly as he could, "We won't open unless those people with tickets form two lines, from . . ." A teenager pressing close to the man tuned his radio. It blasted out as he spun the dial. Mixed with the noise of the crowd came an earnest sounding newscast. ". . . giant poisonous snake . . . still loose . . . false reports . . . city panic . . . mayor's office . . . elementary school closings . . ."

"Will you shut those radios off," the man yelled with exasperation, "so I can be heard?"

"Can't do, man," the teenager next to him declared. "We're listenin' for the snake reports," he shouted to the crowd. They picked up his cry and began to chant "Snake Re-Ports, Snake Re-Ports!"

"What?" the man asked, completely bewildered.

"Ain't you heard about the escaped snake?" the kid asked, incredulous. "Come on, everybody's heard about the giant snake runnin' loose here in San Diego."

"Snake?" the man repeated dumbly.

"Yeah!" the kid shouted over the noise of his radio. "Snake!" He pointed to the twelve-foot-high plywood cut-outs of the members of Sudden Death propped on the roof. The middle figure, clad in a bizarre black, gold, and leather outfit, had a boa constrictor coiled around his neck and arms.

"Snake Re-Port, Snake Re-Port!" the horde demanded vociferously.

*   *   *

Rex Flint, lead singer and founder of Sudden Death, cinched in the third buckle of his black leather belt. He pulled up on his gold lame leotards and straightened the spiked steel poleyns that covered his kneecaps. Rex had been Clarence Dubaniewicz five years ago when he graduated from East Duluth High, but none of his former classmates would have recognized him tonight. He sat down in front of the dressing mirror and grabbed his gold eight-inch-heel boots. As he was tugging them on, he noticed a pair of beautifully tailored suit pants, draped above expensive cordovan shoes, planted to his right. Rex looked up.

"Whaddaya want, Marty?" he asked in a barely civil tone of voice.

"Good house outside, Rex," the well-dressed agent said. "I just stopped by to tell you guys that 'Come, Come, Come' has moved up to the number six slot on the charts this week. You're on your way!"

"Turn around and let me pat your back for you, Marty," Rex said. "I wouldn't want you should sprain anything doin' it yourself. If you're such a great agent, how come we're playing to a lousy fifteen-hundred kids for a six-thousand take?"

Marty wriggled his face into a Kewpie doll smile. "Because, ingrate, until two months ago you guys were nobodys. Be cool! Trust me! In six months you'll be playing the Astrodome." He leaned close to Rex, who had bent over to buckle his boots, and whispered, "I can guarantee it, if 'Come, Come, Come' reaches the number one, even the number two slot."

"Yeah, well, that's kinda out of our hands, Marty, ain't it?" Rex continued to buckle his boots, ignoring the agent. "I mean, the teeny-boppers gotta shell out to make the numbers rise."

"Of course," Marty replied. "But, you see, they don't know they absolutely *must* have your record. Look, Rex, just give me the go-ahead to sink another twelve thousand of your royalties into hyping. The company will spring for the rest if you show good faith. I promise you 'Come, Come, Come' will soar. Minimum four for one return."

"Sheath your fangs and climb back into your coffin, Marty," Rex complained, sitting up. "You're draining us dry."

"But, Rex, baby, you gotta look to the future," Marty responded glibly. "If you hit numero uno, twelve thousand's gonna look like pin money to you."

The leader sighed. "O.K., O.K., you win. Now scram. We've got a show to put on so we can pay you and you can pay your bookie."

"I'm already in L.A.," Marty said with a bland smile, hustling his dapper, rotund body out of the dressing room door.

"Goniff," Rex said, checking his clown white cheeks and forehead and his gold nose and eyelids. He reached across the table for his wig, an immense lion's mane, straight out of Japanese kabuki theatre. It was tawny yellow, bristling out around his ears and over his forehead, reaching down to his ankles in back.

"Hey, Fiona, come over here and help me with this!" Rex called to his curvaceous teenage girlfriend, who had collapsed in a corner of the room like a pile of wetwash. The sclera of her unblinking eyes were rabbit pink.

"I can't. I'm too wrecked," Fiona declared in a husky, trance-like voice.

"Then just sit there. I'll do it myself," Rex replied with disgust.

Beau Cross, the bass guitarist, sat next to Rex, staring into the mirror. Conforming to the star system, his mane was shorter and less magnificent than the lead singer's and pure white. Beau was in the process of gluing bushy white eyebrows above his real ones with spirit gum.

"Phew! I'll never get used to the smell of this stuff!" Beau exclaimed.

Rex sniggered. "With all the coke you snort, you're lucky you can still smell anything. I keep waiting for the roof of your mouth to cave in."

Beau turned. "Hey, I got a change of lyrics in the second verse of 'Snow Queen.' Wanna hear them?" He reached for an acoustic guitar.

Rex stopped penciling his lips black. He threw down the pencil and glared at the bass guitarist. "Why-the-fuck must you keep changing the lyrics? Those asshole kids out there scream so loud, nobody, including me, can hear your words anyway."

Beau shrugged. "We gotta have some words to put inside the record jacket when we record it, don't we?" he asked petulantly.

"No, we don't. We'll put a picture of your old lady's fat ass in there instead. That'll fill both sides." Rex looked at Beau in the mirror. "You wanna know something? I been playing 'Snow Queen' for two weeks now, and I'm still faking half the chords. And you didn't even know it."

"I knew it," Beau replied. "I throw in a few secondary dominants and your fingers go epileptic."

Rex laughed. "Beau-beau, if you're so into being a

quality musician, why don't you join the L.A. Philharmonic?"

"Up yours, Clarence!" the bass player riposted, and turned back to his makeup.

"I'm really wrecked," Fiona announced from the corner, now flat on her back.

"That's nice, baby," Rex replied.

A young, heavily bearded man came through the door. He was dressed in striped pants, a flower-print shirt, and a leather vest; an electric cable wound around his hand and the crook of his elbow. "Hey, Rex!" he said, "the lighting console just blew again. We'll have to do the lighting with the back-up boards."

"Christ, Merrill, I thought you were a qualified electrician," Rex said. "We're paying you eight hundred a week. If I wanted to blow out the lights every other night, I could do that myself for nothing."

"Don't get hyper," the lighting technician said. "I just wanted you guys to know some of the changes might be a little slower than usual. All right?" He raised his arms in a placating gesture.

Rex examined his artwork in the mirror. "Just do it, Merrill. I don't have time to do your job, too." Merrill left the dressing room without further comment. "What else can go wrong tonight?" Rex asked nobody in particular.

"I don't know. What?" Jinks Thompson, the group's drummer said from behind a copy of the *Wall Street Journal*. He was deeply ensconced in a beat-up, shot-spring easy chair at the other end of the room.

Rex turned. "Don't be a wise-ass, Thompson. Instead of doing a dead jellyfish imitation, you could be checking props."

"Why do I always have to check props?" Jinks

wanted to know in a loud voice, not lowering his paper.

"Because you have less shit to put on than we do," Rex shouted at the newspaper.

"Yeah," Reilly Cosby, the fourth member of the group, chimed in.

"I read you," Jinks said, folding the newspaper leisurely. He stood up, letting his Capuchin monk's robe swirl around his legs. His face was made up to look like a skull, the cheeks grey, eye sockets black. White teeth were painted over his lips. Along his fingers and the backs of his hands, white lines were painted to suggest bones. Jinks sauntered to the dressing room door and looked out at the stage area, bustling with last-minute activity.

"They got the smoke bombs out?" Rex asked, combing his wig.

"Check," Jinks replied.

"The chain saws?"

"Check."

"What about the guillotine and the crate of chickens?"

"Double-check."

Rex shook his head. "Christ, I hope they're livelier than the crate we had at the last concert. That bunch didn't dance at all. What about personal props? You have your sickle?"

"Yes," Jinks sighed. "You got your packets of stage blood?"

Rex reached into the hidden pockets of his black cape. "Yes."

"What about your boa constrictor?"

Rex looked around. "No. Where's Bruce? Anybody seen Bruce? Where-the-fuck is the snake?" Rex took off his knee armor and got down on all fours. "Check under that easy chair, Jinks. Remember when he crawled up in the springs of that sofa, and we pulled on him for half an hour?"

"Not here," Jinks announced, after examining the chair.

"This isn't funny any more," Rex said, an edge in his voice. "Where's my goddamn snake? Fiona, you were playing with it before. Where is it?"

"Where's what?" Fiona said through her self-induced fog.

"Bruce."

"Bruce?"

"My snake."

"My snake?" she repeated.

"Ah, shit!" Rex cursed, running from the room. Jinks heard him yell to the stage crew. "Everybody drop what you're doing and help me look for my snake!"

"I'm so wrecked," Fiona said.

° ° °

Harry Jacobi, clutching his microphone, looked down from the stage at the dais. "And so, tonight we honor Aaron and Rose Salkin, a truly beautiful couple who celebrate fifty years of wedded bliss together this week." The crowd applauded lustily. Harry looked back over his shoulder and smiled at the band he always worked with at weddings, anniversaries, and bar mitzvahs.

"Fifty years," Harry repeated. "I asked Aaron before the dinner, 'How did you manage to live with the same woman for fifty years?' He said, 'Easy. The day we were married, Rose said, "Aaron, in this marriage you will make all the big decisions. I'll make the little ones." 'So far,' Aaron told me, 'there hasn't been a big decision.'" The drummer raised his sticks. Ba-dum, bum. Most of the guests laughed politely, those not too drunk or too deaf.

Harry sang, "Oh, how they danced on the night they were wed/If you think they danced, you got rocks in your head." The laughter was lighter. Harry hurried to the next joke. "Seriously, though, folks, I asked a friend who celebrated his fiftieth wedding anniversary last week how it was going. 'All right,' he said. He and his wife went back to Atlantic City and, would you believe it, got the same room in which they spent their wedding night? He's watching the T.V. in his underwear, drinking a beer. His wife waltzes out wearing a see-through nightie. 'Marvin,' she whispers in his ear, 'Remember fifty years ago, when I came out of that bathroom? You were in such a hurry, I didn't even have time to take off my stockings.' 'Don't worry, Esther,' he says. 'Tonight, you'll have enough time to knit a pair.' " Maybe two dozen of the hundred and twenty people at the party laughed. Harry had reached for one of the most sure-fire laughs in his repertoire, and it had bombed. If this group didn't like off-color humor, he was in big trouble. The last two jokes were robin's egg blue, and most of his stuff was dark navy. "What is this," Harry complained, "an audience or an oil painting?" The drummer had heard the "ad-lib" many times before, but he still laughed and touched his sticks to the drumhead. Ba-du-bum.

An old man who had been milling around the tables during Harry's monologue, acting as a self-appointed and unofficial emcee, looked up, and, in a loud voice, said, "That joke is older than I am. Let's dance!" A large part of the group applauded.

Harry pointed at the old fellow and said, "Sir, didn't you heckle me about thirty years ago? I never forget a suit." Ba-dum, bum. Harry turned to the band. "I did better last month at the pallbearer's convention. Who'll give me three to one odds this group is Conservative? Maybe closet Orthodox, even." Harry realized that not only the old man's voice and movement were distracting his audience, but also the low, rumbling noises coming from the other side of one wall.

"What's that noise?" Harry asked a waitress who had started to clear the dais tables.

"It's the crowd coming in for the Sudden Death concert."

"Sudden Death? That's how I feel about my act tonight," Harry remarked to the band. "I'm not gonna compete with jungle music. Go ahead, play!" He turned to the audience. "You win, sir. First we'll dance for a little, then Mr. and Mrs. Salkin will open their presents." He pointed to a large table in front of the dais, laden down with gifts.

The band began to play "David Melech Ysrael." The tables were quickly emptied as the guests scrambled to the edge of the circular dance floor to form the hora. Harry, with nothing else to do, clapped and stamped his feet vigorously.

Beneath the stage, Bruce, the boa constrictor, was frightened by the sudden vibrations. The snake slithered forward, under the gift table and out in the direction of the dance floor. Bewildered by the sudden bright light, it would have turned back to the dark confines of the understage, except that in that instant a thin, normally high-strung woman spotted it and let out a blood-curdling scream. Immediately a half dozen people shouted, "It's the snake! The snake!"

The panic was instantaneous. In their efforts to get off the dance floor and onto the tables, people fell over each other, in several instances, two or three times. Those on the dais and in the band were unable to see the snake. They rushed forward en masse, refusing to panic until after they had seen it. Once they had, they made an even greater commotion. Their stampede convinced Bruce to crawl onto the now-deserted dance floor. Immediately, accompanied by screams in English and Yiddish, the partygoers began to rain down a torrent of debris upon the hapless snake. A hundred hands let loose with plates, ashtrays, bud vases, potato kugel, honeycakes, and anything they considered might have enough weight behind it to maim or kill. Wherever the snake wriggled, missiles fell. Only a small percentage of things struck the snake, but the barrage was so heavy that it was still badly hurt. First one, then another of the younger men ventured out with chairs and sent them crashing down on the stunned boa constrictor. Its smooth skin was split in a half dozen places, and, where a well-aimed chair had struck it, bones showed plainly. A few women continued to scream hysterically. One especially valiant man rushed out and stomped on Bruce's head, which the dying reptile was no longer able to lift.

By the time the Sudden Death troupe burst into the anniversary fiasco, Bruce's smooth body had been mashed into a twisted, blood-smeared pulp. A few of the wide-eyed guests redoubled their screams when they spied the rock group's bizarre outfits.

Clarence Dubaniewicz, alias, Rex Flint, ran to the center of the dance floor. He went down on his knees, oblivious of the broken chairs, shattered glass, and splattered food.

"Bruce!" he cried in a pathetic tone, cradling the mangled body tenderly in his arms, letting the real blood ooze across his two-thousand-dollar costume.

Rex looked up at the shocked revelers, still cowering on the tabletops.

"Animals!!!" he roared at the top of his lungs, tossing back his tawny mane. "You animals!!!"

22

THE STORM clouds rolled nearer to the Mission
Ridge Mountains, shrouding them in unnatural
darkness. Already the moon and many of the con-
stellations had been obscured. Even on clear nights,
Mission Ridge's darkness assumed an almost wil-
derness degree. The federal government owned
much of the land and had kept it virgin. The few
private citizens living there did so on narrow parcels
of flatland tucked into the folds of the mountain
chain. One such piece of property, twelve acres
with a house, a horse barn, a corral and a vegetable
garden, was vaingloriously named the Two Star
Ranch. Its owners, Ben and Clara Henning, were
both native Californians, well into their fifties. Over
the past thirty years they had watched with dismay
as immigrants overran every acre of the state that
was not too ruggedly vertical or too doggedly dry
for habitation. They had bought their property be-

tween the bases of two prominent peaks, secure in the knowledge that no housing development could ever rise around them. They were happy there, surrounded by nature.

Ben Henning worked for the County Highway Department during the week, but his real love, shared by his wife, was for his horses. In the evenings, on weekends, and during Ben's vacations, they gave riding lessons and led trail rides.

Ben's greatest pride and joy was his chestnut standardbred mare, Belle, who was pregnant and due to give birth in three weeks. Belle was having a difficult night. She sensed the continuous drop in air pressure that portended the approaching thunderstorm. Also, the unborn foal inside her swollen belly was restless, kicking every few minutes. Belle eased herself around in the stall to the limits of her tether. The barn stood silently in the sweltering night. The other three horses slept peacefully in the common stall.

Suddenly, Belle heard a faint squeaking and the patter of tiny feet skittering through the hay between her legs. She recognized the sounds immediately as one of the countless field mice who made the barn their home. This mouse, however, was in a great hurry. Belle lowered her neck and drew air into her nostrils with her powerful lungs. Her eyes widened. She caught the scent of something dangerous nearby. Belle whinnied apprehensively and turned her head in the direction of the smell as far as her tether would allow. Her large, rectangular pupils peered through the slats of the stall, searching the near-total darkness. The smell became stronger. The mare pawed the ground and called out to the other horses, who began to stir. She pulled hard on the rope that restrained her.

Her eye caught a rapid movement on her flank, and she felt a sharp pain in her belly. Something had bitten her there and was holding fast. She felt its slight weight. Belle screamed in pain, twisted and kicked out with her hind legs, fighting desperately to protect herself and her foal. The weight dropped from her side, but Belle continued to cry out, causing the other horses to mill wildly within the confines of their stall. The big stallion backed toward the wooden crosspiece that barred their exit into the center of the barn and kicked out. The wood splintered under the force of the flailing iron-shod hooves. A second horse got in the stallion's way and was kicked into the crossbar. It fell against it with all its weight, breaking it in two.

Belle pulled wildly at her tether, jerking at the rope until it threatened to choke. A frightening scent filled her nostrils. As she yanked back once more, the pain returned, this time on her neck. She pawed at the shadowy form that twisted below her, but the rope held her defenseless. Belle raised her head and screamed for rescue.

o   o   o

Ben Henning threw back the top sheet and flicked on the bedside light. "Something's in the barn, Clara!" he said to his wife, instantly awakened by the agonized screams of his prize mare. He struggled into his boots. "You call the police!"

"At least put on your pants before you go out there," Clara pleaded.

"No time," he yelled. Clad only in pajamas, Ben dashed from the bedroom and through the parlor. He grabbed a rifle and a long flashlight he kept behind the front door. His wife followed him, calling through the screen, "Be careful, Ben! Please!" She hurried to the kitchen to make the call, leaving a long trapezoidal beam of light from the hall to illuminate Ben's path across the driveway to the corral.

As Henning opened the corral gate, he called out, "I got a gun, and I'll use. Believe me. You better come out with your hands up." Ben sniffed the air. He smelled no fire, his greatest fear. He waited for the doors to open, listening to the thundering commotion of the horses, crying and bumping against each other and every obstacle in the blackness. Waiting no longer, he tucked the flashlight under his gun arm, undid the crossbar, and threw open one of the doors. Immediately, the stallion shot through, brushing the door hard with his flank, knocking Henning to the ground. The other two horses followed into the corral at a gallop. Henning picked himself up and hastened around the door.

"Belle!" he called as he thrust the flashlight beam toward the mare's stall. He was amazed to see her standing quite still, making only gentle, neighing noises. "Belle, you O.K.?" Henning asked, taking two steps into the barn, playing the beam on the stalls, the bales of hay, and the crates in the loft. Despite the mare's noises, Ben was too cautious a man to rush into a dark barn without first making a careful search. To his relief and perplexity, he saw nothing. He turned the light again to the pregnant mare as he strode to her stall. Her flank quivered as if a dozen flies were annoying her. She shifted nervously in place, kicking weakly with one hind leg. He opened the gate and let it swing into the darkness.

"Whatsa matter, girl? Is your foal trying to get out already?" he said soothingly. Without warning, Belle dropped to her knees, then let her great belly roll to

the side. The tether held her head off the ground
a little way. She rolled her eye balefully, showing Henning the white. He saw a glint of wetness
around her mouth and turned the flashlight. A
trace of foam slavered across her lips. She moaned
deeply.

Henning bent to examine the mare, but, in rolling
over, she had hidden the bite wounds from his inspec-
tion. Henning stood, bewildered. "You just relax, girl.
I'll get the vet." He swung the stall gate and was
about to leave the barn when he heard a rustling
sound. He whirled around and threw the flashlight
beam at the rear of the barn, a separate enclosure he
used as a tack and storage room. Henning listened for
a repetition of the sound, but the horses outside continued to stamp and neigh, making it almost impossible
to hear subtle noises.

Henning cocked his Winchester and pointed it at
the center of the barn. He advanced cautiously on the
tack room, moving out of the pool of light emanating
from the house. Darkness enclosed him. He swept the
flashlight back and forth more rapidly into a semi-
circular pattern.

Henning had fixed rollers to the tack room door and
secured it on a metal track for ease of movement. He
hooked his elbow into the handle, pushed the door
open a crack, then stuck his booted foot in the space.
He edged the door back with the inside of his leg and
rolled it to the limits of the door frame.

The room was a barely organized dumping ground
for all the Hennings' equine paraphernalia. Saddles
sat on saw horses, surrounded by buckets and brushes.
On the walls hung lengths of rope, bridles, bits and
halters. The remaining spaces were crowded with

hoses, water cans, a wheelbarrow, bags of feed, and bales of half-used hay.

Henning raised the rifle and tightened his finger around the trigger. He aligned the flashlight with the gun's barrel. He shone the light to his left. Each object's shadow moved in tandem with the beam, metamorphosizing as the angle of light slowly shifted. Henning held the light steady. Between two boxes. the loose hay on the floor poked up into an elongated mound. He traced the unfamiliar shape past the boxes until it disappeared behind a bale of hay. Even before he had located its continuation on the other side of the bale, Henning's recollection of the six o'clock news melded with the image from his eyes. "The snake!" he whispered. The dark, cylindrical shape stirred beneath the straw. Henning shone the beam to his right, following the snake's body as rapidly as he could. An accomplished marksman, he had shot half a dozen rattlers in the wild. All he needed was to find the creature's head. One shot would do the trick, but Henning decided he would pump three or four more rounds into it in retaliation for its outrageous act of having attacked the mare.

Henning had been tracing the snake's body for better than five seconds. It wound through the layered confusion like an endless mountain road. His heart flip-flopped. He had traced the body all the way across the tack room and still he hadn't found the damned monster's head. He began to understand what the reporter had meant by the word "giant."

Suddenly, the room was alive with sound. From everywhere at once came the rustle of disturbed hay. Henning pulled the flashlight beam back toward his body. Out of its corona he at last caught sight of the snake's head. It was lunging with incredible speed at his leg. Before he could react, Henning felt a blow to his knee, delivered like a boxer's jab. Without thinking, he lowered the rifle in the direction of the attacker and squeezed the trigger. The Winchester's kick popped the flashlight from his left hand. It dropped to the floor, shattered, and went out.

Henning recoiled from the room and simultaneously yanked at the door. As he stumbled backward into the stall area, fighting to maintain his balance and keep hold of the rifle, the door slammed shut. Henning backed into a support beam. He leaned against it and felt his knee. The pajama leg had been ripped slightly. The bite, only seconds old, did not hurt, but the knee felt somewhat stiff.

Henning had been reacting reflexively, but now he stopped to think. He stood in total darkness. The nearest light illuminated the floor some twenty feet behind him, the faint glow from the house. In front of him, the tack room door was securely closed. Henning was not especially heartened by the fact, however. On either side of the door, there were gaping spaces in the walls, which had been constructed only to keep the horses from the feed.

Henning recocked his rifle. He had never heard of a snake attacking so aggressively. For all he knew, it might press the attack again. He hobbled toward the light. Hay rustled to his right. He flinched and fired at the sound. The bullet struck metal and ricocheted noisily into the rafters. He recocked the rifle again, backing more quickly, and began to swing the barrel in front of his knees like a scythe. If the rustling continued, Henning could not hear it, with the increased stamping of the horses in the corral and the mare's death rattle gurgling thickly in her lungs and throat.

Henning was almost to the edge of the light when he heard a heart-stopping hissing at his side. He wheeled and fired, illuminating the area to his immediate right with a spurt of red-yellow flame. Henning turned toward the pool of light and planted his good foot to run. With that movement, he felt the force of a second blow. The sharp fangs ripped into his flesh. Henning raised his leg to kick the attacker and slipped on a mixture of wet hay and manure. He fell hard. The butt of the Winchester caught him under the ribs and drove the wind from his lungs. Gasping for air, he crawled toward the light. The snake attacked a third time, biting through the pajamas where his thigh joined his buttock. He reached back and slapped weakly at the monster while his legs churned wildly in an effort to escape. On all fours, he scuttled forward.

The snake slithered along Henning's back and dug its jaws into his neck. The man struggled to stand, but his knee was no longer obeying his command. He fell again, feeling more and more of the slippery flesh slithering across his bare skin. Henning clawed his way singlemindedly toward the light, possessed by the irrational belief that, if he cleared the barn doors, the snake would be forced to let go. In his fear-crazed mind the barn had been transformed to Hell itself. Outside the barn lay the bright, sane, safe world.

Clara Henning stepped into the doorway of the barn and looked with horror at the fitful struggle of man and beast. Her hands flew to her mouth, but they could not muffle the screams that rang through the little valley. Ben's hand went up, waving her back.

She could not bear to leave him. He waved again, more frantically.

"Get out of the light!" he screamed. Then his face pitched forward into the muck, and he lay very still.

23

THE AIR inside the rented car was getting stale. Miller rolled the window halfway down; the warm, dense night atmosphere rushed in. He heard, far off, the kettledrum roll of thunder, watched the distant displays of lightning. Somewhere overhead in the darkness a flock of birds were flapping their way inland.

"Will it bother you if I turn on the light?" Miller asked Ioka, who had curled up in the back seat, both hands tucked under her cheek. "Ioka?" She slept on peacefully. The fatigue lines on her young face had softened. Miller turned on the dome light and, as quietly as possible, unfolded his soiled and wrinkled topographical map. For more than eighteen hours there had been no trace of the taipan. Miller rubbed his eyes wearily. He looked at the three-inch circle he had drawn on the map at the start of the afternoon, its southern perimeter touching Mission Ridge Road. Outside this circle he now drew another, six inches in diameter. He looked out the windshield at the mountain peaks, but found them indistinguishable in the gloom. The wind had picked up and was swirling through the car. Miller closed the window, turned the car radio on very low, and dialed to a classical FM station. He recognized the music as the gentle, lulling introduction of Ravel's *Daphnis et Chloe*. He sat back, staring out at the darkness, thinking of Marcus Wrightson's harsh words, and of the nerve-shattering situation he had brought upon the young scientist and Ioka. He squeezed his eyes shut tightly, then looked again at the map, crossing out with tiny x's the areas he and Ioka had searched before the waning light had forced a halt. The marks made a trail northward, winding from valley to valley to ever higher elevations. When Miller laid down the pencil, hardly a quarter of the six-inch circle had been lined out. He set the map on the dashboard and snuggled down in the seat. There was nothing more he could do before first light. He didn't want to sleep, but he decided it would do him good to rest his eyes for a while.

°　°　°

The jungle was alive with sounds. Insects buzzed by his head. Invisible birds warbled lustily in the tree branches. A nearby waterfall tumbled down the mountain slopes to the island's gleaming white beach where the frightened natives waited apprehensively by the campsite. Strong as the sounds were, his consciousness was dominated by visual sensations. All morning, his eyes had scrutinized each moss-carpeted branch, each clump of fern, every outcropping of rock and every dark recess large enough to conceal a snake. The air was steamy, the temperature, even within the umbra of the jungle, sweltering. On any other day and in any other place the climate would have enervated him, but the challenge of high adventure drove him forward with uncommon exhilaration. He drew energy as well from the knowledge that he stood in the prime of his manhood.

The terrain had flattened slightly. Ahead lay an elongated clearing where a colossal hardwood had recently crashed to its death, exposing the forest floor. The equatorial sun streamed down on the decaying trunk, surrounded by knee-high grasses and by the sapling trees that would soon supplant them. As he leaned against his capture pole for support, breathing deeply, he thought he heard his friend, Claude, calling him from the lower slopes. He couldn't be sure, since the noise of the waterfall muffled and mixed with every other sound. To be safe, he shouted back. Although he had halted his swinging stride to allow the older man to catch up, his sharp eyes continued to sweep across the jungle, searching for the creature they had come to catch.

Adrenalin coursed suddenly into his veins. On a large rock, beyond the fallen tree, lay a monstrous snake, stretched out full length, soaking up the sun. He could not accurately judge its size, since he stood a good distance from it, but he knew the snake had to measure at least sixteen feet. Its coloration was unremarkable, a uniform brown-black from head to tail. Its length and girth were not especially awe-inspiring either, since he had captured a number of reticulated pythons with Claude. The plain coloring and the long, slender shape, however, were significant beyond visual impression. This snake fit precisely Claude's description of the Naraka-pintu taipan.

Well aware of the snake's total deafness, he turned and called once again down the slope to the tiny figure of his friend. "Hurry up! I've spotted one!" He tested the air and found that he stood crosswind to the

taipan. Anxious that the snake not see him and slither
quickly into the undergrowth, he circled into the
shadows on his side of the fallen tree trunk. As he
neared the motionless reptile, he heard Claude call
out insistently, "Wait for me! Don't try to catch it
yourself!" He would gladly have heeded his mentor's
advice had the snake not chosen that moment to
move, pulling its great length up toward its coffin-
shaped head, threatening to disappear into the grasses
in the direction from which Claude was advancing.

He could afford to wait no longer. It would vanish
in a matter of seconds. "Hurry, Claude!" he shouted.
He dashed around the towering root of the tree with
his Y-pronged pole braced in both arms like a jousting
lance.

The giant taipan caught his movement out of the
corner of one gleaming eye. As the forked pole de-
scended, it used the mass of its athletic body to propel
its head and neck to the side. The instrument missed
pinning it by only inches, but he had so counted on his
speed that the force of his motion could not be redirected in time. His overabundant strength drove the
pole deeply into the damp earth. Claude had warned
him about the lightning quickness of the species. He
knew, moreover, that this particular giant could throw
its head across at least seven feet of open space, not
striking at the feet as did smaller snakes, but aiming
for the arms or even the face. There was not an instant
to be lost. He gave a forceful tug on the pole the second he realized he had not pinned the taipan's head.
The prong had lodged in something weighty beneath
the surface debris, and it resisted as if rooted in place.
He tugged again, harder. The pole snapped cleanly in
two. He hurtled backward over the uneven earth, and,
in so doing, avoided death by inches. The taipan had

drawn itself into a few tight coils, then had lunged forward with all its power. Its gaping jaws snapped shut in empty air, where his head had been a second before. He continued stumbling backward over the yielding soil until he fell into a tangle of parasitic vines that dangled from branches of an immense jungle tree to the ground. The vines were thin enough that his weight and momentum carried him through them to the snarled roots of the tree, but strong enough that, once entangled, he was effectively snared. He looked through the ropy vegetation at the place where the bottom of his pole stuck out of the ground. The taipan had recovered from its unsuccessful lunge and was once again raising its fearsome head. It looked straight at him, tongue darting in and out. One glance at the evil head told him the snake had no intention of retreating, as all ordinary snakes surely would. Slowly, inexorably, it slithered toward the first of the vines. He fought his way to a standing position. The tree roots surrounded him to the level of his waist. The vines coiled around his arms and legs tenaciously. He was about to die, and there was no way he could prevent it.

The taipan's head swung to the right. He followed the snake's changing focus as he shrugged more of the vines from his extremities. Claude had planted one foot on the rotting log and was leaping up with his capture pole extended. The taipan dropped its head back and unhinged its jaws. He watched the snake's smooth flesh ripple as the musculature beneath tensed. As Claude cleared the log, the prong of his pole caught in a branch. The pole was cleanly whisked from his hand. There was no way Claude could halt his headlong drive toward the snake. Weaponless, he charged forward with hands extended, concentrating with all his power on the taipan's neck. Three feet from the creature his left arm swung out quickly. The snake ignored the diversion. Instead of meeting Claude's attack head-on, it brought its center of mass quickly to the right and lunged from the side at his right arm. Miraculously, the man's fine-honed reflexes allowed him to adjust rapidly enough to drop to his knees and grab the taipan around the neck. The maneuver, skillful as it was, was an impossible one, too low to prevent the supple creature from arching its head down viciously and breaking Claude's skin with a sharp blow. He released the neck and yelped in pain. The taipan lashed out again, tearing at Claude's face. Blood shot out from the force of the bite. With a tremendous backhand slap, he whipped the snake into the thick undergrowth. Claude glanced at the younger man who stood almost free of the vines but frozen by fear. "Run! Save yourself!" Claude commanded.

He shook his head in disbelief. This could not be happening to Claude, one of the world's most experienced snake hunters. The vegetation quivered with motion. Claude rose from his knees and gave ground toward the tree trunk, drawing the snake away from the vines.

Shrugging the last of the vines from his legs, he reached to his hip and pulled his machete from its sheath. "No! Run, Scott!" Claude yelled at him. "I'm a dead man. Run!"

He dropped the knife and ran as he had never run, vaulting rocks and bushes in tremendous leaps, falling, rolling, clambering up again, swinging around and between masses of vines. Branches leapt out at his face, raking his flesh. The soft, damp ground threatened to suck the boots off his feet. He impaled himself

in a bramble thicket and was flailing wildly for release
when he heard a sharp, cracking noise. It was Claude's
revolver. The snake hunter must have shot the taipan
with his final conscious effort. He listened to the
echoes of the gunfire, dying away. He looked back up
the slopes. He had not run nearly as far as he had
imagined. He could still see traces of the shaft of light
that poured down into the break in the forest. He
knew he had to return. He could not let his friend rot
in the hostile jungle. Moreover, Claude would have
wanted him to bring the taipan's carcass back to
civilization to prove its existence.

He picked his way back up the slope. Gone was his
bravado, deplored were the foolish boasts he and
Claude had shared in a score of Djakartan saloons. His
progress was slowed by fear and exhaustion. His great
reserves of energy had disappeared. He was still
breathing heavily when he climbed onto the tree
trunk and looked down on the body of his friend. The
taipan was nowhere to be seen. What he had heard
was the sound of Claude ending his own agony. The
revolver lay in his right hand, the barrel close by the
tiny, powder-rimmed hole in the right temple. The
opposite side of his friend's head was a concave shell
of bone, brain, and blood. Flecks of liquid red dripped
off nearby leaves. He doubled over and started to
retch.

＊　＊　＊

The sharp, crackling report of thunder directly
overhead brought Miller to instant wakefulness. Every nerve fiber in his body tingled with the image of
his dead friend, kept fresh by the tormenting, recur-
rent nightmares. He gasped for air, feeling the
claustrophobic confines of the car. He threw the door
open and leaned his head out, willing his lungs to

cease their heaving. In a while he recovered, swung the door shut, and turned back to check on Ioka. She was sitting up, wide awake, and had evidently been watching him for a long time.

"Are you all right?" she asked calmly, as if he'd done no more than choke momentarily on a piece of food.

Miller mopped his forehead, embarrassed in spite of her matter-of-fact behavior. "Yes. Fine." He switched on the light and looked at his watch. "Should be dawn in a bit."

Ioka nodded. "But we may not see it arrive through these clouds." Heavy drops of rain plopped sporadically against the windshield.

"Let's check if there's any news," Miller said, avoiding Ioka's eyes. He turned on the police walkie-talkie.

"And add a 10-79," a voice came in, almost immediately. "There's no hurry. The victim's dead."

Miller waited for more information, but he had apparently caught the tail end of the transmission. "Hello, San Diego Police" he called, using the same channel. "This is Scott Miller. I'm working with Lieutenant Novack on the snake case. Do you have any new information? Over."

"Affirmative, Mr. Miller," the same voice said, crackling with the electrical discharge of the storm. "The snake's killed a horse and another man, in a barn at the Two Star Ranch."

"Is the snake still there? Over."

"Negative. We just finished a search of the property. Over."

"How long ago did the attack take place?"

"About thirty minutes. We've been looking for you. Are you still in the field?"

"Yes, I am. On an unnamed dirt road two miles due north of the university extension campus. Over."

"If you have a topo map, we're about a mile northeast of your position. The house and barn are marked on my map. Two inches southeast of the peak with the 1291 elevation. Over."

Miller unfolded his map hastily. "Yes, I see it. I'll be right there. Out." Miller looked again at the map. As the crow flew, the buildings lay less than a mile from the car. Between the two points, however, lay a broad line of peaks. The circuitous trip would take them back down the Mission Ridge Road and then around the mountains another three miles. Miller slid across the seat to the steering wheel and turned the key in the column. The engine roared to life. Before putting the car in gear, he turned back to Ioka. She sat as stolid as a stone statue, refusing to react.

"Ioka, I'm going to call Marc. We've got to bring this to a swift conclusion."

"He won't help you," she declared quietly.

Miller dropped the shift into reverse. "We'll see."

○   ○   ○

Wrightson pulled himself out of the lounge chair, staggered groggily into the living room, and picked up the telephone. "Hello."

"Marc, this is Scott Miller."

Wrightson looked incredulously at the receiver, then said, as rudely as he could, "What do you want?"

"I want your help."

"Forget it. You've gotten all you're gonna get out of me."

"Marc, the taipan attacked again. It killed a horse and a man."

"You mean you've finally got a hot trail, and you're wasting time talking to me?" Wrightson replied.

"Marc, whatever you think of me I probably deserve. I'm very sorry I got you and Ioka involved in this mess. At the moment all I can do is apologize and promise to make it up to you. I admit I was foolish to think only of capturing the snake. The important thing now is not our wants but just to stop it, to prevent any more killing. If you're truly dedicated to saving lives, you won't get a better opportunity than this."

Wrightson began to listen. Miller sounded sincere. Was the pronounced sense of honor and decency Ioka had credited the man with finally coming to the fore? Wrightson checked by saying, "All right. There are a number of military units willing to go into those hills with bazookas, grenades, flamethrowers, or whatever, Just . . ."

"We don't need them," Miller interrupted. "I know exactly where the snake is heading. I've traced its progress on my map. I only need one more experienced person to form a search triangle so the taipan can't slip by me again. Marc, I can catch it. I *must* catch it."

Wrightson sighed softly with disappointment. He berated himself for having believed Miller was capable of overcoming his obsession. The best plan of action now lay in pretending to go along with the man, find out his intention and his idea of the snake's location, then call the military authorities for assistance.

"Marc, the sooner you get here, the more certain the catch will be."

"O.K., O.K., Scott. I'll come. Tell me where you are." Wrightson picked up a pad and pencil near the phone.

"The taipan came through a valley with a little place called the Two Star Ranch. Take Mission Dam

Road. It's the second turnoff on the right after Navajo Canyon. The snake is climbing, as I expected, but it's moving much faster than I thought it would. It's trying to reach an altitude identical to its native habitat."

"Mission Dam. Second turnoff after Navajo Canyon," Wrightson repeated as he wrote.

"How soon can you get here?"

"Not for a good thirty minutes," Wrightson lied. "I was having some idling trouble last night, and I left my carburetor half assembled when I went to bed."

"Call a cab," Miller said anxiously.

"No need. It's just a matter of reconnecting things. I'll be there soon."

"It'll be light before you get here. Ioka and I will take the road that leads up into the canyon and start without you."

Wrightson knew better than to argue. It was enough that Miller had bought his story. "You make sure Ioka stays safe," Wrightson admonished.

"Don't worry about Ioka, Marc. I've been taking care of her for a long time," Miller said, then hung up.

Wrightson put down the phone. He decided that the best way to contact the military was through police headquarters. Somewhere under the mess on the kitchen table lay the slip of paper with Novack's work number on it. He looked toward the kitchen and jumped partway off the sofa with fright. Standing in the doorway was a man with a pistol in his hand. The gun had a silencer on the business end, and it was pointed between Wrightson's eyes. The shocking apparition was intensified by the fact that the owner of the pistol wore a rain-drenched mackintosh, a dripping southwester, galoshes, and silvered sunglasses.

"Who are you?" Wrightson gasped.

"Why don't you call me Frank Buck."

"What do you want?"

Crowley giggled. "I'm collecting for the animal shelter. Got any used snakes you'd like to contribute?"

Wrightson's eyebrows furrowed. "You—you must be a partner of the man who was bitten in my laboratory."

"Bullseye. You're a fast thinker, Doc. I really liked the way you made up that lie about your car. Why'd you do that to your old buddy?"

"To give me time to call the military in," Wrightson answered, his eyes fixed on the silencer.

"Oh, no. I don't want that any more than Miller does. I'm so glad he called you. I was getting tired of watching you sleep. For a while I was afraid maybe you were out of this free-for-all, but I guess you're still officially playing. Good thing. There's so many cops up in those mountains, I couldn't get near Miller. Now you're not only my ticket in, but you've got us exact directions to the snake."

"And if I refuse?" Wrightson asked, wanting to know immediately just how serious the man was.

"Well, that's your option, Doc," Crowley said, the smile fading from his face. "You can stay here, but only one way." He pointed his pistol at an easy chair three feet to Wrightson's side and squeezed the trigger. The suppressed noise of the bullet was drowned out by the sound of splitting plasterboard. Wrightson looked at the chair's back cushion. A small hole had been drilled through its middle. Behind the chair, a fistful of stuffing had burst across the floor, and the wall had a hole in it the size of a nickel.

Wrightson stood slowly, arms held out slightly from his side. "Why did—why do you want the snake?"

"I got mice in my attic." Crowley burst into an abrupt paroxysm of giggling. He was back in charge again, feeling like his old self. Just as suddenly, he discarded his smile. "Let's go. We'll take your car."

24

"I'VE GOT some questions for you, Doc," Crowley said from the back seat as Wrightson steered carefully onto rain-slick Mission Dam Road.

"Why should I answer any of your questions?" Wrightson asked, sorry that the man had interrupted the silence and his half-formed plan for escape. "Whenever I ask you one, all I get are flip retorts."

"O.K., fair enough," Crowley said. "I promise to answer one of your questions for each one you answer for me. Deal?"

"We'll see," Wrightson said, glancing in the mirror at the pistol still pointed in his direction. The man held it like a natural extension of his arm.

"My first question is: Why did you let the snake out of the crate? Miller told you specifically not to open it or feed the snake two days ago."

"I called him from the airport the next day, and he changed his mind. He thought the snake might need feeding."

"So that explains it. It was Miller's fault, not yours.

See, I've got a tap on your phone, Doc, but that couldn't help me if you called him from a public phone booth, could it? Too bad you did. If that crate had stayed shut, by now me and my friend would have been long gone and the snake also."

"Yeah, too bad," Wrightson agreed. "My turn. Why did your partner untie the bag inside the crate?"

"What bag?" Crowley asked, puzzled.

"Oh, come on, buddy. Are you gonna answer my questions or not?"

"What bag?" Crowley repeated.

Wrightson sighed. "If you've got no answers, there's not much point in this game. What shall we play instead?"

Crowley waggled the gun across the backrest of the front seat. "We play 'You slow down and turn right.'"

Wrightson pushed his foot to the brake. "There's no road here."

"Correct. Turn anyway." Wrightson looked over to the highway's shoulder. They had just passed between two steep hills. To his right lay a field in fallow, with a rough tractor path running parallel with the hill's base.

"We can't drive over that," Wrightson protested. "We'll get stuck in the mud."

"Not if you keep your foot to the pedal," Crowley answered. "The rain hasn't been heavy enough to wet the ground deep down." He nodded with pleasure as Wrightson turned the station wagon and bumped over the first of the ruts. "Those dark shapes over to the left are the buildings where the real turnoff is. But there's bound to be cops swarming all over. Now, if I were you, and somebody was holding a gun on me, I'd love to drive into a nest of cops. We're going around to avoid trouble. If a cop gets nosy, you say I'm a professional snake hunter helping you. Otherwise, I'll blast him first and you next."

Wrightson had no doubt the man meant what he said. Although he couldn't read through the sunglasses, the edge in the man's voice bespoke a psychopathic personality. Wrightson concentrated on the tortuous track, praying the gun would not go off as they bounced over the larger holes. His vision was reduced to less than two hundred feet in the gloomy dawn light. Overhead, through the slapping wipers he regarded the solid sheet of grey clouds, scumbled with streaks of black. The rain had dwindled to a light drizzle. The man in the back seat was probably no mental giant, but he had brains enough to foresee Wrightson's best chance for escape. Wrightson had planned to bring the car as close to a crowd of uniforms as possible and hop out the second it rolled to a halt. As he drove toward the end of the field, the furrows bent toward the canyon road. Wrightson looked in the direction of the house and barn, barely visible through the steaming miasma. No vehicle had followed after them. His mind discarded the first plan and sorted through alternatives. If he tried to jump the man alone, there was a definite chance he would die. If he waited until they found Miller and Ioka, he could certainly rely on Miller to help him overpower the madman, but then Ioka would be in danger. Wrightson decided not to decide—that a spontaneous action would serve best at the right opportunity.

Wrightson's thoughts had diverted his attention from the dirt road. Suddenly, opening in front of the right tire was an immense pothole. He turned the wheel sharply, but the station wagon slid through the mud, out of control. He hit the brakes. The car's motion carried it forward at a slight angle to the road until the right rear tire dropped into the pothole and churned futilely. Wrightson reshifted to first and gunned the engine. The car was stuck fast. "So much for your prediction about the mud," he said acerbically.

"I didn't ask you to drive into a hole," Crowley replied. "O.K., get out. Slowly."

Wrightson gestured timidly at the loaded rear end. "I've got my capture pole back there."

"Get out, so I can watch you," Crowley said, as he opened his door.

Wrightson climbed out, swung open the rear door, and reached slowly for the sturdy steel capture pole. As an afterthought he grabbed the metal-tipped umbrella that lay next to it.

"You afraid of getting your head wet?" Crowley sniggered.

"No," Wrightson replied, deadpan. "We can use this to ward off the snake if it attacks." Crowley seemed impressed by the ingenuity. Primitive as they were in comparison to the pistol, Wrightson now had weapons. As he slammed the door, he nodded at the gun and said, "How can I be sure you won't use that on me, Miller, and the woman when we hand the snake over to you?"

Crowley took two steps backward, then wiped a handkerchief around and under each of the silvered lenses, clearing away the accumulated moisture. " 'Cause I don't want to go to the electric chair for a fucking snake, that's why. You just be a good doctor and behave, and you'll all be fine. Let's go."

They trudged up the steep, mud-clogged lane with Wrightson in the lead. Despite the man's words of assurance, Wrightson was convinced he might kill all of them. A true psychopath would indeed be afraid of dying, but would never admit to himself that he was stupid enough to get caught. Wrightson certainly had no intention of letting the man know his opinion. That would only make him more vigilant. Better that he thought he was dealing with a sheep.

"There's a car ahead," Crowley observed. Around a bend in the road Wrightson could see the tail end of a late-model sedan. "Give a shout!" Crowley commanded.

"Scott! Ioka!" Wrightson yelled. The dense foliage swallowed up the sounds.

"Again," Crowley urged. Wrightson obliged. There was no response. "It's got to be their car," Crowley said as he angled to the edge of the lane to get a better look.

"I wouldn't get too close to the brush if I were you," Wrightson cautioned. "Unless you're sure the snake isn't there."

Crowley jumped as if touched by a live electric wire. He hurried nervously to the middle of the road and motioned Wrightson forward with a wave of his weapon. Wrightson now had another piece of information. The man was terrified of the snake. He didn't blame him.

The car was empty. There was no evidence as to who owned it. "Maybe I should keep quiet," Wrightson suggested. "This might be an unmarked police car or some curiosity seekers."

"Yeah, right," Crowley said skeptically. He didn't urge Wrightson to shout again, however.

Wrightson pointed to a path recently beaten through knee-high grasses close to the car. "Whoever they are, they went this way," he said as he stepped into the meadow, not waiting for Crowley to order him in that direction. The man seemed quite capable of protecting himself, Wrightson discovered. He hung back a dozen paces, far enough that no snapping branch would put him out of commission.

The path became steeper and more difficult. It led toward a sheer precipice of rock, jutting some thirty feet above the local terrain. When they crossed a stretch of bare earth, Wrightson's trained eyes told him that the path had probably been beaten by a man and a woman. There were two clear sets of footprints, one considerably smaller than the other. Wrightson pointed urgently to the trees that thickly patterned the meadow. "Listen, as long as we have two pairs of eyes, let's use them. I can't watch the trail and the trees at the same time. You check the trees."

Crowley eyed Wrightson with suspicion. "Are you trying to tell me that snake can climb trees?"

"Goddamn right I am. It almost killed me that way in the university greenhouse." He looked straight at Crowley, knowing the truth of his statement would be easy to read. Crowley glanced nervously from branch to branch. With the man further diverted, Wrightson moved forward. He tried to obliterate the footprints as much as possible. Suddenly, he discovered the faint impression of a snake's sinuous trail. As they neared the cliff, however, the ground turned to rock, and all the tracks disappeared.

Wrightson paused, listening intently, and put his arm up for silence.

"Now what?" Crowley said, with exasperation.

"Now shut up!" Wrightson commanded. "I thought I heard something."

Crowley listened for a second, then said, "I don't hear anything."

"Shut up, dammit!" Wrightson snapped. "Didn't you hear it? The snake is very close to us."

Crowley stepped away from Wrightson two extra paces, glancing around the meadow slowly. "That's the leaves dripping. Cut the crap, Doc! Quit tryin' to spook me." He dipped his pistol in the direction of the cliff. "Let's . . ."

Wrightson pointed urgently behind Crowley. "Look!" The taipan's head had cleared the grasses for a moment, then dropped down.

Crowley was two-thirds convinced that Wrightson was about to attempt some heroic action, but his overwhelming fear of the taipan forced him to turn around. The creature's head had disappeared, but Crowley recognized the powerful hissing that had echoed off the laboratory walls. He jumped closer to Wrightson. The taipan was near, but he wasn't at all sure it was where the scientist had pointed. "Get it!" he shouted, pointing at the capture tongs.

Wrightson threw the pole to the ground. "You get it," he said quietly.

Crowley looked at him with shock. "Pick that up!" he barked as he struggled vainly to watch all sides simultaneously. Wrightson stood motionless, the pole lying at his feet. "I said pick it up!" he screamed madly and sent a bullet crashing into the ground at Wrightson's feet. The taipan hissed again. Crowley whirled around. The snake was racing through the grassy cover toward him, exactly from the direction where Wrightson had pointed. Crowley pushed out his pistol and fired. The slender taipan's violent, zig-zag progressions, half concealed by vegetation, made it a difficult target for even a steady-handed marksman. His hand twitched like a leaf in a wind-storm. He held his ground and squeezed off two more useless shots as the snake closed the distance between them. Stubbornly, he refused to believe that his weapon would not momentarily bring down the beast.

The taipan was almost upon Crowley, concentrating on the man's outstretched arm. It lunged. Crowley fired point blank, but the snake's head had twisted to the right at the last instant and clamped its fangs firmly around the outside of his wrist. Crowley screamed out in pain and dropped his weapon. With the snake still riding his wrist, chewing fiercely, he squatted to retrieve the pistol, the source of his confidence. The taipan released, recoiled, and drove its open jaws into Crowley's face, knocking the sunglasses into the brush. Crowley sat down hard, flailing at the snake.

"Help me!" he yelled, trying impossibly to divide his attention between warding off the snake's onslaught and searching for his gun and glasses. His pathetic, blind gropings told Wrightson that the man either had prescription lenses or that he was extremely sensitive to light. The taipan backed off and prepared to strike a third time, but Crowley jumped to his feet and ran for a tree. Powered by the energy of fear, he swung easily into the lowest branch, then climbed as high as he could. The snake pursued, winding almost leisurely toward the tree.

Although both men had survived harrowing experiences with the taipan just the day before, their reactions were totally divergent. Crowley had cracked the instant he heard the hissing of the snake. Wrightson, even taking into account the fact that he was for the moment not the object of the snake's fury, found himself watching it in the process of killing with a bizarrely detached sangfroid. So much so, in fact, that he glanced down and realized he was still holding the unopened umbrella like a commuter calmly awaiting the 7:35 from Westport. Somehow, he could not think of the taipan doing anything else but kill, so, while the scene unfolding before him was undeniably gruesome and revolting, it also seemed totally, insanely natural. This was what he had come to expect from the monster. He had boiled its relationship with humanity down to the simplest of survival formulas—kill or be killed.

Wrightson dropped the umbrella and lunged forward toward the pistol. The taipan spotted his movement. It changed direction rapidly. He realized he would reach the weapon with barely enough time to point it at the snake. Moreover, he had seen how easily a small calibre bullet might miss the narrow, perpetually weaving target. He turned and ran toward a line of boulders that had tumbled off the face of the cliff, surrounding a shallow dome of white rock. The taipan followed, surprising Wrightson with its speed. He ran toward the largest of the boulders, a smooth, nine-foot-high monolith. His choice seemed a mistake. He couldn't spot a foothold in the surface. But as he ran directly up to it, he found one vertical split, about three feet up. He wedged his sneaker in tightly and boosted his body against the wet-slippery rock. Wrightson looked back. The taipan was closing on him quickly and showed no sign of flagging. He tested a tiny protrusion on the surface with his free foot, planted it, then pushed off. His hands clawed into the top of the boulder. His muscles contracted, drawing him slowly upward. His mud-caked sneakers kicked furiously for extra ounces of upward thrust. With a spasmodic contortion, he yanked himself onto the flat surface and kicked his legs over. He rolled on his belly and looked down at the taipan. It was still closing on the rock without slackening its speed. Had Wrightson fallen, he would probably not have recovered in time to avoid death. He stood and watched the snake, arms akimbo. The taipan drew itself against the base of the boulder and set its head up along the near-vertical surface. Wrightson readied his foot in case the monster succeeded in performing the impossible. Two feet short of the top, however, its body could no longer support the extension. It hissed wildly at Wrightson and allowed itself to sink back slowly toward the damp earth.

Wrightson heard a pitiful sound coming from the meadow. He looked out and saw the shadow of Crowley sitting in the crown of an oak tree, yelling for help. How long he had been calling, Wrightson could not guess. His mind had been too preoccupied to register sounds. He stared down at the taipan. It had stopped hissing and had drawn itself into a tightly packed series of coils, its head rising about a foot above. It held itself amazingly motionless, considering the frantic exertions it had just accomplished; only its tongue flickered in and out ceaselessly. Physically defeated, it seemed to be concentrating its mental powers on Wrightson, beckoning him down with its hypnotic, seductive eyes.

Crowley's noises drew Wrightson's eyes from the creature. They were weaker now, more like sobs. Wrightson looked at the shadow. It wavered in the tree uncertainly. Abruptly, the man fell silent. Wrightson watched the shadow lurch, attempt to catch itself, then plummet down through the branches like a ripe apple, crashing violently toward the ground. The body landed with a heavy thud, followed by a cortege of shorn-off branches and gracefully fluttering leaves.

Wrightson took one last look at the taipan and ran, leaping from bouldertop to bouldertop, well beyond the snake's ability to follow.

A little more than a minute later, Miller and Ioka appeared, looking down on the boulders, unaware that Wrightson had just disappeared from their line of vision. They stood at the top of the cliff, having climbed to gain a perspective on the narrow valley. They had been climbing the more horizontal, reverse side when they heard Crowley's cries. They had debated quickly whether to turn back or to continue up. Miller decided to go on, and Ioka followed silently. He arrived at the edge first, steel capture pole in hand. About twenty feet below lay the top of the boulder Wrightson had clambered upon, and, nine feet below that, the taipan Miller had so long sought.

"There it is!" Miller cried out, his voice breathy with excitement. Crowley's cries and all else in the immediate world were forgotten. Miller's stomach muscles tightened as he felt the adrenalin pouring into his veins. His tongue flicked out to moisten his lips. The moment of expiation he had anticipated for six interminable years was finally at hand. Not in the sterile Rotarium, as he had expected, but in a setting quite similar to that in which he had first encountered the taipan. The adoring crowd would be missing, but that scarcely mattered. He was only concerned that

Ioka be present to witness the confrontation and to understand that it was not Scott Miller's cowardice that had caused her father's death.

The taipan was unaware of the two hunters. It turned and started to slither into the grasses of the meadow. "It's getting away," Ioka said dejectedly, her voice snapping Miller's reverie.

"We won't let it," Miller vowed. He bent and scooped up half a dozen stones. He handed two to Ioka. "Throw them at it! Get its attention!" Miller's aim was better than the woman's. His first toss hit the ground a foot from the reptile. The taipan didn't notice. The second, however, struck an inch from its tail. It recoiled instantly. Miller threw his last two stones. The taipan pivoted its head in confusion, testing the air with no success, lashing its tail with vexation. It chanced to raise its gaze in the direction of the cliff. Miller flapped his arms wildly, hoping to attract its attention. It seemed to respond, but probably could not see more than a soft blur at that distance.

"What now?" Ioka asked.

"We can't go back the way we came," Miller said, staring down at the taipan. "It took us almost ten minutes to get up here. By that time it'll have disappeared again. We'll have to go down the face of the cliff." Ioka fluttered the white bag in the air to hold the snake's attention but made no comment on Miller's plan. "Look, Ioka, there's a mound of rock below us perfect for our purpose. We'll handle it just as we would in the Rotarium. You climb down first, staying right over that largest boulder. Once you're down, hold its attention while I follow. Grab that tree root to start!"

Obediently, Ioka tucked the capture bag into her

belt, knelt down, and swung off the tree root over the edge of the cliff. Miller held her left arm securely. "Got a hold?" he asked.

"Yes." She looked down to a foothold two feet below her and gingerly lowered her weight. Miller alternated his attention between the woman and the taipan. He longed to yell for Ioka to hurry. The taipan seemed perfectly willing to wait for the humans to descend. Ioka edged along an outcropping, searching for an easy access to the next level.

"You're going too far right," Miller yelled.

"I can't go straight down," Ioka yelled back. She was now directly over the white mound of rock and halfway down the cliff face. She set her foot on a jagged protrusion and tested it. It seemed strong enough. When she set all her weight on it, however, it snapped off, wrenching her from the cliff and into space. She dropped fifteen feet to the hard rock, landing heavily on her right leg. Even from the top of the cliff, Miller heard the sharp snap of breaking bone. Ioka's other leg hit, then she threw her arms to ease the shock of the landing. Her arms and ribs took terrible punishment from the unyielding surface.

Miller acted without a moment of hesitation. He knelt, lowered the capture pole as far as he could, then let it fall. He swung off the root and scrambled down, using an entirely different path than Ioka had chosen. "Don't move, Ioka!" he yelled, listening to her first moans of pain. "Don't move!" He glanced down at the taipan. It had seen the woman land on the summit of the mound and was already slithering toward her. Miller found himself without a foothold. He swung acrobatically across a gaping crevasse, and, with one huge hand, pulled himself over.

The taipan's path to Ioka was not straight or easy, but, by rapid trial and error, it was purposefully working toward her. Miller realized that only by taking a desperate risk would he be certain to reach her before the taipan could. The largest of the giant boulders lay directly below him. Although he was too high to jump down safely, he carefully squatted and planted his hands outside his feet. One at a time, he wormed his legs down the cliff, until all his weight rested on his arms and shoulders. He pushed off, landing like a professional gymnast, his knees absorbing the initial shock, then, by tumbling, distributing the rest of the sudden force along his shoulder, arm, and the length of his side. While his bone structure survived intact, his muscles were badly bruised, and his arms and face had sustained a number of deep gashes that immediately welled with bright streams of blood. He picked himself up painfully from the rock and retrieved the capture pole. His heart sank as he saw that the left pincers had snapped off in the fall. The instrument, with only two rubber-coated prongs curving off its end, was now little more than a glorified stick.

Miller looked across to Ioka. She sat up halfway, clutching her broken leg with both hands. The taipan had already found a path through the stony rubble and was sliding onto the base of the mound. Miller leapt from the boulder to the top of the smoothly convex rock. He placed himself six feet to the right of the woman so the snake would be able to see both of them.

"I'm here Ioka," he said calmly, his black eyes aglow with excitement. Almost ritualistically, he rolled back the tattered remnants of his shirtsleeves, displaying his formidable forearms.

The taipan opened its jaws and hissed demonically. It was annoyed by the slippery inclined surface. Miller could see the taipan's total length as it struggled up the barren rock. It stopped its hissing, concentrating on the slope, consolidating its streamlined length, then slithering out from the coils, working its way upward with savage determination.

Miller set his feet in two depressions. He held the broken tongs close to his chest. Ioka began to croon her sing-song chant. Miller looked lovingly at the woman. Although barely able to maintain consciousness, she had pulled her body upright and was waving an arm mechanically at the snake, trying to aid Miller by distracting it.

Miller allowed the taipan to advance within eight feet. When it had reached that point, he flicked out the tongs in a clear gesture of defiance. The snake's head and neck reared into the air. It drew up its great bundles of reptilian muscle, barely concealed under the shiny, brown-black skin. The taipan spread its ribs, puffing out its body. As Miller wiped the water and the blood from his forehead, he studied the red, speckled flesh beneath the pale, yellow belly scales. He looked at the snake with a cold, dispassionate stare, almost identical to the look the taipan was giving him.

The taipan drew the middle of its length at right angles to its advance, ignoring the woman's gestures. It had at last brought itself within striking distance, and Miller knew it. He concentrated on the muscles of the snake's neck, which he knew would telegraph its intention. It tensed. With blurring speed, it shifted its center of gravity to Miller's right and launched its head at the man's flank. The tactic did not surprise

Miller. He had seen it a hundred times in his dreams. With a deft coordination of muscle and eye, his arms swung out, not swiftly but accurately. He concerned himself merely with guiding the taipan's lunging head into the curve of the broken tongs. Just as the snake launched half its great body into the air and its head passed beyond the pincers, Miller gave a lightninglike twist, flipping the snake sideways and down, pinning the head precariously to the rock. Miller set the pole down and pressed his foot on it. Step by step he worked his way down the pole, praying the hold between the pincers and the uneven rock was tight enough to keep the squirming taipan trapped. Finally, with the snake coiling into an ever tighter ball, he reached down and calmped his powerful fingers around its equally powerful neck. Miller took his foot off the pole and lifted the taipan's head. With his free hand he stretched down along the neck and straightened its smooth skin as far as his reach would allow. He had intended to pull most of the snake off the ground to render it helpless, then march it over to Ioka and the capture bag, but more than half the creature lay beyond his reach. He looked down. The snake's tail wrapped itself swiftly around his legs, seeking a purchase by which it might wrest itself free. Miller raised his leg to clear the flailing tail, but the snake contorted violently and lashed hard against Miller's earthbound foot. The smoothly curved, rain-slick rock caused him to lose his balance. He fell awkwardly, unable to release either hand from the taipan's fiercely jerking neck. The snake hissed malevolently. It tensed its elongated musculature, and, with every ounce of power it possessed, thrust its head toward the man's face. Miller, flat on his back,

flexed his arm muscles, increasing the pressure around
the squirming monster's neck. His action forced the
mouth open almost to its limit. Venom dripped from
the fangs and plunged onto Miller's rain-bedabbled
forehead and cheeks. As the drops fell, he squeezed
his eyes shut and forced the head back toward his
stomach. He opened his eyes and smiled grotesquely
at it, his clenched teeth bared, lips curled back. He
shook the snake violently for a minute, then held it
patiently in his viselike grip. Well aware that reptiles
have little reserve of energy, he let the enraged
monster thrash and flail, throwing its coils uselessly
across his supine body. As he squeezed, Miller felt a
tingling sensation spreading across his forehead. He
rolled his head against his upper arm and rubbed it up
and down. For the first time he became aware of the
deep wounds he had sustained when he dropped from
the cliff. His sleeve was soaked with blood. He knew
then what caused the bubbly, dizzy feelings just under his hairline. A minute amount of the liquid
death, diluted by the life-giving water, had worked
its way into his open wounds and was beginning to
numb his nervous system. The tainted vessels
flowed directly into his brain. He knew he would be
spared the nausea and the vomiting, the spitting up
of blood and thick mucous excretions. His death
would be clean and mercifully swift. The taipan,
then, would also die, and in agony. Indifferent now
to the gleaming fangs, half-concealed beneath the
cream-white sheath of flesh, Miller brought the
taipan's head close to his own. He tightened with
all his strength, watching the snake's frenzied reactions as he crimped shut its air passages. He
squeezed tighter and tighter, until at last the

taipan's neck relaxed. The forked tongue ceased its darting. Its head lolled listlessly. The lidless eyes seemed to dull. Below the neck, the snake's body twitched spasmodically, but Miller was not concerned. He knew that a snake's primitive nervous system might send meaningless impulses long after the head's death. He had no idea, however, that his own nervous system was so near to complete nonfunction. He had thought he was squeezing with all his might, but he had already lost command of his awesome musculature. With a final, superhuman effort, he sat up, pulled the snake into a convoluted mass, and hurled it down to the base of the mound.

Miller turned to Ioka. She lay on her side, eyes half open, watching him. He tried to tell her with a serene smile that she was safe, and that he was, at last, at peace. The circle had closed. Her father had sacrificed himself to save Miller, and now he had done the same to save the daughter. Ioka returned his smile, her beautiful, young face for the moment devoid of pain. No longer able to hold his head up, he lay back. He looked up through the scattered raindrops at the formless white clouds. He retreated within himself, feeling his vital functions ebbing away, life contracting upward from his limbs and torso into his head. There was no sound, no feeling of the hard rock beneath him. Only the clouds above, darkening from grey to black.

Ioka looked apprehensively at the limp pile of reptilian flesh. She told herself that if Scott had strangled it, it was certainly dead. She drew her eyes away and regarded Miller. He seemed to be barely breathing, totally drained.

"Scott," she murmured through the fiery pain of

her broken leg. Inch by inch, she crawled laboriously toward Miller, whose heart and lungs had not yet surrendered to the taipan's poisons.

The taipan, stunned and gravely injured, watched the woman crawling slowly across the top of the mound. Oxygen had begun to circulate again in its brain. It turned its bruised and battered neck a fraction to follow the woman's movement. When it was satisfied that she was incapable of charging down the rock and mistreating it as the marr had, it started up the incline. This time it did not rush. It stalked, silently and stealthily, pushing its head flatly along the surface. Foot by foot it advanced, drawing its length into tight esses, then unwinding slowly and deliberately.

Ioka had crawled to within a few feet of Miller, close enough so that she could see raindrops bouncing off his unblinking pupils. Before the man's death had fully registered in her mind, she found herself staring at a second set of unblinking eyes. The taipan had pushed itself halfway up the mound and was slithering in slow motion directly at her. She opened her mouth to scream, realized the utter futility of the act, and watched instead in silence as the snake undulated nearer. It did not hiss or make any erratic movement. All its energies were concentrated on reaching the woman, as it worked patiently against the slippery incline. Its malevolent eyes were fixed on her face. Ioka had no doubt that it was the serpent of Satan.

The taipan drew close enough to strike. Unhurriedly, it raised its head from the rock. Its flesh rippled with demonic anger. Ioka closed her eyes and turned her face to the heavens.

A thunderous blast ripped across the face of the cliff and out into the valley. Ioka's eyes snapped open. In front of her lay the quivering body of the taipan. The head and neck had been blown across the white mound, staining it with a hundred rivulets of blood. The fearsome head had disappeared.

Ioka looked across the mound. Wrightson stood with his legs spread apart, a shotgun raised in both hands, its butt pressed into his shoulder. He lowered the weapon slowly, looking at the carnage he had wreaked. The shredded body of the taipan had been blown almost into Miller's outstretched hand. Wrightson set the gun down and walked quickly to Ioka. He knelt and cradled her in his arms. She began to sob, at first softly, then in greater and greater spasms.

"It's over, Ioka," he whispered tenderly. "It's all over."

78a

DON'T MISS
THESE OTHER
FICTION BESTSELLERS
FROM ACE!

☐ **Borderline** Keener 07080-9 $2.50
A fast-paced novel of hijacks and hijinks!

☐ **Casino** Lynch 09229-2 $2.50
Blockbuster in the bestselling tradition of AIRPORT and HOTEL!

☐ **Charades** Kelrich 10261-1 $2.50
A yacht-filled marina is a private pleasure oasis for the rich and beautiful, where survival depends on how well they play the game.

☐ **Plague** Masterton 66761-9 $2.25
Millions succumb—others must wait to die.

☐ **Diary of a Nazi Lady** Freeman 14740-2 $2.50
Riveting confessions of a young woman's rise and fall in Nazi society.

Available wherever paperbacks are sold or use this coupon.

ACE BOOKS WAREHOUSE
P.O. Box 400, Kirkwood, N.Y. 13795

Please send me the titles checked above. I enclose _____.
Include 75¢ for postage and handling if one book is ordered; 50¢ per book for two to five. If six or more are ordered, postage is free. California, Illinois, New York and Tennessee residents please add sales tax.

NAME_____

ADDRESS_____

CITY_____STATE_____ZIP_____

78E